MARVEL

A NOVEL OF THE MARVEL UNIVERSE

GUARDIANS OF THE GALAXY

ANNIHILATION: CONQUEST

NOVELS OF THE MARVEL UNIVERSE BY TITAN BOOKS

Ant-Man: Natural Enemy by Jason Starr
Avengers: Everybody Wants to Rule the World by Dan Abnett
Avengers: Infinity by James A. Moore
Black Panther: Panther's Rage by Sheree Renée Thomas
Black Panther: Tales of Wakanda by Jesse J. Holland
Black Panther: Who is the Black Panther? by Jesse J. Holland
Captain America: Dark Designs by Stefan Petrucha
Captain Marvel: Liberation Run by Tess Sharpe
Captain Marvel: Shadow Code by Gilly Segal
Civil War by Stuart Moore
Deadpool: Paws by Stefan Petrucha
Morbius: The Living Vampire – Blood Ties by Brendan Deneen
Spider-Man: Forever Young by Stefan Petrucha
Spider-Man: Kraven's Last Hunt by Neil Kleid
Spider-Man: The Darkest Hours Omnibus by Jim Butcher, Keith R.A. DeCandido, and Christopher L. Bennett
Spider-Man: The Venom Factor Omnibus by Diane Duane
Thanos: Death Sentence by Stuart Moore
Venom: Lethal Protector by James R. Tuck
Wolverine: Weapon X Omnibus by Marc Cerasini, David Alan Mack and Hugh Matthews
X-Men: Days of Future Past by Alex Irvine
X-Men: The Dark Phoenix Saga by Stuart Moore
X-Men: The Mutant Empire Omnibus by Christopher Golden
X-Men & The Avengers: The Gamma Quest Omnibus by Greg Cox

ALSO FROM TITAN AND TITAN BOOKS

Marvel Contest of Champions: The Art of the Battlerealm by Paul Davies
Marvel's Guardians of the Galaxy: No Guts, No Glory by M.K. England
Marvel's Midnight Suns: Infernal Rising by S.D. Perry
Marvel's Spider-Man: The Art of the Game by Paul Davies
Obsessed with Marvel by Peter Sanderson and Marc Sumerak
Spider-Man: Into the Spider-Verse – The Art of the Movie by Ramin Zahed
Spider-Man: Hostile Takeover by David Liss
Spider-Man: Miles Morales – Wings of Fury by Brittney Morris
The Art of Iron Man (10th Anniversary Edition) by John Rhett Thomas
The Marvel Vault by Matthew K. Manning, Peter Sanderson, and Roy Thomas
Ant-Man and the Wasp: The Official Movie Special
Avengers: Endgame – The Official Movie Special
Avengers: Infinity War – The Official Movie Special
Black Panther: The Official Movie Companion
Black Panther: The Official Movie Special
Captain Marvel: The Official Movie Special
Marvel Studios: The First 10 Years
Marvel's Avengers – Script to Page
Marvel's Black Panther – Script to Page
Marvel's Black Widow: The Official Movie Special
Marvel's Spider-Man – Script to Page
Spider-Man: Far From Home: The Official Movie Special
Spider-Man: Into the Spider-Verse: Movie Special
Thor: Ragnarok The Official Movie Special

A NOVEL OF THE MARVEL UNIVERSE

GUARDIANS OF THE GALAXY

ANNIHILATION: CONQUEST

AN ORIGINAL NOVEL BY

BRENDAN DENEEN

TITAN BOOKS

MARVEL

GUARDIANS OF THE GALAXY – ANNIHILATION: CONQUEST
Hardback edition ISBN: 9781803362519
E-book edition ISBN: 9781803362533

Published by Titan Books
A division of Titan Publishing Group Ltd
144 Southwark Street, London SE1 0UP
www.titanbooks.com

First edition: April 2023
10 9 8 7 6 5 4 3 2 1

FOR MARVEL PUBLISHING
Jeff Youngquist, VP Production and Special Projects
Sarah Singer, Editor, Special Projects
Jeremy West, Manager, Licensed Publishing
Sven Larsen, VP, Licensed Publishing
David Gabriel, SVP of Sales & Marketing, Publishing
C.B. Cebulski, Editor in Chief

MARVEL

A CIP catalogue record for this title is available from the British Library.

Printed and bound by CPI Group (UK) Ltd, Croydon CR0 4YY.

This novel is dedicated to my parents Irene Murray and Rich Deneen
For always supporting my dreams and encouraging my imagination

PART ONE

THE SAVIOR

CHAPTER ONE

HALA, THE HOMEWORLD OF THE KREE EMPIRE—TODAY

PETER QUILL was feeling pretty good.

It was a hot day, especially in the metal jungle that was Hala's capital city. Even though he was sweating, Peter had a big smile on his face as he walked towards the planet's largest spaceport.

His current mission was going better than expected. It was always a gamble to go into business with a race as self-interested as the Kree, but the money was good, and he was enjoying being a hero for a change. Instead of his usual 'job' of being chased across the galaxy by someone who had accused him of something he may or may not have actually done, this time he was acting as a freelance defense network advisor following a series of intergalactic combat triumphs that had surprised even him. He could get used to being on this side of the law.

The defense network upgrade had been Ronan's idea, and the Kree leader had reached out to Star-Lord first, impressed by Quill's escapades during the seemingly never-ending conflicts that had been raging across the galaxy for the last several weeks. Months? Years? Peter wasn't even sure anymore. It felt to him like he'd been jumping from massive battle to massive battle lately, and he was glad they were finally over.

In a few minutes, he'd be meeting up with the Space Knights, an elite group of cyborg warriors created on Galador to battle a race called the Dire Wraiths.

Peter had faced off against a Dire Wraith once in a dark alley back on Earth. It hadn't been the prettiest confrontation in his life, but he'd come out victorious (and covered in Dire Wraith guts, but that was a whole other story).

After this job on Hala, he was going to finally take some time off. He had more than earned a little peace and quiet. And money. Well, he hadn't exactly earned the money just yet, but he was pretty darn close.

"Quill!"

Peter looked over and saw Ten-Cor approaching. The Kree suns reflected gently off her blue skin and Peter found himself smiling. She'd become a good friend in the last few weeks, and he really enjoyed spending time with her while they worked together on Hala's defense network.

"I'm impressed," Ten-Cor said, looking at Peter appraisingly.

Peter checked out his outfit and nodded. Yep, this new outfit was pretty sweet—even he had to admit it. He'd recently purchased it on credit from a Kymellian trader on Deneb-7. He'd soon have more than enough to pay him and the Rigellians back. And then some.

"Right? I just bought it. Nicest threads I've ever owned."

Ten-Cor looked at him as if he'd just insulted her puppy. "I was not talking about your clothes, you ridiculous Earthling," she responded, grinning back at him. "I meant this mission. Negotiating a deal between Lord Ronan and the Space Knights. That was no small task."

"Aw shucks," he said.

"Please do not pretend to be humble, 'Star-Lord,' and just admit that you worked your donkey off to improve the defense capabilities of Hala, all for a very reasonable price."

Peter cocked his head at her.

"Donkey?"

"That is the word, is it not? I am still figuring out the nuances of English."

"Donkey works for me," Peter admitted. "I just hope this Galadorian technology does what the Space Knights are promising it will."

"As do I and the rest of the Kree Council. This defense network upgrade will make a significant difference, especially after the damage we have incurred with the ceaseless wars. What it will do for the fleet, the sentries, the surface systems. It is a new day for Hala, and I cannot thank you enough."

"My pleasure," Peter said, tipping an imaginary hat. Confusion creased Ten-Cor's face. Peter started to explain what tipping one's hat meant on Earth, but then stopped. He'd never seen a single Kree wearing a hat, other than the helmets the warrior class donned before battle. "Once today's initial demonstration is over, we can integrate it fully into Hala's grid, and then I can go on vacation."

"Vacation," Ten-Cor huffed. "Such a *human* concept."

"Darn straight," Peter replied.

PETER ARRIVED at the central landing pad on the spaceport rooftop with a full cadre of stone-faced Kree warriors. He grinned at their leader, an especially emotionless man named Tur-Van, who gave no indication that he'd seen the smile or shared in Quill's excitement for the imminent arrival of the Space Knights.

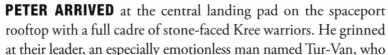

After a moment, the five cybernetic warriors touched down a few feet in front of Peter and the Kree honor guard. Quill wasn't easily awed, and even less likely to show it when he was, but he had to admit to himself that the armored cyborgs were impressive. Each one was a different color, with slightly different armor, and he could practically feel the power radiating from their metal shells. He didn't know a ton about the Space Knights, no one did, but their reputation as fierce fighters seemed well-deserved, at least at first glance.

"Gentlemen!" Peter practically shouted, a little too eager, then toned himself down. "A-hem. My name is Peter Quill, though perhaps you know me as… Star-Lord."

He waited for a reaction. There was none.

Probably because they're cyborgs, he reasoned to himself.

"I'm the Special Advisor to the Kree government," Peter continued. "And I'm pleased to formally welcome you to Hala."

One of the Knights, the silver one, stepped forward, its eyes glowing red. It was the tallest and broadest of them all, and Peter swallowed nervously. He'd gone up against all kinds of enemies, large and small, humanoid and… not-so humanoid, and this was one entity that he was glad was an ally.

"I am Daystar," the Space Knight said, its voice mechanized and completely devoid of emotion. Peter had heard that some of the Space Knights could imitate emotion, but it was clearly not an attribute Daystar possessed. "I serve the Space Knight Restitution Initiative. In my travels across the galaxy, I have heard nothing but positive comments about the Star-Lord."

Aww yeah, Peter thought, nodding appreciatively. Dude already knew my codename.

"We are pleased that the Kree are working with you," Daystar finished.

"Yeah, they're not so bad when they stop fighting the Skrulls for two seconds, amirite?" Peter joked, then realized he was surrounded by a bunch of cyborgs and Kree soldiers, neither of which was known for their sense of humor. The soldiers behind him shifted awkwardly.

"I… suppose," Daystar responded, apparently attempting to process the comment.

Good job, Peter, you're the only person in the galaxy who can make a cyborg feel awkward.

"If Galadorian technology can improve Kree defenses, especially after so many intergalactic conflicts, we are pleased to be of help." Daystar glanced at its companions. "There are not many Space Knights left after our seemingly endless battles with the Dire Wraiths. We appreciate that Hala is one of the most important lines of defense in this quadrant, and we recognize the need to bolster those defenses, for the sake of all innocent life. This technology benefits the Kree Empire, and thus all of us."

Peter fought against an urge to give Daystar a high five.

"I agree wholeheartedly," he said stiffly instead. Just finish this job and then you get to go on vacation, he reminded himself.

There was a long moment of silence and Peter looked around, confused, then realized that everyone was waiting on him.

"Oh!" he said, smiling and holding his arms out. "Okay! Time for the demonstration. Of course."

Peter looked at Tur-Van and nodded. The commanding Kree officer opened a small compartment on the forearm of his armor and punched in a series of commands on a screen hidden there. For a moment, nothing happened.

Uh-oh, Peter thought after almost uttering it out loud.

However, a moment later, a section of the large metal floor began to move nearby, revealing dozens of shadowed figures that grew in clarity as Hala's suns showcased their details.

Another platform below raised the figures fully into the light and Peter smiled at the sight. Fifty huge Kree sentries, fully robotic: silent, implacable, unmoving.

The Space Knights glanced at each other, as if saying, *That's it?*

Peter nodded at Tur-Van again, and the latter punched in another series of commands. The sentries' eyes blazed to life, an eerie green that cut through the intense daylight, and a deep hum filled the air. Peter smiled as he felt the sentries booting up through the ground. There was some serious power being displayed here... and they hadn't even really gotten started.

"Okay, let's go," Peter uttered confidently, and Tur-Van punched in the final commands. The sentries suddenly shot into the air in unison, a perfect and clearly deadly formation. Peter watched the Space Knights' faces and noticed what almost looked like satisfaction flash across their metallic visages.

The sentries performed several complex drills in the sky, showcasing their power and firing capabilities. Several Kree surface-to-air ships also performed impressive moves on the outskirts of the demonstration, further showcasing the Kree's renewed might.

Peter moved forward, removing the most important item of the day from inside his coat. It wasn't large, not much bigger than a cell phone on Earth, but its importance could hardly be understated.

This device, which Peter himself had helped conceive, design and create, would connect the Space Knights to the Kree defense network, allowing the two races to coordinate their moves the next time someone was foolish enough to mount a large-scale attack on multiple star systems. This kind of cooperation was unprecedented for either race, and Peter stood at the center of this groundbreaking moment. He realized he was beaming as he held out the device but just went with the feeling instead of concealing his pride. He'd never been good at shielding his emotions anyway.

"Kree leadership is aware that we will be accessing their mainframe, correct?" Daystar asked mechanically.

"Yep!" Peter responded. "Lord Ronan himself is watching the demonstration from his flagship. I know we can't see him, but I can feel his eyes burning a hole in the back of my neck. Not gonna lie, that guy still kind of scares me!" Peter laughed but the laughter died when the Space Knight just continued to stare at him.

Star-Lord cleared his throat and continued: "We're going to upload your Galadorian upgrades through the lead Kree ships, as well as the sentries that are doing their best to impress you very-difficult-to-impress Space Knights. Then we can run some threat scenarios. Cool?"

Daystar stared at him. An awkward moment of silence stretched out as the air show continued above.

"Would you like to do the honors?" Peter asked, holding the device up in front of Daystar.

Peter had never seen a Space Knight smile, had heard from multiple people on multiple planets that they never showed emotion to outsiders—and probably never showed it, period. But if you'd asked him to place a bet in that moment, he probably would have put down a sizable one that Daystar had must smirked.

But no, that was impossible. It must have been the way the light was hitting the cyborg's metallic face.

"With pleasure," Daystar replied, showing no actual pleasure other than that mirage of a smile.

While the Kree sentries continued their impressive defensive dance above, surrounded by the nimble airships, the lead Space Knight punched a series of commands into Quill's device, connecting his network to the Kree defense system. Daystar cocked his head for a moment, as if he'd heard something in the distance, and then took a step back.

"Connection complete," the Space Knight announced.

"Fantastic," Peter responded.

He let out a long breath. It had worked. Now he could relax.

Finally.

CHAPTER TWO

THE OUTWORLD OF LAMENTIS—AROUND THE SAME TIME

THE TRAIL of dark purple blood shimmered in the snow.

The hunters followed it slowly, gripping their assault weapons tightly in their gloved hands. Everything was silent except for the crunching noises their military boots made while walking through the wintery wasteland.

After a few minutes, the lead hunter, a Chitauri named Kraddus, held up his fist and the party halted noiselessly.

They'd been hunting the family of frost minx for days. The matriarch was wounded— badly, judging by the amount of blood on the ground—but she and her pups were still moving at an impressive clip. The animal's meat was useless, poison to almost every race in the known universe—but the gold and green fur would fetch more than a fair price on Deneb-7.

The hunting party was made up of multiple aliens, and in a different time, they might have found themselves pitted against each other in an intergalactic conflagration. But for now, they all shared a common characteristic that bonded them together despite the intense cold.

Greed.

"They're in there," Kraddus whispered into his headset, pointing his gun at a copse ahead of them. The other hunters nodded, fanning out just liked they'd discussed at the beginning of the hunt.

The guns they clutched were overkill, they all would have admitted that if pressed, but this excursion wasn't about a fair fight. It was about making money and making it as fast as possible.

They'd started the hunt as equals, but since Kraddus had drawn first blood, he was now the unofficial leader, and the other mercenaries grudgingly followed his orders.

Moving forward in a unified semicircle, the hunters entered the small forest. It was even quieter in here, the ground somewhat protected from the constant snowfall by the large, multicolored trees that rose into the sky.

Kraddus continued to follow the blood, clocking the rest of his party in the corners of his eyes. If he could finish the kill by himself, perhaps he could claim a larger portion of the eventual credits.

Or perhaps he would be the only one to leave this deity-forsaken planet after a series of unfortunate but ultimately beneficial accidents. Stranger things had been known to happen to some of his former partners.

He inched forward as quickly as possible without giving himself away to his quarry. *There.* Just behind a small bush and tucked away between two rocks. He could see the animals' breath rising through the branches.

Kraddus glanced over. The other hunters were far enough away that he could finish this—and then maybe finish them. He smiled as he slowly aimed at the small hidden crevice and placed his finger gently on the trigger. It was almost too easy…

The whining sound of an energy blast filled the air, followed a millisecond later by a concussive attack that hit Kraddus square in the chest, throwing him back twenty feet, where he crashed into the snow, his breath ballooning out of his lungs with a pained grunt.

“What in the name of the Celestials…?!” he spat, quickly grabbing his gun from where he’d dropped it and scrambling to his feet.

A lone figure descended from the sky. A woman. Wispy silver hair. Wearing a skintight red-and-yellow suit complemented by a black cape that swirled in the wind as she touched down in front of the rock where the frost minx had been hiding. Kraddus had no doubt the animals were long gone, and cursed his luck, and the woman as well. They’d have to take care of her, then start their hunt all over again.

He blinked snow out of his eyes and got a better look at her. She had what looked like a scar running down the right side of her face, above and below the eye, and the socket there was just a glowing orb. Likewise, two luminous bands were wrapped around each wrist, one of which was still pulsating from the energy attack it had clearly just delivered. It took a second for his brain to register the weapons on her forearms, but then it clicked.

Those were the Quantum Bands.

“Quasar…” he uttered, his stomach dropping.

“Well,” she said, an angry smile appearing on her face, “my friends call me Phyla-Vell, but I don’t think we’re quite there yet.”

The bands were beginning to glow again when Quasar was suddenly hit in the back and sides by multiple energy attacks. The other hunters had completed their circle and were just as annoyed as Kraddus at the loss of their prey.

Phyla-Vell collapsed to the ground, her hands pushing into a pile of snow between two trees, the bands glowing eerily under the white powder.

“More!” Kraddus shouted. “She’s Quasar! If we bring her in… dead or alive… we’ll all be very rich men!”

The other hunters didn’t need to hear anything else. They doubled their attack, moving closer as they did so. Kraddus pulled his trigger with glee, adding to the violent barrage.

Quasar was clearly in pain, but she managed to stand and raise an energy barrier, shielding herself from the assault. Snarling, she took to the air again and fired power beams from both arms, sending two of the hunters crashing into large trees. They landed at the bases of the trunks, unmoving.

The other hunters fired wildly at her, but she moved through the air like she'd been born to it, smashing her energized fists into another hunter, burying him in the snow. Without even looking, she blasted another man behind her and grabbed yet another's weapon as he closed on her, and broke it in half over her knee. She punched the surprised hunter so hard that he spun a hundred and eighty degrees and collapsed onto the snow-dusted ground.

Quasar quickly turned and hit the second-to-last hunter with what could only be described as a 'rope' of energy that lashed out from the Quantum Band on her left hand. It caught the snarling man in his face and sent him snapping back into the shadow of a large tree.

Turning slowly, she faced off against Kraddus, her breathing slow and steady. She'd fought all kind of intergalactic threats since taking on the mantle of Quasar, but this conflict felt particularly satisfying. She'd always despised those who preyed on the weak and innocent.

The Chitauri leveled his weapon, aiming it between her eyes as she walked calmly towards him. At this range, he was confident he could blow the interloper's head clear off, despite her seeming resistance to the earlier attacks.

"Go ahead," she said, her right eye glowing, "Do your w—Arrrrrgh!"

A bolt of pain exploded inside Phyla-Vell's head, making her see literal stars and a very specific planet. The pain was so intense that she fell to her knees and blinked rapidly, trying to clear the unexpected images out of her mind.

"*You must reach him before they do*," a voice intoned within her mind.

She was vaguely aware of the hunter placing the muzzle of his weapon against her temple, but she was unable to do anything about it. Waves of dizziness and nausea racked her body as the images pulsed in and out of her brain. It was almost as if it was a message, an SOS, repeating itself over and over again.

"I'd make more if I brought you in alive," Kraddus said through a cruel grin, "but I'm going to enjoy killing you so much that it's more than worth it."

Just as he started to pull the trigger, a green boot came flying out of nowhere and smashed into his face, throwing him to the ground. His weapon slipped out of his hands and landed nearby.

"What now?!" he shouted, wiping yellow blood from his mouth.

Another woman stood between him and Quasar, dressed all in green, her bald head gleaming softly in the little light that made its way through the gently swaying branches overhead.

"Heather…?" Phyla-Vell whispered, confused, unsure if this was part of the hallucinations that were playing out in her mind.

Kraddus grabbed for his weapon and brought it to bear as quickly as possible. "I don't know who you are, 'Heather,' but I'm sure you will fetch a pretty penny on the slavers' block."

"I am Moondragon," she answered, dodging the hunter's attack, and leveling him with a nasty right hook, sending him back down to the ground a final time. "And I fetch for no man."

Heather Douglas stood for a moment, surveying her surroundings. All the hunters were clearly unconscious, but she reached out telepathically to confirm that none were about to wake up. Satisfied, she quickly made her way to Quasar's side, her knee crunching small sticks and snow as she knelt.

"Phyla, are you okay? Talk to me."

Quasar blinked rapidly as the images finally started to fade.

"I… I don't know what just happened. Something invaded my mind during the battle," she said, allowing Moondragon to help her to her feet. "Whatever it was, it almost got me killed."

"May I?" Heather asked.

Phyla-Vell nodded. Though they were as close as two

people could be, they had agreed early in their relationship that Moondragon would never peer into her mind without her express permission.

Heather placed her hand on Quasar's cheek, more an act of tenderness than a necessity to unlock her telepathic powers, and gently probed.

"Strange," she muttered. "I don't recognize that planet, but I know exactly who spoke to you." She withdrew her mind from Phyla-Vell's. "It was the High Evolutionary."

"Seriously?" Quasar said, starting to feel like herself again. "What is he doing, sending me messages? I mean, I know he's constantly playing dice with the universe, so to speak. But why me? Why now?"

"I... do not know," Moondragon responded. "But I sense no deception in the message. Something is happening. And he needs our help. I just wish I knew where he was trying to send you."

"That's the easy part. That planet I saw was Morag IV." She stared down at the Quantum Bands, which glowed softly. "I'm still getting used to these, but I think you're right. Those images aren't random. I suspect something important is happening there… or is *going* to happen." The bands pulsed brighter, as if responding to her words. "I know we came here for some peace and quiet after everything we've both been through. But we're needed on Morag, Heather. I just don't know why, or what dangers we might face."

Heather took Phyla-Vell's hand in her own.

"Based on what I saw in your mind, what the High Evolutionary said, I agree," Moondragon replied. "I sense that there is someone there who needs our help. Whatever it is, we'll face it together. But first, let's drop these hunters off at the local authorities. If I was a betting woman, I'd guess that these are wanted men somewhere in the galaxy."

Quasar smiled and began gathering the men up in an energy sphere while Moondragon made short work of their weapons, smashing them into so much garbage, which Phyla-Vell then incinerated.

Despite the sunlight that peeked down through the leaves and the sound of the now-safe frost minx skittering in the distance, Phyla-Vell couldn't shake the imagery that echoed in her mind. Something big was on the horizon, something that she suspected could threaten every living thing in the universe.

CHAPTER THREE

THE CAPITAL CITY OF HALA—SEVERAL MINUTES EARLIER

STAR-LORD NODDED his head, satisfied.

Glancing over at the Kree soldiers, who still stared into the sky with blank expressions, he laughed and took a step closer to them. "It's okay, Tur-Van, you're allowed to celebrate now."

None of the Kree soldiers celebrated or indicated that they'd even heard Peter. However, Tur-Van's eyes suddenly widened.

"Quill..." he uttered, his voice barely more than a whisper.

Peter felt his smile fading as he looked up, just in time to witness one of the sentries smashing into a Kree airship, both exploding in a massive fireball. After a moment, the sound of the crash reached the ground.

"What happened?!" Peter shouted at Tur-Van.

The lead Kree soldier flipped open his control module again, and his face quickly went dark. "I'm completely locked out!" He looked up at his fellow soldiers and nodded pointedly as debris began raining down around them. They understood his silent command and scrambled in an orderly fashion, their training kicking in immediately.

"This... this isn't possible," Peter said, looking at the device he had created to initiate the defense grid upload. The screen, which should have been full of data, was blank. "What the hell?" He smacked it against his palm, but the rudimentary fix had no effect. He looked over at Daystar.

"I need you to remove the Galadorian programming from the Kree network *immediately*! I don't know if that was just a one-time error, but we can't—"

"There was no error," Daystar interrupted coldly.

"What are you talking about, 'no error?' Didn't you see what just..."

Peter's words trailed off as he looked at the Space Knights, at the subtle difference in their posture since before the explosion. And their eyes. Their eyes were now practically swimming with what looked like living technology.

"*You*," he spat. "You did this. But why?"

In response, the Space Knights began to flank around Quill, who quickly pulled a communicator out of his inside jacket pocket.

"Ronan! We've been double-crossed by the Space Knights! Shut it down! Shut it all down!"

Daystar's metal hand wrapped around Peter's fingers and crushed, the communicator splintering into pieces. Blood ran down Quill's arm and he screamed in agony, his brain cycling through his next steps despite the pain.

"*Free will* is the error," the metal voice intoned. "You and every other living being will join us. Or die."

"Sounds kinda boring. I'll pass," Peter hissed through the pain, quickly unholstering his laser pistol and shooting Daystar directly in the face. The cyborg stumbled back, releasing Quill's hand, and Star-Lord rolled away, blasting another Space Knight as he made it back to his feet.

"Tur-Van!" he shouted at the Kree warrior. "Target the Space Knights! Maybe if we take them out now, we can avoid any more casualties!"

Tur-Van and his Kree warriors began firing on the Galadorians, but the Space Knights had already started firing on anyone who resisted.

"Destroy any that will not join us of their own free will," Daystar commanded.

"Processing," the other Space Knights said in unison, continuing the carnage.

Quill barreled through the firefight towards the elevator, trying to ignore the throbbing pain in his left hand, shooting the Space Knights when he could get a clear shot. Based on what he was witnessing, he would be outnumbered in a matter of minutes.

A series of explosions above him halted his progress for a moment and he looked up.

"My god…" he uttered.

The sentries were destroying Kree ships en masse now, violent fireballs lighting up the sky as if it were a firework display.

Looking back down, Peter grimaced as he watched Daystar mow down Tur-Van, the Kree's eyes making contact with Peter's before closing in unconsciousness.

In a surprising moment of silence during this sudden warzone, all the Space Knights turned and faced Star-Lord, their hands glowing with deadly energy.

"Yeah, no thanks," Peter said, then slammed through the stairwell door, deciding he didn't want to risk his life by getting into a magnetically supported elevator.

As Quill raced down the steps, shaking his left hand, thanking whatever gods were watching that it had already stopped bleeding and that none of the bones were broken, he chuckled mirthlessly to himself.

"I guess that vacation is gonna have to wait…"

STAR-LORD BURST out on the ground floor, out of breath, laser pistol held in front of him. Sweat ran down the back of his neck and he blinked against the light of Hala's suns, which blazed even brighter than when he'd been on top of the building just minutes earlier.

He hid in a small nook in the facade and inhaled huge gulping breaths, taking in everything around him while he recovered.

The streets of Hala, which only a little while earlier had been in pristine condition, the result of generations of cooperation and governmental spending, were covered in rubble and dead bodies. Dogfights continued to scream overhead but just a glance up confirmed Quill's worst fears: the Kree ships were losing, and losing badly. To their own robotic troops.

Peter took a deep breath—what must have been pure adrenaline making him feel at the top of his game, at least temporarily—and ran out into the maze of concrete. He still wasn't sure what the Space Knights were doing, what possible motive they could have, but he knew he had to get off the planet and reconvene with Ronan. And then hopefully get the hell out of this star system. He'd had more than his fill of battles lately.

AFTER A few relatively uneventful minutes, Peter was stopped in his tracks by the sound of someone calling his name. Weakly, but nearby.

He crouched down low, like he'd been doing repeatedly, just in case a rogue sentry suddenly showed up, then quickly and quietly searched for the voice. After another minute, he found it. Part of him wished he hadn't.

"Ten-Cor!" he yelled, a strained sound, since he was both trying to contain his voice but also unable to control his emotions.

Ten-Cor lay on the ground, her body half buried in rubble, blue blood leaking out the side of her mouth. As Quill approached, she gave him a weak smile, which he tried to mirror. His stomach twisted painfully as he kneeled next to her, started pulling rubble off her.

"You must be... very excited about that... vacation," she managed to say between pained grimaces.

"I am… and you're coming with me," he said, that dumb smile still plastered on his face. He felt like an idiot, helpless, but he kept pulling jagged pieces of concrete off her body.

She placed her hand against his face and he felt its fading warmth, fought back tears. He'd learned a long time ago that tears never helped in life-and-death situations.

"It's okay," she barely whispered, breathless. "I have to go now. But I'll… I'll see you soon, Peter Qui…"

She didn't finish her sentence, her final word falling away into nothingness, and her hand fell away from his cheek, her face going slack, eyes lifeless.

"Damn it," Peter whispered, then closed her eyes. "I'm sorry, Ten-Cor. I'm going to make someone pay for this."

He stood, didn't look at her again, couldn't, and dashed off into the growing shadows of an increasingly chaotic day—and a deeply ravaged city.

STAR-LORD COULDN'T believe his eyes.

The sentries had destroyed every single Kree ship in the planet's atmosphere and were now flying in formation towards the capital's main power generator. Below them, the city burned.

There were way more sentries than Star-Lord had ever remembered seeing. Where had they come from? The other quadrants where they sometimes worked as protectors? Had the Space Knights built more themselves? After what Peter had seen today, anything seemed possible.

Quill wiped the seemingly never-ending sweat from his forehead and watched from his position in the shadowy room with its huge windows. This massive suite, at the top of a military building, had once been an opulent location for the Kree's many celebrations following any number of victories. Now, it was dark and empty except for overturned tables and chairs, multiple windows cracked or shattered entirely. But it gave Peter a bird's-eye view of everything that was happening.

Thankfully, there were no Kree citizens on the streets anymore. He hoped the survivors of the initial assault had found safety in some of the small towns that surrounded the city, or had even made it off-planet. He needed to start thinking about doing the same thing. But first, he wanted to find out what the hell the sentries were doing. And where were the Space Knights? He hadn't seen one in at least an hour. This fact probably should have given him comfort, but it just made him even more nervous than he already had been.

Outside, the sentries continued to mass together above the power generator, huge jags of electricity shooting into the sky through and around them. Quill had to look away several times as the brightness of the energy bursts increased.

As more and more of the robots came together, Peter had a sudden realization.

They were fusing together. Building something.

"This is impossible," he whispered to no one.

Despite their incredible size, strength and battle capabilities, the sentries were relatively simple machines by Kree standards. Their existing technology would never allow them to do what he was clearly witnessing.

Their *existing* technology.

Maybe the Space Knights gave them an upgrade, he thought, shaking his head in disgust and wonder.

The sentries continued to merge as Peter watched, exhausted and helpless.

After a few more minutes, he realized the sentries were collectively forming a tower above the power generator, one that stretched so far into the sky that he couldn't even see the top anymore. Energy radiated up from its newly formed walls, continuing to throw off massive bolts of electricity into the air. He was forced to look away again but tried to keep his eyes on what was happening, knew that something very bad was occurring right in front of him.

Finally, the last of the sentries joined the tower and the energy blasts slowed, and then stopped altogether. It grew eerily quiet on Hala.

"This can't be good," Quill said.

As if in response, a colossal shock wave, seemingly brighter than the Kree suns themselves, burst outwards, bathing the city in a strange glow but also shooting up and into space, and in uncountable directions.

What was left of the windows in front of Star-Lord burst inwards, slicing him open in multiple spots. He screamed and fell to the floor, dragging himself to safety behind one of the overturned tables, streaks of blood spreading out on the floor behind him.

Grunting, he ripped parts of his new clothes into shreds and pressed the cloth against the worst of his wounds. Luckily, the broken glass had missed all his arteries.

"Nope. Not good at all."

CHAPTER FOUR

HEMPSTEAD, NEW YORK, EARTH—AROUND THE SAME TIME

RICHARD RIDER carefully hid his peas beneath the pile of mashed potatoes.

Even though he was in his twenties, whenever he was around his parents, especially back here in this house, he felt like a little kid again. It was somehow both awesome and terrible at the same time.

"I see you," his mom said, not even looking at him. Across the table, his father chuckled and placed a forkful of peas into his own mouth, smiling at his son as he did so.

Richard laughed, too. He'd been attempting this same trick his entire life and had not once been successful. He grimaced and picked a single pea off his plate, forcing it down his throat followed by a giant gulp of milk.

"Gloria, our son has saved the universe more than once. I think he's allowed to go a night without vegetables."

"Charles, even the great and mighty Nova needs his greens," she countered, levelling a loving stare at her husband. "I hear that Thor eats broccoli with *every* meal."

"Oh my god," Richard said, laughing again. It felt good to laugh after what he'd been through. He hadn't seen his parents in months, had been in outer space dealing with a series of intergalactic threats and had barely made it out alive. He'd also witnessed the deaths of the rest of the Nova Corps—*all* of them—and was now the last living Nova. The entire history and knowledge of Xandar, the Nova Corps' home world, was now his constant companion in the form of the Worldmind artificial intelligence. Since the death of the Corps, Richard had been pushing himself harder than ever, trying to prove himself worthy. But now? He was beyond exhausted. He needed bad jokes from his mom more than ever.

"There is *no* way Thor eats broccoli. He's more of a leg of mutton and flagon of ale kind of guy."

"Speaking of which, have the Avengers invited you to be on the team yet?" his father asked, raising an eyebrow. It was a question he asked often, sometimes as a joke, sometimes not. This time seemed to fall into the latter category. "They really could use someone with your speed and power. In fact, just the other day, I was telling Mr. Zito that…"

A loud noise from outside, like a muffled explosion followed by a slight tremor in the floor, caught their attention and Charles's words trailed off into confused silence.

"Get somewhere safe. Now," Richard whispered, grabbing his star-adorned helmet from where it waited on the seat next to him, like a very quiet dinner guest, and placing it on his head. His consciousness instantly connected with the Xandarian Worldmind and his battle armor began unfolding itself onto his body, the three energy plates on his chest immediately pulsing with power.

"Richard… what… what's happening?" Gloria asked as she and Charles backed towards the living room and the basement stairs. Richard knew they had a panic room down there—knew because he and his parents had built it together shortly after he had been given the powers of the Nova Corps by a dying alien. Just in case.

Richard opened his parents' front door and walked through, eyes narrowing at what he found standing on his childhood front lawn.

It was Garthan Saal. A former Nova who had, at one time, also hosted the Worldmind, and had gone insane with grief and power. Richard had heard that Garthan had possibly died during an attack on Xandar, but was relieved to see that wasn't the case.

Saal had fluctuated for years between doing the right thing and crossing the line into questionable behavior. Based on the anger on Garthan's face and his glowing hands, Richard suspected the former Nova wasn't here to join them for dinner.

"Garthan!" Richard said, forcing a smile onto his face. Whatever was happening here, he wanted to de-escalate it immediately. His parents were probably safe in the basement, but he didn't want to take any chances. "I'm so happy to see you. I thought you were dead."

"More like you *wished* I was dead," Saal hissed back. He wore no helmet, and his Nova Corps uniform had been altered, either intentionally or otherwise—now looking battle-damaged and somehow deeply troubling.

Richard kept his breathing even. "What are you doing here? Is everything okay? Anything I can do to help?"

"Everything is *not* okay, Rider! I have been trying to catch up with you since the destruction of the Corps. You do not *deserve* to be the host of the Worldmind! Only *I* am worthy!"

Saal quickly raised his hand and Nova was pummeled by a powerful burst of energy.

Luckily, the attack sent Nova into the street, rather than into his parents' house, and he counted his meager blessings as he got back to his feet as fast as possible.

He quickly accessed the Worldmind's scanning capabilities as Garthan began to run towards him, and read the data that showed up directly in front of his eyes.

Saal's energy levels were higher than seemed possible. If the former Corpsman truly had been following Richard around the cosmos since the destruction of Xander, who knew what kind of upgrades he'd given himself.

"Worldmind, call S.H.I.E.L—" he started to say as Garthan

suddenly rushed at him, faster than he expected, and slammed a fist directly into his face, sending him flying farther down the street and into a fire hydrant—which immediately ruptured and shot water into the air, and all over Richard.

"Great. Mr. Manne's dog loves that hydrant," he groaned, wiping blood from his mouth. "He's going to kill me if I survive this."

Nova quickly blasted what was left of the hydrant, sealing the metal and stopping the flow of water, and then took to the sky, feeling the frustration and anger building. He hadn't had a home-cooked meal, let alone a home-cooked meal with his parents, in forever. And his dad had even made his favorite meal (except for the peas). Garthan Saal had crossed a line.

Hovering several dozen feet in the air, Richard unleashed a blistering blast of energy at his enemy, snarling as he did so. In the past, this amount of power had dispatched more than its fair share of opponents.

The powerful beam encased Saal and everything around him, creating a cloud of pulverized concrete and dirt. When Richard was convinced the former Nova had to be defeated, he let up with his attack and watched as the cloud settled and began to dissipate.

A loud voice suddenly ripped into his mind, and he nearly doubled over in pain from the psychic invasion.

"*Richard Rider. You are needed. Come to me.* Now."

And then it was gone.

As a rattled Nova attempted to regain his wits, Garthan suddenly shot up through the dust and into the sky, and slammed directly into Richard's solar plexus, knocking the wind out of him and pushing them both higher into the atmosphere and the diminishing sunlight of evening.

Richard struggled to catch his breath as Garthan grappled with him, mumbling angrily and getting his hands around Nova's arms and back, and squeezing almost instantaneously. Richard's already ragged breath suddenly vanished altogether, and he quickly started seeing stars as they rose higher into the air, the oxygen in both his lungs and the space around him diminishing rapidly.

I am not *going out like this*, said a voice inside his brain, though it sounded far off, and he wondered if it wouldn't be easier to just go to sleep.

"No!" he shouted, intense energy erupting from the three circular plates in his chest armor, and he threw his arms out with all the strength he had, breaking Garthan's grip. He could feel the rage pulsing through his body.

Nova grabbed his enemy's arm and flew in a lightning-fast circle, evading desperate blows from the disoriented Saal. The helmeted warrior spun faster and faster, and at the apogee of the spin, he hurled Garthan back towards the Earth at blinding speed.

Richard shook his head and watched as the former Nova hurtled downwards, attempting to halt his descent and fly back up towards his enemy.

"Nope. Not happening," Richard said through gritted teeth, and rocketed down towards his adversary.

Just as Saal was starting to take control of his direction, Nova slammed into him, fists first, and sped towards the ground. Every instinct in his body told him to slow down, that he was about to commit very painful suicide. He shut those warnings off and increased his speed.

"You don't... deserve the Worldmind..." Garthan managed to say as the ground grew closer and closer.

On some level, Richard suspected Saal was right, which made him speed up even more.

The two combatants hit the ground with what felt like the force of a megaton bomb, shattering glass for miles in every direction. The road's concrete broke apart and went flying, fragments finding purchase in trees, homes, and anything else that stood in their way.

Slowly, the chaos settled, and silence asserted itself on the scene. All was still for several minutes.

A blue-and-yellow gloved hand rose from the giant hole that now adorned the small town's main street. Richard pulled himself up and collapsed on the road which he had driven since he was sixteen years old.

"Ow," he murmured, staring up at the bright blue sky.

After a moment, he clambered to his feet and looked back down into the hole. Garthan Saal was unconscious but alive.

There wasn't another human in sight, so Richard quickly accessed the Worldmind and did a thermal search. It didn't look like anyone had been killed or even injured by the superhuman crash. A small miracle.

I'll take any miracles I can get, he thought.

The Worldmind suddenly spoke, the sound filling his helmet.

"*S.H.I.E.L.D. agents are en route and will arrive in six minutes. Garthan Saal is uninjured other than superficial wounds, and will not regain consciousness for eighteen minutes.*"

"Great, that's more than enough time for S.H.I.E.L.D. to bag and tag him." Richard thought back to the battle for a moment. "Worldmind, did you... happen to hear that weird voice during the battle?"

"*I heard no voice,*" the Worldmind responded, "*but a set of coordinates deep in space was downloaded directly into my mainframe.*"

"Seriously? How did it bypass your security protocols? Who sent the message?

There was a long moment of silence. The Worldmind was one of the most advanced artificial intelligences in the universe. Nova wasn't used to it being stumped.

"*I do not know the answer to either question,*" it finally replied.

Richard sighed. He wanted nothing more than to go back inside his house and eat those potatoes. Heck, he'd even eat the peas. He hated them with the passion of a million burning suns, but even that was better than what he knew he needed to do.

Something serious was happening out in space. Deep in his heart, he knew it. And he was the last living Nova, which meant it was his responsibility to find out what it was. He owed it to the rest of Corps, to the ones who had not survived.

Taking a last look around at the small town in which he had grown up, and which he still loved, Richard Rider blasted off into the air and was already deep into outer space within a matter of minutes.

GLORIA AND Charles Rider watched as their street appeared on the local news.

A news reporter stood in front of police tape, reporting on what she believed was a meteor strike, while police officers and agents dressed in black worked quickly in the background.

"Do you think we should go up… see if he's doing okay? That explosion was *so* loud. I'm worried," Charles said, nervously picking at his fingernails.

"I… I don't think so," Gloria answered, letting out an exasperated sigh. "He'll be okay. He's always okay. I hope."

The television set suddenly went fuzzy, and a dome-shaped head began to appear behind the snow.

"Is that…?" Charles said.

"Yeah," Nova answered, his ghostly image suddenly appearing on their television set. "Sorry to barge in like this. I needed to hack your cable so I could talk to you."

"Richard!" his parents both shouted.

"Are you okay?!" Gloria said, quickly standing up and stepping closer to the screen.

"I'm a little banged up, but yeah, I'm good. You should see the other guy. Well, I guess you can't. S.H.I.E.L.D. probably already threw him down a hole. I'll check on him when I get back."

"Where are you?" Charles asked, standing next to his wife and putting his arm around her shoulder. They were both trembling.

"I just passed Saturn. Wish I could slow down enough to appreciate how beautiful it is."

"Richard. What's happening?"

"Sorry, Mom. I think I'm just trying to distract myself. Based on the very little information the Worldmind has been able to glean, something serious is happening. Hala—that's the Kree home world—it's gone totally silent. Which means whatever is happening out here is very real, and it's very big. I don't know what I can do, but I have to try. I have to help."

There was a long moment of silence.

"Mom? Dad? I can't see you... are you still there?"

"We're here, Richard," Charles said.

"And we're so proud of you," Gloria added. "Go. Do what you do best. Be a hero, and save the universe."

"And then come home and finish your peas," Charles joked, even though the words were strained in his throat and tears were rolling down his cheeks.

Richard laughed, but it was a sad sound.

"Sounds like a deal. I love both of you."

"We love you, too," they echoed at the same time, their bodies moving even closer together as the image of their son, hundreds of millions of miles away, began to fade.

"Now back to your regularly scheduled programming..." Richard said.

And then he was gone.

CHAPTER FIVE

THE CAPITAL CITY OF HALA

PETER HEARD the Space Knight before he saw it.

He was slower than usual; probably due to blood loss, or maybe he had a concussion (wouldn't be his first), but he somehow still got the drop on the cybernetic warrior, choosing to roll as he fired—which probably saved his life.

As it was, the attack grazed Star-Lord's shoulder but he barely felt it. The pain just joined in with the rest of the bruises and cuts across his body, a surreal mélange of misery that he pushed deep into the back of his mind. He'd been hurt worse before, and he'd probably be hurt worse again.

His blast, however, landed square in the middle of the Space Knight's chest, knocking it back. Before the robot had a chance to recalibrate its attack, Peter fired again, hitting it in the exact same spot, and then pulled the trigger again and again and again until the machine blew apart.

Peter let out a long breath and holstered his laser pistol.

It was time to get the hell off this planet.

As he took a step towards the emergency exit door and more stairs (*Please, no more stairs after this*, he thought grimly), a group of figures appeared in the archway to the next room. It was dark in there, the new arrivals at first existing only as silhouettes. In the amount of time it would take someone to blink, Peter had his weapon back in his hand.

"Okay, nice and easy. Come out into the light."

After a moment they complied, in unison, and he saw their uniforms before he saw their faces. They were Kree soldiers. Battered and dirty, but alive. He let out a relieved breath.

"Thank god it's you. We need to get up to Ronan's ship ASAP—if it's even still there. Then we can hopefully access the data core and pull the plug on... whatever this is."

The soldier in the lead was the first to reach the light and Peter's spirits were lifted even further. It was Tur-Van.

The Kree officer and Star-Lord hadn't been fast friends—far from it; Quill had sometimes wondered if the soldier hated him—but they had a common enemy now.

"Tur-Van! You survived. Like I said, I'm not sure exactly what's happening, but I do know that..."

Peter's words died away as he noticed Tur-Van's eyes. Or his *lack* of eyes.

In their place were hundreds of tiny shards of metal, spliced together, moving, almost as if the technology was alive. It looked like Tur-Van had been eaten from the inside out by a machine. And perhaps he had.

As the other Kree warriors advanced into the light, Peter saw their eyes were all the same. Whoever they *had* been, Quill suspected they were no longer those people.

"We must join together," the Kree officer said, as if to punctuate the fact. His voice was cold, metallic. Yep, that definitely wasn't Tur-Van anymore.

The warrior moved towards Quill and raised his hands. Peter could see small metal filaments extruding from Tur-Van's fingertips, getting longer as the Kree got closer and closer.

"Join us," the metallic voice echoed.

"Uhh... no thanks," Star-Lord replied, and started firing.

He hit two of the soldiers with blasts that should have incapacitated them, but they barely flinched. The attacks revealed circuitry where flesh should have been, wrapped in and around skin and muscle and internal organs.

"That can't be healthy," Quill muttered, continuing to fire.

"If you will not join us, you will die," Tur-Van announced, then tilted his head. The gesture must have been some kind of message, because his soldiers opened fire on Star-Lord.

"Damn it!" he shouted. "Haven't I been beat up enough today?!"

He glanced behind him, then at his boots. The Kree soldiers continued to advance, firing indiscriminately. Whatever technology had taken over their bodies also made them less than perfect markspeople. Or maybe their Kree selves were fighting back from within. Whatever the reason, their blasts hadn't killed him. Yet. But it was just a matter of time.

"This is possibly the dumbest thing I've ever done," he said. "And I've done some spectacularly stupid things in my life."

Star-Lord punched a command into his wrist control while ducking beneath a barrage of laser blasts.

And then he jumped out of the hundred-story window.

THE JET boots had been designed for short jumps.

And they'd worked, every time. That Shi'ar jewel heist on Korbin. The hostage rescue on Sszardil. That time he'd helped the Silver Surfer get his board back on Elanis. Those were just the highlights, and the boots had done their job.

But those had been mini flights, often more showboating than necessity.

These jets hadn't been designed for a leap from the top of a perfectly good building.

Star-Lord fell, fast.

For a moment, he was disoriented as the oxygen was sucked from his lungs and every cut and abrasion on his body screamed out in protest. Then his mind cleared, and he realized he only had about thirty seconds to live unless he acted quickly.

He punched in the secondary commands for the jet boots and they roared to life, fighting a failing battle against gravity. Still, Quill's descent slowed.

He increased the power past the red line, something he had been warned never to do.

"I mean, you could blow your legs off," the Kree salesman had said casually. Peter had rolled his eyes back then. But he wasn't rolling them now.

He started flying slightly forward instead of just plummeting down, and he inwardly celebrated. If he could make it a few more seconds without blowing his legs off…

As the ground continued to approach at a dismaying rate, Peter searched frantically for options. He silently cursed Kree architecture—it was so sleek and angular, nothing to break a fall from an unexpected height.

But then, just as hope started to dwindle, he saw it.

The destruction that had rained down on the city had also provided a glimmer of hope. Down below, jutting out from a jagged hole in one of the buildings across the way, were two large pieces of metal that had once been part of the edifice's infrastructure. More importantly, a series of wires were strung haphazardly between the two steel rods, almost like a net. Or part of one.

Star-Lord steered himself as best he could in that direction.

He knew there were a lot of 'what ifs' at play here. What if the wires snapped as soon as he hit them and he plummeted to his death anyway? What if the wires were electrified and he went out in a literal blaze of glory? What if he hit the wires and they sliced and diced him like a Calurnian steak?

I guess we're about to find out, he thought and increased the rocket boots to full power. He could feel them start to vibrate and he added another 'what if' to the list.

What if I land safely but don't have legs anymore?

Smoke started to pour out of the rockets and then they just…

stopped. He was so close to the wires, but did he have enough momentum?

At least my legs didn't blow up.

He laughed and closed his eyes. This was it.

The landing, if it could be called that, knocked the wind out him, and he felt himself testing the limits of the wires' tenacity.

Okay, I'm still alive, so at least they aren't electrified.

The thought flashed instantly in his mind, and then he realized that the wires had reached their limit and were now snapping him back in the other direction.

His imagination created a scenario where the wires repelled him directly into the side of the adjacent building, where he'd end up like a bug on a windshield back on Earth. Quickly, he opened his eyes and wrapped his arms around the wires, grimaced as they ate into his flesh and drew blood. *More* blood.

But it worked. He bounced harshly and then gently, and then stopped altogether.

Looking down, he realized he wasn't all that far away from the ground, so he pulled out his gun, adjusted the setting with his teeth, and sliced one of the wires. The tension releasing in that one wire, Star-Lord swung to the ground, but lost his footing on impact and tumbled, eventually rolling to a stop, his arms and legs jumbled up in every direction.

"Take *that*, Spidey," he joked, slowly getting to his feet, then limped as fast as possible in the direction of Hala's main star port. He didn't have the launch keys for any shuttles, but he'd been hotwiring spaceships for as long as he could remember.

THE ELEVATOR at the space port was still working.

"Thank god for small favors," he murmured, hitting the button for the launch pad on the roof of the building. Hopefully the ships there were untouched as well.

As Quill ascended, he took deep breaths and looked over his many wounds. Luckily, all were survivable—though he'd be feeling them for a quite a while—and most of the bleeding had stopped. Kree elevator music played in the background, and he rolled his eyes at how bad it was. He'd pay every last galactic credit he owned (which wasn't very many, admittedly) for a little Zeppelin.

Finally, the elevator glided to a halt and the doors opened. He stepped out, pistol at the ready. But the weapon wasn't necessary. The place was a ghost town.

Through the giant windows, out on the launch pad, he saw a number of Kree ships, all of which looked ready to fly. But just to be sure, he sat down at the command computer console and ran a full diagnostic on them. It would take a few minutes, which he didn't love, but he wanted to make sure he got on board a ship that would actually get him out of there in one piece, and as fast as possible. Just because a ship *looked* like it was in good shape, didn't mean it necessarily was.

As he punched keys and scanned data on the main consoles, several other screens caught his attention. They were surveillance feeds, and they showed scenes from across the city. Someone had tuned them to the key spots in the battle that had just taken place.

Quill knew he should ignore them, that he should focus on getting the hell out of there, but he couldn't stop watching.

On one of the screens, Daystar suddenly appeared, on top of the original building where this had all started. His eyes, if they could be called that, were still crawling with that strange living wiring, and he was speaking, his voice amplified to an incredible degree.

"...will join us!" the Space Knight was saying. "There is no need to be afraid! Together, as one, we will make the galaxy safe against the flesh-and-blood virus that has for too long spread their infection from world to world. We are one!" he screamed.

"We are one!" a chorus of voices echoed.

Peter looked at another screen, which showed a street somewhere below the other scene. Gathered there were hundreds, if not thousands, of Kree citizens. Peter leaned in closer and squinted. Yep, all their eyes had been replaced by that wiring, too. Whatever happened, it had apparently consumed the entire city.

"We must join together!" Daystar yelled.

"We must join together!" they agreed.

Giant metallic tendrils, writhing in the dying light of day, suddenly stretched out from the tower that had once been thousands of individual sentries. The tendrils, as big as the largest tree branches Peter had ever seen on Earth, reached out and began entering windows and doors in every building in the city.

"Do not be afraid!" Daystar continued, his voice reverberating all over the city. "We do not wish to destroy you. We wish to *save* you. We wish to save the future. By giving yourselves over to us, you are helping bring order to the universe. And in return, we, the Phalanx, thank you for your sacrifice."

"*The Phalanx*? What the hell is *that*?" Peter mumbled, then realized one of the tendrils was heading straight towards the window.

He'd gotten so caught up in watching the computer screens, watching the invasion that was taking place in real time, it hadn't occurred to him that those metallic probes were probably going to check out this building too. Looking for people to infect.

He stood up, his mind spinning and his body aching, as the tendril exploded through the glass. He only had a matter of moments before he became part of the Phalanx, whatever the heck that was. And he liked his eyes just the way they were, thank you very much.

Quill hadn't finished his diagnostics of the available ships but there wasn't time for that anymore. He just had to go with his gut, pick whichever one seemed sturdy enough to get him off this increasingly dangerous planet.

He burst out onto the launch pad, scanning the ships, running mental calculations on each one without even realizing he was doing so. For some reason, one that he would never be able to articulate, one of the vehicles crystallized in his mind as the obvious choice.

It wasn't the nicest looking, it wasn't the largest, but it had personality—and that went a long way for Star-Lord. After all, he had personality, too.

Behind him, he heard a second window smash open, heard a weird chittering sound that could only be the Phalanx tendril.

"Come on… come on…" he said breathlessly as he punched in the command code to open the vehicle's door. Luckily, the Kree had trusted him enough to give him this kind of data—otherwise, he'd be trading in his eyeballs for some alien wires right about now.

He barreled onto the ship, the terrifying alien noise growing in volume behind him. He ignored it as best he could, slamming down into the seat and punching in codes as fast as his fingers could move. Ten-Cor had been teaching him Kree and he couldn't wait to thank her.

His heart sank as he remembered holding her lifeless body, then pushed the image out of his mind after vowing vengeance against whoever was responsible for the death of his friend.

The door quickly closed and the engines roared to life—those may have been the two greatest sounds he had ever heard in his entire life.

As the ship lifted into the air, Quill saw the tendril shooting towards him out of the corner of his eye. He quickly turned the control stick to the right, causing the entire vessel to shudder as it suddenly swerved, but the tendril shot past, missing its target by inches. He engaged the thrusters and the ship shot up at incredible speeds, shoving Star-Lord back into his seat.

"All right, I'll admit it," he said to the ship. "I'm impressed."

As if in response, the ship beeped back—clearly a warning signal. He scanned the video feeds and saw that the tendril hadn't given up. It was stretching closer and closer, despite the speed of his ascent.

"Unbelievable," he whispered. Then he smiled, punched in a few codes, and sat back in his seat as the stars above started to appear. "Sayonara, sucker."

A single missile shot out from the ship's rear hatch and connected with the tendril seconds later, blowing the upper part of the Phalanx probe into pieces, which rained down all over the capital city.

Star-Lord piloted out of the atmosphere and into Kree space. Or at least, what used to be Kree space.

DAYSTAR WATCHED as the ship disappeared.

"Do not concern yourselves," he said, turning to the other Phalanx-possessed Space Knights. "No matter where he goes, eventually he will join us. They all will. Now, let us continue to prepare the tower for the Master's arrival."

CHAPTER SIX

KREE COMMAND SHIP

ADMIRAL GALEN-KOR was in a bad mood.

He had been part of Kree law enforcement his entire adult life—lived and breathed the laws of his people, protecting them from all threats both foreign and domestic, most notably the Skrulls, a race he could barely stomach.

But those threats seemed almost quaint now, following the catastrophic attack that had just taken place on his home world. He blamed himself. It was his responsibility to protect his planet and his citizens. And he had failed.

Sitting on the bridge of his command ship, his officers scurrying around, trying to find answers, he vowed vengeance on whoever had orchestrated such a deadly blow to a seemingly invulnerable empire.

"Sir!"

Galen-Kor turned to Ko-Rel, one of his younger soldiers. Part of him wanted to kill the cadet for interrupting his brooding contemplation, but he thought better of it. He needed every Kree possible for the coming retaliation. Their ranks had been decimated by the Phalanx.

"Speak."

"Star-Lord just docked in bay seven. The guards there are asking what to do with him."

Quill. So, the human had survived the attack. Galen-Kor felt some grudging admiration and immediately shoved the emotion away. He looked at the data that had come in from Hala. It was dire—but he had an idea.

"Tell Captain Chan-Dar to meet me on the prison level, and have Quill brought there as well," Galen-Kor barked, standing and moving towards the elevator.

"The... the prison, sir?" Ko-Rel asked, clearly confused by the unexpected command.

Once again, Galen-Kor fought an urge to blast the young officer into particles and instead hit the button that would take him to the ship's lower levels.

To Peter Quill. The so-called Star-Lord.

And perhaps to salvation.

PETER FELT like he was going to throw up.

Now that things had slowed down—only momentarily, no doubt—all his many wounds were screaming, not least his injured hand. He was being led to a deep part of the ship, an area that didn't bode well, if you judged these kinds of things by the kinds of Kree soldiers he was seeing. They were grizzled down here. He smiled at them anyway, if for no other reason than to annoy them.

The person leading him was Captain Chan-Dar. He'd met her once, briefly, a few weeks earlier, when he had first arrived on Kree and had begun his work on the security upgrade. That encounter felt like years ago and he wondered if she even remembered him. Not that it mattered. He had a bad feeling about this. And that wasn't even counting the nausea.

"Right in here," Chan-Dar said, stopping at a closed door and nodding at it.

"Please tell me there's a bar in here, or a bed. Or both," he quipped as the doors slid open at his approach. He would have preferred if she had gone in first, but what did it matter at this point? If they'd wanted him dead, they would have blown him to bits when he'd first approached the command ship.

This isn't good, he thought as he took in the room he'd entered. Or more accurately, the hallway. A hallway full of armed guards.

He'd been inside enough cells to know a prison wing when he saw one. So, *that* was the plan. Throw him in the brig for allowing Hala to be destroyed, followed by a big show trial probably, and *then* kill him. In a big, public way. It made sense on some level. And honestly, he was too exhausted to care.

"Okay, which room is mine? Just please tell me it has Wi-Fi."

"None of them," a new voice intoned.

Peter turned and saw a Kree he didn't recognize. But he did recognize the man's insignia—he was an admiral. And the scars on his face made it clear that this Kree had seen battles. A lot of them.

"I am Admiral Galen-Kor. I wish we were meeting under different circumstances. Supreme Commander Ronan speaks highly of you."

"So, you're not going to throw me into prison for… you know… destroying your planet?" Peter asked, even though he knew he shouldn't. But he was genuinely curious.

"The betrayal at the hands of the Space Knights was not your fault, Quill," Galen-Kor said, and Peter suddenly noticed how tired the Kree commander looked. Clearly the last several hours had not been easy for anyone. "You were hired by Ronan himself to help upgrade Hala's defense net. You did your job. No one could have predicted the arrival of the Phalanx."

"What exactly *is* the Phalanx?" Peter asked.

"We… do not know. We're still piecing together information based on what the corrupted Space Knights have been broadcasting, and the information we were able to extract from our central computer network before it was shut down entirely. Right now, pretty much all we have been able to figure out is that they appear to be a techno-organic race—no one knows if they even have corporeal form or if they're more like a virus. But they're intelligent, there's no question about that. It's clear to us, based on everything we've learned, that they infect the populations of worlds, taking over the populace and apparently feeding on people and other energy sources until all of the... *nutrition* is gone. I can only surmise that their ultimate goal is to consume the whole universe."

"Oh," Quill said after a charged moment of silence. "Is that all?"

"We have attempted to breach the defenses they've put in place on Hala, but nothing has worked, and we've only lost more soldiers as a result. Their technology is incredibly powerful and unbelievably advanced. And even if we *could* get through, any sentient being or technology is corrupted and taken over—becoming part of the Phalanx hivemind. They are apparently seeding planets, one at a time. Based on what we've learned, we believe that eventually the consumed planets will be connected to the host via that tower they've created, and at that point, all will be lost."

"Okay, so we just need to figure out who the host is, and then chop off the head of the Phalanx. Maybe literally," Peter mused.

"Exactly," Chan-Dar confirmed. "Which is why we've brought you here."

"I... don't get it."

"The Kree armada, or what's left of it, relies heavily on technology to achieve its goals," Galen-Kor continued, stepping over to a command console. "At least, that's what we've done in the past. Based on the current situation, however, we are at a loss regarding how to proceed. Or we were. I have an idea on how we can maybe save the universe. And I think you're the man for the job."

Peter blinked several times, wondering if he had heard correctly. Everyone continued to stare at him, deadly serious. Yep, he had heard correctly, and apparently Galen-Kor wasn't joking.

"What are you thinking?" Star-Lord asked.

"We need to send a small, tech-limited group of combatants

on a mission to discover the central hub of the Phalanx, and to destroy that hub, its leader, and anything that stands in the way of the completion of said mission."

"Makes sense," Quill mused. "But why not send in your best Kree soldiers?"

"First," Chan-Dar said, stepping forward, "many of our finest warriors were killed or taken by the Phalanx. Second, as one of the Kree officers who trains them, I can tell you that our soldiers are taught to rigidly follow orders, no matter what.

"We need a small, aggressive task force that thinks a little more… *independently*," the Kree Admiral concluded.

"So, you want a bunch of expendable loose cannons, led by a notoriously loose cannon." Peter looked around. "I'm starting to understand why we're in the prison wing."

"We must do anything and everything needed to save the Kree Empire," Galen-Kor confirmed. "We are *all* expendable."

"But some of us are a little more expendable than others, right?" Galen-Kor didn't respond, but Quill saw the stony look in his eyes. "Okay, let's see what you've got."

The Admiral nodded to his subordinate and Chan-Dar punched a complex code into a keypad set into the wall. After a moment, one of the steel doors in the hallway hissed and then began to open. Quill waited, simultaneously nervous and excited to see what kind of deadly warrior would emerge from the cell.

Nothing happened.

Galen-Kor cleared his throat. Chan-Dar rolled her eyes and strode forward, entering the cell in a frustrated huff.

"Wake up!" her voice echoed from within. "It's time!"

"All right, all right," a scratchy, annoyed-sounding voice responded. "No need to be such a jerk about it!"

A small creature slowly ambled out of the cell, scratching its left ear and yawning. Chan-Dar followed, her jaw set, eyes locked on the furry prisoner below her.

"Is that a… *raccoon*?" Peter asked, extremely confused. The Kree weren't known for their sense of humor, but maybe this was a practical joke? Maybe they were just trying to ease some of the tension that had been building since the attack?

"Your first conscript is Rocket. Despite his stature, he has an impressive array of abilities."

"You're gonna make me blush," the raccoon muttered.

"A *talking* raccoon," Quill said, realizing this was no joke.

"Rocket showcases impressive intelligence and tactical ingenuity," Chan-Dar said, rejoining Star-Lord and Galen-Kor, "despite being often foul-mouthed and always belligerent."

"And you should see me at parties," Rocket responded, smiling.

Chan-Dar nodded at one of the Kree soldiers, and Rocket was led to the side of the hallway, where he stood impatiently, watching and waiting.

Chan-Dar punched another code into the keypad on the wall. "Up next is Mantis. You may find her a little… strange. She believes she is the 'Celestial Madonna.'"

"I am *so* not going to make the obvious joke here," Peter said, bumping Chan-Dar's arm with his elbow. She was not amused.

Another steel door whooshed open and a woman with antennae stepped out into the hallway. She was slight and graceful, and Peter had to wonder if the Kree officers had lost their minds. A raccoon and this delicate-looking woman? Not much of a strike force so far.

"Ooooo-kay," he said, his head tilting in confusion. "What's her story?"

"Mantis is one of the most powerful psionics we have ever encountered."

"That's all well and good, but why exactly choose her over a more… classic warrior?"

"She told me about this mission before I had a chance to inform her about it," Chan-Dar answered.

"Fair enough."

As Mantis was led by a Kree soldier past Star-Lord, she looked directly into Quill's eyes and smiled. It was not a comforting smile.

"You will love and you will hate what is to come, Peter," she whispered.

He felt chills run up his back as she was positioned next to Rocket, and Chan-Dar punched in another code.

A third door opened, and after a moment Peter watched as branches appeared, traveling along the floor.

"Uhhh... are you all seeing what I'm seeing?"

"This is Groot," Chan-Dar said simply.

What Quill could only have described as a walking tree came lumbering out of the cell. It was by far the tallest creature in the hallway and its skin was made of wood, its head crowned by small shoots of branch-like appendages. Its eyes seemed kind, which worried Star-Lord immediately.

"It looks... *nice*?" Peter said to Chan-Dar.

"Don't let his current demeanor fool you. He put many Kree soldiers in the hospital when we first arrested him. And many since."

"Hi," Peter said, "I'm Star-Lord."

"I am Groot," the creature responded, its voice low and rumbly. It was pretty much exactly the way Peter thought a tree might sound if it could talk.

"Great to meet you. Are you ready for the mission?"

"I am Groot."

"So you mentioned. Has anyone explained to you how dangerous this is going to be?"

"I am Groot."

"Um... yes. Yes, you are. And you're also quite the conversationalist." He glanced at Chan-Dar as Groot walked past. "This strike team is... *interesting* so far. I'm almost afraid to ask, but who's next?"

"I think you'll find Drax a bit more impressive," the Kree captain said confidently, punching in a new code. Another steel door opened and a green-skinned alien came bursting out. He was large and muscular, his chest and back covered in dark red tattoos.

Drax grabbed the closest Kree warrior by the throat and lifted the choking man into the air, then threw him against the wall, which resulted in an unsettling cracking noise and the man slumping to the ground, unconscious.

Several other Kree guards immediately leapt on top of the muscled prisoner and a chaotic brawl broke out as Drax pummeled his captors mercilessly.

"You told me he had been sedated!" Galen-Kor shouted at his subordinate.

"He *was*!" Chan-Dar barked back.

Drax finished off the last of the guards and rushed forward towards Quill and the two Kree officers. Peter tensed for battle, even though he was exhausted and in a considerable amount of pain. Based on the way Galen-Kor and Chan-Dar were staring at Drax, they hadn't expected to be dealing with any hand-to-hand combat while giving a tour to their guest.

Just as Drax was about to reach them, Mantis stepped forward and gently placed her hand on his shoulder. He flinched at the touch, and turned to face her, rage burning in his eyes, his fist cocked. He was clearly confused when he found himself staring at Mantis, and his slight hesitation was all the time she needed.

She moved her fingers up to his cheek and gently said, "Please calm down, Drax."

The fight left him immediately. His entire body went slack, and he even smiled slightly, staring into Mantis's eyes with what almost looked like affection.

"Get up!" Galen-Kor shouted at the Kree warriors on the floor, and the ones who were still conscious quickly got to their feet, shooting daggers at Drax with their eyes. He didn't seem to notice.

"How long can you keep him like that?" Quill asked his new teammate.

"As long as you need me to," Mantis replied. "He is especially susceptible to my psionic commands."

"Okay, great. I don't want him to be a pushover for the entire mission, but if you could keep him on a mental leash until we take off, I would appreciate it."

Mantis nodded, and Quill turned back to Chan-Dar.

"Is that it?" he asked.

"No," she replied, punching in another code. "There's one more."

A final door opened, and another green-skinned prisoner emerged, though this one looked nothing like Drax. It was a woman, and Peter immediately knew exactly who she was. Her very impressive and very dangerous reputation preceded her.

Gamora. The daughter of Thanos. And one of the most dangerous people in the entire galaxy. Also? She was beautiful. Her dark eyes looked Quill up and down as she pushed past him.

She took her place with the rest of the strike force, and Peter quietly surveyed his team as he did some mental math.

Gamora and Drax would be useful warriors as they tracked down the Phalanx and took them out. Groot was big but also seemed kind and gentle, which was an obvious concern. He'd been worried about Mantis's demeanor, but the way she'd handled Drax made him feel a lot better about having her on the squad. Even the strongest opponent was helpless against a powerful enough psionic. Rocket, however, was probably the one who made Peter most uneasy. Chan-Dar had talked about how brilliant the raccoon was, but he was currently picking his nose and mumbling to himself.

It wasn't the squad Star-Lord himself would have necessarily chosen… but like it or not, this was his team.

And he was going to make the best of it.

CHAPTER SEVEN

KREE COMMAND SHIP—SEVERAL MINUTES LATER

THE ATRIUM was tense.

The strike force stood in a semicircle while Admiral Galen-Kor faced them, grim-faced and tightly coiled. Chan-Dar stood nearby, glancing between her superior officer and the motley collection of individuals that had been thrown together. Surrounding them were Kree soldiers, armed to the teeth.

Mantis had reduced her mental control of Drax, but he was still docile. Regardless, he eyeballed everyone in the room with obvious suspicion.

"So, are we gonna dance or what?" Rocket said, rolling his eyes. "If not, put me back in my cell. I was in the middle of an awesome dream when you woke me up and I wanna get back to it."

"I am Groot."

"See? The talking tree agrees with me."

"You can understand him?" Gamora asked.

"Of course I can," the raccoon said, laughing. "You *can't*? He just said I'm totally right and that I should be the leader of this mission."

Now it was Quill's turn to laugh. "I sincerely doubt he said that."

Rocket sneered and stepped towards Star-Lord, the fur on his back rising. "You questioning me, pink skin?"

"Enough!" the Kree admiral shouted, and everyone in the room went silent. "You are teammates for the foreseeable future. Act like it."

Each member of the task force had a snarky response at the ready, but in what could only be considered a minor miracle, none of them said a word.

"The six of you are not our first choice for this mission, but considering our options, you are absolutely the *best* choice. Now, I know what you're thinking. As soon as you leave, you can find a nearby planet and go your own separate, merry ways. That's what *I'd* be thinking if I were you."

Rocket made a face that seemed to say, *You're not wrong.*

"What I'll tell you is this: good luck finding a planet that hasn't already been infected by the Phalanx, or soon will be. We're hearing reports of infestation across the entire Empire. They may not get you right away… but if something isn't done to stop them, eventually they *will* get you. They'll get *all* of us."

"I'd like to think we're all on board," Quill said, eyeballing his new team. Despite his words, he couldn't get a read on any of them.

"I hope so," Galen-Kor responded. "You will be fitted with the most low-tech weapons possible—nothing with a computer chip or any other technology that the Phalanx can lock on to. You'll be virtually invisible to their scans. I hope. We're also working to cloak your vessel, though we're not sure how effective that will be. Star-Lord has insisted on using the ship that he… *borrowed* from Hala. Which is fortunate, because it's one of our older models, thus easier to recalibrate based on our needs."

"What can I say?" Peter shrugged. "Ship and I bonded. I guess that's what a near-death experience will do."

"You are *so* odd," Gamora muttered.

"*Ship*?!" Rocket said, shaking his head. "You named a spaceship *Ship*?"

"Kinda meta, right?" Peter said proudly.

"Oh good lord," Rocket responded.

Galen-Kor turned to the wall behind him and touched it, causing a built-in screen to suddenly light up. A grainy image appeared after a moment, showing several Phalanx-infested Kree warriors and Space Knights approaching a massive glass tank. Behind the glass was a giant green head that had tentacles jutting out in multiple directions. The tank was flanked by and connected to numerous computer banks, which the compromised Kree were accessing.

"As you all probably know, this is the Kree Supreme Intelligence, the single most important entity on our planet. Normally, I would never show you this image, but it's essential that you understand the gravity of the situation and the importance of what I'm about to tell you. The Supreme Intelligence was created more than a million years ago by our ancestors. Over the past multiple millennia, it has been imbued with the brain power of the greatest, most profound Kree minds, which they agreed to give over at the time of their deaths."

"Grody," Rocket mused.

"I am Groot," the large flora agreed, his wooden face mirroring his friend's disgust.

"Before the Supreme Intelligence was taken captive by the Phalanx," Galen-Kor continued, ignoring the comments, "our holy leader was able to send a message, though it was garbled due to malevolent interference. But enough of the transmission survived to give us hope."

Galen-Kor pressed another button, and a recording filled the room. No one on the strike team could understand the language being spoken but they all recognized the sound of desperation when they heard it.

"What is it saying?" Mantis asked quietly.

"We're not entirely sure," Chan-Dar said, stepping forward and taking her place next to Galen-Kor. "But the Supreme Intelligence seems to have indicated that the best chance of success against the Phalanx is a 'savior' on Morag IV. The message cut off before we were able to learn the nature or identity of this so-called savior, but we were able to triangulate what we believe are general coordinates on Morag based on the message."

"Even though the message was scrambled," Galen-Kor continued, "we have to assume the Phalanx will eventually decode it, if they haven't already. We need you six to get to Morag as fast as possible and find this savior, if it even exists."

"What happens if you got the message wrong? If this savior is, like, a five-year-old kid?" Quill asked.

"Then you'll let us know and we'll figure out a new way forward. If we're still in one piece," the Kree Admiral said quietly. "But intergalactic communication must be kept to an absolute minimum. Every use of technology will be like a beacon to the Phalanx. For all intents and purposes, you are on your own."

"I can live with that," Gamora said with a grim smile.

"Okay, so we need to leave as soon as possible," Quill reasoned. "What's the next step?"

"The next step?" Chan-Dar said, smiling too. "We're going to get you all some new clothes, since we don't want you going on this mission in those prison outfits. And Star-Lord, you need to stop by our medical facility. You look terrible."

"Thanks," Peter responded, frowning. "And after that?"

"Why, weapons, of course," the Kree captain said.

"I knew I liked her," Rocket said, elbowing Groot.

THE KREE weapons room was massive.

"Now this is more like it," Rocket said, whistling in appreciation.

"I am Groot!" his new friend agreed.

The entire task force was now wearing new clothes that suited their upcoming mission, except Groot, who looked just as bemused by everything that was going on as ever.

Peter eyed the high-grade artillery suspiciously. This seemed too good to be true.

"What's the catch?" Gamora asked, echoing Quill's thoughts.

"My apologies," Chan-Dar said, walking down a row of almost comically large machine laser guns. "These weapons are unfortunately too high-tech for your mission. The embedded computer chips could draw the Phalanx to your position if they were within range. No, *your* weapons are back here."

The strike team followed the Kree captain to the back of the large room, the armaments becoming less impressive as they went.

"So, what do you think?" Peter asked Gamora as they walked behind the rest of the team. "Can we pull this off?"

She gave him a moment of side-eye and then turned her head fully towards him. "*You* tell me. Galen-Kor and Chan-Dar seem to think you're the leader here."

"Leader? Me? I… I guess so. It's funny—I haven't been a leader in a long time. Seems like a lifetime ago. I hope I can step up and deliver."

Gamora increased her speed, walking away from the frowning Star-Lord.

"You're not exactly inspiring me with confidence here, Quill."

"Me neither," he muttered.

At length, they arrived in a poorly lit back area. The weapons they had passed were all displayed in pristine racks, painstakingly organized, presumably by Kree grunts—even the ammunition was organized by size.

However, back here, the munitions were *not* impressive. And they were strewn across multiple tables, as if someone had dumped them there in a hurry.

The members of the strike force stared at them with disdain. Rocket kept looking at them, then back at Chan-Dar, then back at the tables.

"This is a joke, right?" the raccoon asked, genuinely perplexed.

"I wish it were," the Kree captain said, circling the tables and facing the strike force. She sighed, worried about what she was seeing. This group was the universe's last hope—and they looked very, very confused. "As I mentioned, you need to bring only what you can carry, and the more low-tech, the better."

"I prefer low-tech," Drax said, an eerie smile crossing his face. He picked up a double-bladed sword, its edges curved and serrated. He hit a button on the wooden shaft and the blades retracted, then hit the button again and the blades appeared again with a satisfying sound. Drax smiled and turned to face his supposed comrades. "I'm going to enjoy this," he concluded.

"Um... Mantis?" Quill whispered near one of her antennae.

"Drax, put those away," Mantis ordered.

He scowled at her but did as she said, hitting the button again and grabbing a long sheath from the table, securing it over his shoulder and chest, and sheathing the wooden shaft across his back. He smiled, clearly enjoying the feel of the weapon against his skin.

"Thank god your mind control is still working on him," Peter said to her.

"I didn't use mind control that time," Mantis admitted.

Star-Lord looked at her appraisingly, then at Drax, who walked over and stood stoically next to Mantis. "Huh."

The rest of the strike force examined their choices without much excitement. Peter picked up twin Kree horseshoe blasters and a belt holster, feeling glad to have fully charged weapons again. Still, looking at the others as they pawed through the weapons with disappointed looks on their faces, he couldn't help but feel like their chances of success were quite low. Chan-Dar's voice, right next to him, shocked him out of his reverie.

"Star-Lord."

"Geez, I didn't even know you were there."

"My apologies. I did not mean to startle you. I just... there is something I wanted to tell you."

"If it's about how risky this mission is, trust me, I already know," he responded darkly.

"No. And in fact, I do not think this mission is hopeless."

He turned to her, surprised. "You don't? Why not?"

"Ten-Cor was a friend of mine," the Kree captain answered, and Quill's gut twisted when he heard his murdered comrade's name. "You did not know her for a long time, but I did. She was an excellent Kree warrior, and more importantly, an excellent judge of character. She *believed* in you. She told me there was much more to you than you let on. And based on what I have observed, I believe the same thing. I just hope you come to see that as well."

Without another word, she approached the rest of the strike team, answering any questions they had. Each former prisoner took a weapon or multiple weapons—except Groot, who watched the proceedings with that same look on his face. He seemed so serene, which made Peter smile but also filled him with absolute dread. What use was a gentle tree creature going to be during a battle?

Come to think of it, could he trust the snarky raccoon? Or a woman who apparently thought she was a celestial goddess? And then there was Drax, who was known for his brutality.

Ten-Cor may have believed in Quill, but Quill wasn't sure he could ever believe in himself enough to save the entire galaxy.

But I guess he was about to find out.

They all were.

CHAPTER EIGHT

ABOARD SHIP—ON THE OUTSKIRTS OF KREE SPACE

"I STILL can't believe you named our ship *Ship*!" Rocket mocked.

"It's not *our* ship, it's *my* ship, since I'm the one who stole it from under the Phalanx's nose," Star-Lord retorted, glancing at his small co-pilot. He wouldn't admit it out loud, but the raccoon could fly. Quill was seriously impressed.

Behind him, Gamora was sharpening one of the two knives she had chosen, the sound simultaneously unsettling and encouraging. Peter had tried talking to her while they were picking weapons—she and Drax were the only ones who had picked both laser and hand-to-hand weapons—but she had apparently been too focused on her selections to respond. Or maybe she was just ignoring him.

On the other side of Gamora sat Drax and Mantis. Drax sat completely still, staring at the back of the seat in front of him, his eyes wide open, while Mantis had her eyes closed and giggled every now and then for no apparent reason. In the back of the ship, Groot had folded himself in as best he could, clearly too large for the space he currently inhabited. Despite this, he didn't seem annoyed whatsoever, which only deepened Star-Lord's concern about the living tree's potential contribution to this mission.

"Whatever," Rocket answered, punching data into Ship's computer console. "As long as it has weapons and gets us to Morag, I don't care what you call it."

They'd been flying for hours, and they were no closer to behaving like a team than when they'd left. If anything, Peter surmised, the tension had only increased in the cramped quarters. He wondered which of these self-serving criminals would turn on him first. After all, he knew how they thought—he'd been a self-serving criminal himself for a while. He put his money on Drax. The minute Mantis was out of psionic range, Drax would probably try to kill them all, and he might just succeed.

The console Rocket was working on suddenly chirped and the raccoon laughed triumphantly.

"Yes!" he shouted, looking over at Quill. "I did it. Found a shortcut to Morag."

"What are you talking about?!" Star-Lord said, his eyes widening in disbelief. He punched codes into the computer but was unable to change their now-altered course. "Rocket, let me back into the system. There's no 'shortcut' to Morag."

"There's *always* a shortcut to *everywhere*, ya numbskull. You just don't know about 'em."

Peter tried again but Rocket had somehow locked him out of the navigation system. He felt the anger rising in him but breathed deeply and felt his body relax after a few minutes. He was the unofficial leader of this group of galactic guardians, as ragtag as they were, and murdering one of them before the mission had even really started probably wasn't the best way to christen the team.

After another hour, Morag appeared on their long-range sensors. Peter grumbled to himself in annoyed admiration—Rocket's shortcut had totally worked. He ignored the fact that the raccoon was chuckling.

"Okay, team, we're going to arrive in about fifteen minutes. Morag is devoid of sentient life. Gamora, can you scan for anything bigger than a breadbasket?"

"A what?" Gamora asked dryly.

"Sorry. Earth-ism," Quill said, turning around in his seat and smiling at her. She didn't smile back.

Gamora sighed heavily, sheathed her blade, and engaged the computer that was built into the ship's wall next to her. After a moment, she said, "There's a lot of ionic radiation in the atmosphere, so it's hard to get a lock on anything. But I *can* tell you that the coordinates Ko-Rel got from the Supreme Intelligence are in the middle of an ocean, so I'm guessing they misinterpreted what he was trying to tell them."

"Great," Peter said, dispirited.

"Hold on," Gamora continued. "I'm getting some strange readings in the northeastern hemisphere. Inside a huge cluster of caves. They're so numerous and deep, the computer can't get a good read on them."

"Also, the computers on this ship kinda suck, so..." Rocket mumbled.

"Hey!" Peter snapped.

"I mean, he's not lying," Gamora countered. "But I think there's something in those caves that doesn't belong on this planet. And whatever it is, it's throwing off incredible energy."

"Okay," Quill said. "Let's set down as close to that cave cluster as possible. But not *too* close. There's no guarantee the Phalanx didn't decipher that message and get here before us."

"Nah," Rocket mused, tapping commands into Ship's computer. "They don't know my shortcut."

"I am Groot," a voice rumbled from behind all of them.

"Thanks, buddy," Rocket said, nodding his head in appreciation.

Star-Lord rolled his eyes and started working on his computer module as well. Rocket had been gracious enough to let him back into the system. He'd have to reconfigure the security protocols while the raccoon wasn't looking—he couldn't afford to be locked out of his own ship during a battle.

Soon, Rocket set them down on Morag, though the planet's intense winds made it a less than pleasant landing.

"Let me out of this tin can!" Drax shouted as soon as the

ship had safely set down. Quill punched in a code and the door opened. Drax burst out into the buffeting winds, disappearing almost immediately.

And that's the last time anyone ever saw Drax, Peter thought.

"Okay," he said out loud, unbuckling and standing up. "Everyone double-check your gear and then let's head out. We have no idea what we're going to find out there. So, stay frosty."

"Earth-ism?" Mantis asked, smiling up at Star-Lord.

"Exactly, Mantis, exactly."

As Peter checked his guns, he allowed himself a smile. Maybe this team was actually going to do it—was actually going to save the universe.

A moment later, Gamora walked up to him and crossed her arms, staring at him with squinted eyes.

"What's up?" he asked.

"You bark orders like you're the leader, but everyone here would gut you just as soon as look at you. So, watch your back, 'Star-Lord.'"

"Oooo-kay," he responded, then watched as she turned and exited the ship, followed by Mantis, Rocket, and finally Groot, who barely squeezed himself out of the door.

Maybe we won't be saving the universe after all, he thought.

"WHERE'S DRAX?"

Peter scanned the bleak, hilly terrain as they marched towards the shadowy caves in the distance. He hadn't seen any evidence that Drax had come this way. Based on what he knew about the grim warrior, Quill wouldn't be surprised if Drax had somehow figured out a way off this planet. Drax was infamous for being highly resourceful, especially in combat situations.

"I cannot sense him," Mantis said. Did she sound… *sad*? Star-Lord wasn't sure, but he really needed her attention fully focused on the mission, not distracted by the absence of the deadly, tattooed warrior.

"Well, I'm sure he'll be back soon. He probably had to go to the bathroom or something," Peter said, not believing his own words.

"Yeah, that makes complete sense," Rocket said, then laughed. Peter frowned.

The five remaining members of the strike force continued their push through the intermittent, blistering winds, toward caves that seemed just as far away as when they'd first left the ship.

After several more minutes, Rocket stopped abruptly, his ears turning slightly, his head cocked.

"What is it?" Gamora asked.

There was a burst of blurred movement and a scaly creature slammed into Star-Lord, knocking him to the ground, hard. His one unholstered blaster went skittering across the rocky landscape. Gamora and Rocket instantly opened fire, but the lasers ricocheted off the creature's scales, one of the misdirected attacks hitting Groot and sending him flying backwards.

"Sorry, buddy!" Rocket shouted.

"I am Groot!" the tree creature called back from where he landed, supine.

"These weapons are useless!" Gamora shouted.

Mantis stepped towards the creature, her fingers at her temples, antennae swiveling. "I cannot get a lock on its mind. It either has natural defenses… or its brain is simply too small."

As the creature's teeth got closer and closer to Quill's face, he got a better look at it. He was barely holding it back and could see that it had multiple eyes that were set deep in its face and a mouth that showcased several rows of razor-sharp fangs. It had six legs: it was using four of them to get a better grip on him, the other two keeping itself planted on the ground, an impressive use of leverage. Gamora was charging forward, her knives drawn, but Peter's hands were slipping on the sleek scales, and he knew she wasn't going to get there in time.

Save the universe? Heck, he couldn't even save himself.

A bellowing war cry suddenly echoed around the battlescape and Drax appeared in the middle of the air, having apparently jumped from a nearby rockface. He had his massive double-bladed sword clutched in both hands and lodged one end of it deep in between the multiple eyes of the dragon-like creature, which screamed in agony, rolling off Star-Lord and facing off against its new enemy.

It drunkenly slashed at Drax with its claws, but he easily dodged the swipes and withdrew the sword he had buried in the creature's skull, and quickly jammed the weapon into its throat, killing it instantly. Drax pulled his weapon from the carcass and wiped the black blood on his pants.

"Drax! You saved my life," Peter said, shocked, getting to his feet.

"Of course I did. You are the leader of this mission."

"But you just… *took off* after we landed."

"I had to relieve myself."

Peter looked over at Gamora and Rocket and waggled his eyebrows. The two of them looked at each other and both rolled their eyes.

"That's right," Quill said, dusting himself off. "I'm the leader of this mission. Thank you, Drax. Now let's go find this savior."

CHAPTER NINE

THE CAVES OF MORAG—TWENTY MINUTES LATER

THEY APPROACHED with caution.

This general location was where the limited computers aboard Ship had indicated there may have been some kind of life form, but nothing was moving anywhere, other than the natural detritus being whipped around by the planet's occasionally intense winds. Peter shook his head, looked around.

"Anyone see anything?"

"I see a giant waste of time," Rocket said and sat down on a large rock, scratching his armpit. "This place is totally deserted. And it has been for centuries."

The raccoon wasn't wrong. Quill had read up on it during the trip here: Morag had once boasted a technologically advanced society, but massive wars—waged over race and religion—destroyed not only every single inhabitant, but also all their impressive architectural achievements. All that remained was a desolate wasteland.

"I… sense something," Mantis said, staring into the distance with a blank look in her eyes.

"Where?" Drax asked, moving closer to her, hitting the button on his weapon once again. The blades sprang out immediately.

"This way," Mantis continued, walking as if blind, her eyes now half-closed. Drax gently took her arm to make sure she wouldn't trip on the many rocks that littered her path.

Peter and Gamora looked at each other and both shrugged. It was comforting to see Drax like this—and also deeply discomfiting.

After several minutes of unsteady, uphill walking, Mantis stopped, as did her compatriots behind her. She closed her eyes fully, her antennae now rotating furiously. The wind had slowed again, causing an unsettling silence to descend.

"This isn't totally creepy," Rocket said.

"I am Groot."

Mantis's eyes suddenly opened, and she pointed at a nearby cave mouth, large but unremarkable. "There!" she said.

"The savior?" Quill asked, stepping forward, raising his gun.

"I don't know," Mantis admitted. "But there is something inside that is radiating incredible psionic power."

"Okay, Guardians, let's take this nice and slow."

"Um, what did you just call us?" Gamora said, walking next to Peter, her own blaster gripped in hand.

"Well… I was thinking that we're… you know… kind of guarding the galaxy, so…"

"So, we're the *Guardians of the Galaxy*? *That's* what you're naming us?"

"Yeah, I guess…? I mean, I don't know," Star-Lord mumbled.

"You are a truly ridiculous human," she said, then fell back, completing the team's protective semicircle as they approached the darkened cave.

Quill sighed, felt his stomach clench as he thought about Gamora, then refocused on the mission. There could be anything inside this cave.

When they were a hundred feet from the opening, Star-Lord halted his troops and grabbed the small but high-powered flashlight from his belt. He clicked it to life and shone it into the cave. He was waiting for a dozen more scaly dragon creatures to come scuttling out, but luckily the cave was empty, except for a single entity. They all stared from just outside the entrance to the dark cavity, not daring to enter just yet.

It was a large, dark cocoon.

"What is *that*?" Rocket said, his patented snark vanishing for a moment.

"I am Groooooot," the tree being practically whistled, obviously impressed by the large structure that was clearly out of place in this desolate cave.

"Could the Kree savior be... *inside* that?" Gamora wondered out loud.

"There is only one way to find out. I will simply cut it open!" Drax exclaimed, rushing forward with his sword gripped tightly in his right hand.

"Drax, no! We don't—" Quill started to say. A massive energy beam suddenly hit Drax square in the chest, sending him flying far into distance, sword still clenched in his fist.

The Guardians stepped back and looked up, towards the source of the attack. A woman in a red outfit with a dark cape and an extremely serious look on her face descended, her right fist and one opaque eye glowing with pure energy.

"Back away from the cave and leave this place. It is under *my* protection," Quasar intoned darkly, landing in front of these new interlopers.

"Yeah, but who's gonna protect *you*?" Rocket said, withdrawing a strange-looking piece of metal from within his tunic.

"Uh, Rocket, what is *that*?" Peter asked, suddenly nervous.

"Just something I borrowed from the weapons room when Chan-Dar wasn't looking."

Rocket pushed a button on the device, and it suddenly made a clacking sound, unfolding itself into a massive energy weapon which dwarfed the raccoon that was currently holding it.

"Heh heh," Rocket laughed, taking aim.

"Rocket!" Quill shouted. "That thing is going to give our location away if the Phalanx are anywhere nearby!"

"Then I'll make this nice and quick!" the raccoon yelled back, firing a volley of massive energy bolts at Quasar, one hitting her in the stomach. She flew back and hit the rockface just above the cave entrance, causing it to shatter and partially obstruct the opening.

Quasar tumbled to the ground but managed to land on her feet, the bands on her wrists glowing with power.

"*That* was a mistake," she hissed.

Quasar formed her energy into a rope and shot it at Rocket, grabbing the massive Kree weapon out of his hands and sending it skittering across the landscape.

"Hey!" the raccoon shouted, clearly offended.

"I have got this," Mantis said quietly, and stepped towards their enemy. Her antennae shivered slightly, and she cocked her head as she stared at Quasar, who suddenly crumpled, grabbing her temples.

"Get… out of… my head!"

"Nice work, Mantis!" Peter said, stepping forward. They needed to subdue this woman immediately, and also destroy Rocket's purloined weapon before things escalated. It was clear she was very powerful, but luckily she didn't have the mental defenses necessary to combat a powerful psionic like—

Mantis suddenly doubled over, shouting in pain.

"What now?!" Peter said, looking around.

A bald woman was approaching slowly, her eyes focused solely on Mantis. "Leave. Her. Alone!" she commanded. Mantis stood up shakily and turned her attention to the new combatant, her antennae pointing directly at this unexpected arrival. The bald woman winced at the mental attack and the two squared off in silent battle.

Recovered, Quasar shot an energy beam towards Rocket, who quickly realized there was no way he could dodge in time.

"Uh-oh," the raccoon said quietly.

At the last possible second, a branch shot out and pushed Rocket out of the way, the attack severing the wooden appendage in half. Groot screamed in pain as he stared at the stump where his arm used to be.

Gamora exploded forward, landing a massive punch to Quasar's jaw, rocking her back on her heels. Quill noted that Gamora could have gutted her enemy but chose not to—Quasar's eyes were normal, weren't metal-enshrouded, which meant she wasn't under Phalanx control. There could be other factors at play here.

Quasar locked eyes with Gamora and a smile played on her face. "I see how it is."

She threw her own energy-encased fist at Gamora's chin, but the latter ducked and landed a boot in Quasar's midsection, momentarily knocking the wind out of her.

"I'm going into the cave to secure the cocoon!" Gamora shouted back to Star-Lord, who nodded, glancing over at Mantis and Moondragon. The two stood stock-still, staring at each other, but a small amount of blood leaked from each of their nostrils.

Quill took aim at Moondragon, but a shout from Gamora distracted him. Looking over, he saw his teammate get hit by an energy blast from Quasar and slam into the rockface next to the cave's half-collapsed entrance.

"Gamora!" he screamed, with more emotion than he expected or intended.

Drax appeared from the direction where he'd gone flying earlier, yelling some kind of warrior curse, and slammed into Quasar, though Peter noticed she threw up an energy shield at the last possible second. He had to grudgingly admit that she was very impressive. She was taking on five-sixths of their team by herself and had barely broken a sweat.

While Quasar and Drax battled each other, Peter ran over to Gamora, who was angrily getting to her feet.

"Are you okay?" he said, looking her over.

"I'm fine. I should have killed her."

"I… don't think so," he responded, looking over at Drax and Quasar. Drax slashed at her frenetically, but Quasar blocked each attack with small bursts of energy, her eyes locked on her enemy's. "Her uniform and those wrist bands are so familiar. I think that's—"

Before Star-Lord could finish his sentence, an immense explosion rocked the entire area, throwing all the combatants to the ground.

Dazed, trying to figure out exactly what the hell was happening, Quill watched as a giant humanoid figure descended from the sky, small circles in the center of its palms glowing, and landed in the middle of what had turned into a massive battleground.

In his peripheral vision, Peter could see everyone scrambling to get to their feet, so he did the same.

Mantis and Moondragon suddenly appeared on either side of him, both wiping the blood from their noses, and he glanced at them, confused.

"Um… hi. What's going on?"

"I believe we have misjudged Moondragon and Quasar," Mantis said, pointing at the shadowed creature that was still hidden within the massive plume of dust it had kicked up with its arrival. "*That* is our real enemy."

"Oooo-kay," Peter responded, smiling sheepishly at Moondragon. She didn't return the grin. "Fine. But who exactly *is* that?"

The rest of the Guardians—and Quasar—emerged from the dust cloud, flanking Star-Lord and the two psionics.

"Heather?!" Drax said to Moondragon, who stared back at him with what looked like anger.

"You two... know each other?" Quasar asked, clearly shocked.

"I do not wish to discuss it," Moondragon replied, her tone clipped.

Peter noticed that Groot's arm was starting to grow back, the small appendage sprouting tiny leaves as it formed.

"That's a *handy* power," he deadpanned.

"Are you ever serious?" Gamora asked.

"Sorry, I make bad jokes when I'm nervous," he responded to her quietly.

As the dust settled, the new combatant began to take shape in their eyes. The creature was holding what looked like a bow in one hand and a hammer in another. Its head was covered by some kind of mask that pointed up on two sides of its head, and there was a star on its chest, with what appeared to be a shield strapped to its back.

"Aw crap," Rocket said, looking around for the weapon he'd smuggled into the mission.

"What's the matter? Or should I be afraid to ask?" Peter asked, squinting at the unmoving figure in the mist.

"I know what that is, and we're in a *lot* of trouble," the raccoon continued, unholstering his relatively low-powered Kree weapon with a depressed sigh. Another moment passed.

"Well?!" Gamora shouted at Rocket. "What is it?!"

"That, ladies and germs, is none other than the Super-Adaptoid."

CHAPTER TEN

"THE SUPER *what*?" Quill said as their enemy stepped out into the murky light of Morag's multiple moons.

It was clearly a robot and it looked like it had been cobbled together with leftover parts from other robots. But it was huge, even taller and wider than Groot, and most disturbingly, its eyes were writhing with Phalanx technology.

"That stupid gun brought it directly to us!" Gamora shouted at Rocket.

"We don't know that!" the raccoon countered. "It might have followed us here!"

"I am Groot!"

"You don't *have* to agree with him, you know!" Gamora reprimanded the tree creature. Groot just shrugged.

"Wait, that looks like..." Quill started to say, tilting his head, confused and a little intrigued by what he was looking at.

"Yep," Rocket confirmed. "It can mimic all the powers of all the Avengers. It may look ridiculous, but that thing is one of the deadliest entities on Earth."

"*All* the Avengers?" Peter said, shocked. "Even, like... Dr.

Druid and Gilgamesh?"

Before Rocket could respond, the Super Adaptoid burst forward at incredible speed, slamming into the group with its arms outstretched, sending them all flying.

"Let me guess," Peter said, picking himself up from the ground as quickly as possible. "Quicksilver."

"Yep!" Rocket replied, shooting the robot repeatedly with his laser pistol. The attack slowed the Adaptoid slightly, causing small burn marks on its silver exterior, but otherwise the robot seemed unbothered. "Gahh! This gun is *terrible*!"

Moondragon and Mantis both stepped forward, hands at their temples like mirror images of each other. After a moment, the Adaptoid let loose with the deadly replica of Thor's hammer, which hit both of them and sent them sprawling before returning to the robot's grasp. Drax was at Mantis's side within moments.

"What happened?!" he shouted.

"It has no brain…" Mantis gasped.

"So our mental attacks were useless," Moondragon finished.

A hole opened up in the Adaptoid's chest and it withdrew an arrow from within.

"Gross," Quill and Rocket said at the same time.

Nocking the arrow at incredible speed, the android released the arrow at Groot, who was charging towards his enemy. The arrow hit the tree creature directly in the chest and at first made no apparent impact, though Groot did stop and look down, then smiled when he saw that no damage had been done. He raised his undamaged arm in a nasty-looking wooden fist.

"I… am…"

The arrow suddenly burst into flame.

"Groooooooooooot!!" he screamed in absolute fear, dropping to the ground and rolling frantically.

"I'll help you, buddy!" Rocket shouted, running over and patting out the flames as best he could.

Gamora appeared behind the Adaptoid, slashing at the android's back with her knife, causing gaping rifts in its armored shell. The creature moved forward in surprise, but the lacerations closed up almost as quickly as Gamora caused them. It turned and stared at her with what almost seemed like anger, then backhanded her with the fist that held the imitation—but still heavy—Mjolnir, sending her stumbling backwards, though she maintained her footing.

She went in for another attack but had to dodge one of Quasar's blasts, which exploded right next to her, also missing the Adaptoid.

"Watch it!" Gamora shouted.

"I had to alter my aim because you were in the way!" Quasar yelled back from where she floated above the fray.

The robot took advantage of the momentary confusion and whipped its circular shield at Quasar, hitting her hard, and sending her towards the ground at an incredible speed. She regained her senses just in time to create an energy shield below her, which diminished the impact only slightly. The shield bounced off a nearby rock and then returned to the Super-Adaptoid's arm, which mechanically replaced it on its back.

Gamora shot the android directly in the head, but the low-energy weapon did nothing more than rock the Adaptoid back, barely, before its fist turned a slight shade of green and landed a massive punch to its enemy, knocking her to the ground.

"Gamora!"

"I… I'm okay," she answered, scrambling away.

"So, this thing can just casually summon Hulk-level strength. Nothing to be concerned about."

"You are our leader, Peter," Mantis said. "You must lead us."

"I'm trying!" he shouted back, though he knew she had a point. But his team was in disarray and the huge robot was now stomping towards the cave and the cocoon within—and perhaps the savior, if such a thing really existed. The Adaptoid wasn't even bothering to try and turn them into Phalanx. It clearly had one mission: get the cocoon and whatever was inside it.

Star-Lord had been a leader, once, but those skills were only memories now, and he felt his confidence falter. Had he made a mistake by accepting this mission, this leadership?

Just as he opened his mouth to utter some semblance of a plan, another eager voice interrupted.

"Assemble *this*!" Rocket yelled from a rocky outgrowth just above the cave entrance. The raccoon had recovered the smuggled Kree weapon, but Peter noticed it appeared slightly different. It almost looked like it had been turned inside out and was somehow even larger than it had been. Had Rocket… *reconfigured* it on the fly, in the middle of a battle?!

"Wait…!" Quill shouted, running forward.

Before Peter could say another word, a cackling Rocket fired just as the android looked up to see what the commotion was.

Two things happened simultaneously: the Super-Adaptoid was hit by an incredibly bright and powerful burst of pure energy from Rocket's makeshift weapon; and the gun itself exploded in a blinding flash, causing a huge amount of rubble to collapse on top of the android. As the dust began to disperse, the smallest Guardian was nowhere to be seen.

"Rocket!" Peter shouted, looking around.

Quill and Gamora carefully approached the pile of rocks, each silently hoping that the Phalanx-controlled Adaptoid had been destroyed by the combination of the blast and the collapse of extremely heavy rocks. Once they were sure, they could search for their missing teammate.

Drax and Mantis joined them, while Moondragon and Quasar stood on the fringes, waiting to see what battle might erupt next. Everyone looked beaten down and exhausted.

"Is it…?" Mantis started to say.

The rocks in front of them began to move, and then exploded outwards as the Super-Adaptoid rose from its would-be grave. It had suffered severe damage that even its formidable healing power couldn't handle, and it looked a little wobbly as it made its way down the pile of rocks towards its adversaries. Despite its compromised condition, its eyes were glowing and it started twirling the hammer in its hand at an incredible speed.

"Here we go again," Star-Lord said, nodding at his team and

gritting his teeth. They might lose this battle after all, but they would go down fighting.

Just as the massive robot was about to let loose with the hammer, a charred wooden appendage appeared out of nowhere and wrapped around the Adaptoid's waist. The robot looked down in apparent surprise despite its otherwise emotionless face, but before it could even turn to its attacker, it was raised off its feet and into the air.

Groot, a portion of his body blackened by the now extinguished fire, stalked closer to their assailant, which was suspended in the wooden creature's extended arm. The Adaptoid began to struggle against its captor, but Groot slammed the robot down against the rocky ground with incredible strength, further damaging the Phalanx lackey. Quill noticed the look on Groot's face and remembered what Chan-Dar had said about the hospitalized Kree soldiers. This was a far cry from the gentle creature Peter had first met.

Groot slammed the Adaptoid down onto the ground again before the robot could retaliate, then again and again and again and again, angrily screaming, "I! AM! GROOT!" as he did so. The other Guardians could feel each impact in their teeth.

Star-Lord lost count of the number of times Groot smashed the Adaptoid onto the unforgiving Morag terrain, but finally all that was left of the android was its head and limbs, scattered across the landscape. Groot withdrew his arm back to its normal length, nodded, and then wandered off, presumably looking for Rocket.

"We need your help to find our raccoon!" Peter shouted at Quasar and Moondragon as Drax kicked at the Adaptoid pieces, nodding appreciatively at Groot's handiwork.

For good measure, Quasar stepped forward and incinerated the damaged pieces, which were literally crawling with living technology, no doubt the remnants of the Phalanx infestation.

"Um... a little help here!" a voice shouted from above just as Quasar was about to take to the air.

Everyone looked up and saw Rocket climbing his way across the nearly sheer rockface. His fur looked singed, and his usual snarky expression had been dulled somewhat when his cobbled-together weapon had literally blown up in his face.

Star-Lord and Quasar locked eyes, then Phyla-Vell nodded and rocketed into the air, gently plucking the frazzled raccoon off the outcrop. She landed, gently placing him onto the ground in front of her.

"I am Groot?"

"Yeah, I'm okay, buddy. But looks like we both got barbecued a little bit there," Rocket said, patting a now-kneeling Groot on the shoulder.

The rest of the Guardians squared off with Moondragon and Quasar.

"I get the feeling that maybe we're on the same side here," Quill said finally, after a tense moment of silence.

"Same here," Quasar replied, smiling. "Sorry about attacking you. It's been a… weird day."

"Tell me about it," Peter said.

"I'm glad we're all getting along now," Gamora said, pointing at the cave opening, which was almost completely covered by rocks following Rocket's impromptu attack, "but what are we going to do about *that*?"

Quasar pursed her lips as she took in the obstacle, her one eye and wrist bands starting to glow.

"No problem," she answered with an assured smile.

"My love… no," Moondragon said, putting her hand gently on Phyla-Vell's shoulder. "We must not risk the cocoon."

"I agree," Mantis said dreamily, her eyes half-shut. "Whatever is inside it is stirring. We must get to it quickly."

Drax rushed forward and picked up a couple of large rocks, throwing them to the side. After repeating this several times, he had barely made a dent in the rubble.

"I can do this!" he shouted, straining with even larger rocks. Quill was impressed by the man's strength, but this would take far too long. The Super-Adaptoid had the speed of the fastest Avengers, which explained how it had gotten here before any other agents of the Phalanx, but it wouldn't be long before others arrived. Gamora locked eyes with Peter and shook her head. She clearly agreed.

Groot suddenly stood up and approached the group, gently parting them with his once again elongating arms as he walked.

"I am Groot," he said sadly, clearly still hurting from the fire. As he stretched his arm out, his hand became larger and larger, and he began scooping huge boulders up from the blocked entranceway, depositing them on either side. His face showed an incredible amount of strained effort, but he worked soundlessly for several minutes, until there was enough room for them to clamber over and through.

Then, Groot passed out.

"Buddy!" Rocket shouted, rushing to his friend's side.

"Is he okay?" Gamora said, stepping next to Rocket, concern creasing her face.

"He's breathing," the raccoon said quietly. "But I don't know if…"

Mantis appeared next to them as well. "I am in his mind, and he is okay. He is just… tired."

"Same," Peter said. "All right, Guardians, let's go find out what's going on with this cocoon. Rocket, stay here and guard Groot."

One by one, they climbed the rubble that still stood in their way, and then made their way into the dark, quiet cave.

CHAPTER ELEVEN

THE COCOON was cracked.

They stood in a semicircle around it, Quasar's raised and glowing fist lighting up the cavernous space. Other than the cocoon and a few dozen stalactites arching down from the ceiling, the cave was entirely empty.

"What exactly is this thing?" Quill wondered out loud.

"And who put it here?" Gamora added.

Moondragon and Mantis stepped forward, flanking the slightly pulsating object. They each placed their hand gently on the cocoon and, after a moment, spoke at the exact same time in a low, hushed tone.

"It is alive. It is not time. But the time has come. It must not emerge and yet it will now see the light of day. It is both savior and destroyer. It is time."

"Worst. Duet. *Ever*," Quill whispered to Gamora. He was surprised and just a little thrilled to see the slightest smile appear on her face at his joke, then vanish as if it had never been there in the first place.

The two empaths placed their other hands on the pulsating

mass and closed their eyes fully, their faces looking strained, sweat beginning to form on their brows. Drax stepped forward with his sword at the ready.

"Let me slice it open!" he shouted, barely containing the excitement on his face.

"No!" Quasar shouted, her Quantum Bands starting to glow brighter.

Quill stepped forward too, and got in between them. The last thing they needed was for another fight to break out. He had no intention of getting buried alive in a Moragian cave.

"Okay, okay, I know we're all looking for answers, but please, let's just give them a minute to communicate with... the savior," he said, turning his Quill charm up as far as possible. It seemed to work, because Drax lowered his sword and Quasar's bands powered down, though there was still enough light emanating from her wrist so they could see what was going on.

"Nice work," Gamora said quietly behind him, sounding genuinely impressed.

He felt his stomach twist but didn't turn around. The two psionics were starting to shake, especially their arms, which seemed glued to the cocoon.

Quasar cautiously stepped towards them.

"Heather?"

"I'm okay... for now..." Moondragon responded, barely getting the words past her clenched teeth. "The power within is... *significant*."

The cocoon began to pulsate with light, slightly at first and then growing quickly in brightness.

"Heather," Phyla-Vell repeated, stepping forward. "I think it's time to let go."

"We... *can't*..." Mantis and Moondragon said at the same time, clearly struggling to withdraw their hands from the cocoon, which began to radiate even brighter.

The two empaths suddenly screamed in pain but were unable to free themselves. They, too, began to glow, their forms being lost within the light of the cocoon.

"Mantis…?" Peter said, stepping closer to her. He barely knew this woman—thought she was odd, to say the least—but she was a part of the team, and he would fight for her.

"No!" Quasar shouted at him, her eye and hands powering up again. "Stay back. I've got this."

Setting her jaw, Phyla-Vell stepped between Mantis and Moondragon and placed a palm on each of their backs. Despite the look of absolute concentration and determination on Quasar's face, after a moment she shook her head angrily.

"It's not working!" she shouted.

"It's… dying…" Moondragon and Mantis whispered at the same time. "Do… something. Please…"

Phyla-Vell lowered her head and closed her eyes, then abruptly screamed as her entire body was engulfed in light.

The Guardians who were present in the cave attempted to watch what was transpiring but it soon grew too bright, and they all turned away. Quasar's scream died away and the cave was bathed in seemingly impossible brightness and silence.

Then an unnatural burst of brilliance exploded outward from the cocoon, freeing the two psionics, and knocking everyone off their feet.

After a moment, the radiance faded, and darkness asserted itself within the cave.

Other than everyone's shocked breathing, all was silent and dark. Then, Quasar held up a glowing fist again. "Is everyone okay?" she asked, blinking as if clearing her senses. "Heather?"

"I'm okay, Phyla. Are *you*? What happened?"

"I'm still getting used to being Quasar, but I tried to absorb all the energy so it wouldn't kill you. I guess it worked."

"The cocoon!" Gamora shouted, pointing at the large object.

Everyone looked and saw that the crack in its surface had grown but its surface color had dulled, blackening as they watched.

"The savior is dying!" Mantis cried.

Before anyone else could move, Drax leaped forward and took hold of the cocoon on either side of the split. He pulled with all his strength—for a few agonizing seconds, nothing happened.

Then there was a deep ripping sound and the crack in the cocoon began to increase in size. Drax yelled determinedly, his massive muscles flexing as he did so.

Finally, the rip increased so much that it ran from the top of the cocoon to the bottom, and Drax fell back, clearly exhausted.

The assembled team watched as a figure slowly slumped out of the cocoon, covered in a mucus-like film. He was tall and his skin was golden, a black skintight uniform covering his chest and legs, with what looked like a glowing lightning bolt pulsating on his chest. His longish hair was golden as well, though lighter than his skin.

"Is that…? Moondragon said.

"Warlock," Gamora answered her unfinished question.

"Who?" Quill asked, looking around, clearly confused.

"Adam Warlock," Moondragon continued. "A being created to be 'perfect,' though no such thing is possible, of course. He has had encounters with Thor, the Hulk, Thanos, and many others. He is a being of incredible power."

"He mostly just looks confused right now," Peter observed.

They all looked back over and saw that Quill was correct. Warlock was sitting up, but his face betrayed absolute befuddlement as he looked at each of their faces.

"It's okay," Quasar said gently, stepping forward, shining more light on him. "You're with friends on Morag."

"That may be *where* I am," he said, his voice cracking from clear lack of use. "But I have no idea *who* I am."

"*That* doesn't seem good," Star-Lord mused.

"I should have recognized this cocoon," Moondragon said, approaching and kneeling next to the dazed man. "Warlock uses it to regenerate after sustaining damage. May I?" she asked Adam, slowly bringing her open hand close to his head.

"I… guess?" he said, still looking confused, and now slightly fearful as well. But he didn't recoil as she placed her fingers against his temple and closed her eyes.

Another long moment of silence filled the cave as they watched the motionless encounter. Mantis shut her eyes as well and Peter wondered if she was listening in on the silent 'conversation' that was happening.

Finally, Moondragon opened her eyes and glanced at Phyla-Vell with a distressed look. "His mind is a complete blank. The memories are in there, deep, hidden, and I cannot access them. Which means he cannot either."

"The cocoon's regenerative process was interrupted during our fight with the Super-Adaptoid," Mantis added, her eyes open now, too. "I cannot access the sealed areas of his consciousness either. His body is healed but his mind is not."

"Correct," Moondragon confirmed, helping Adam to his feet.

"Some savior," Drax said. "He can barely stand."

"The Supreme Intelligence must have had a reason to imply that he's the solution to our little Phalanx problem," Star-Lord mused.

"Are we sure of that?" Gamora challenged. "The message was compromised, and the Supreme Intelligence is known for speaking in riddles at the best of times, let alone during a galactic invasion."

"Hard to argue," Quill conceded. "Look, why don't we get out of this cave and discuss this in the… I don't want to call it 'fresh' air because it's pretty awful out there, too—but let's get out of this cave and see how Groot is doing. Then we can figure out our next steps."

Gamora looked at him with what seemed like even more appreciation for his growing leadership skills, then climbed up the rocks that partially blocked the entrance. After a moment, the rest of the team followed, with Moondragon and Quasar helping Warlock navigate the treacherous path.

Peter took a final glance back at the now completely blackened remnants of the cocoon as Quasar's light faded.

Maybe they had come to the right coordinates. Maybe they had done the right thing by breaking Warlock out after they themselves were responsible for damaging it. And maybe he really was the savior they were all betting on.

That was a lot of maybes.

But for now, *maybe* was pretty much all they had.

CHAPTER TWELVE

"OKAY, WHO is *this* dude?!"

Rocket stared at Adam Warlock with distrust in his tired-looking eyes. Behind him, Groot sat on the ground, contemplating his reunited team with the same kind of gentle tranquility that Quill had seen the first time he'd met the tree creature.

"Amazing," Gamora said, kneeling down next to Groot and looking at where he'd been burned. "The skin… bark?… is almost completely healed. I'm glad you're okay." She patted him gently on the shoulder.

"I am Groot," he responded quietly, appreciatively, smiling and looking Gamora in the eyes.

"I believe this is your savior," Moondragon said to Rocket, helping Warlock sit down on a large rock. "But unfortunately, he has no memory of his life whatsoever, so he is unable to confirm if this might be true."

"Sounds about right," the raccoon replied, shaking his head.

"I am no savior," Warlock said suddenly, his eyes beginning to regain focus and clarity. "I do not know much… but I know that."

"You may or may not be the savior they seek," Moondragon said, "but you are Adam Warlock, and that is no small thing, even if your powers are diminished. Either way, I think finding you, despite the calamitous nature of our meeting, is significant."

"That may be," he said, staring Moondragon in the eyes. "But who is Adam Warlock?"

Everyone waited for Moondragon's words, which came after a thoughtful pause.

"I don't know who Adam Warlock is now," she admitted, "but the Adam Warlock I knew, albeit older than you appear to be, was a hero. A man who fought for the lives and the rights of the weak and the downtrodden."

Warlock held her gaze for a moment longer, then stared down at himself with unrecognizing eyes. He shook his head slightly, looked back up at the stranger standing in front of him.

"I… do not think I am that Adam Warlock at all," he responded quietly.

"Oh great," Rocket mumbled, but quieted after a pointed look from Star-Lord.

"We need your help against the Phalanx, Adam," Mantis said softly, approaching him, her antennae trembling slightly as she did so. "Please. I—"

"No!" Warlock shouted, causing her to flinch. Drax stepped closer and Quill put his hand on his holstered gun. They couldn't afford another pointless battle between allies. Their enemies would probably be there any minute. "Stop pleading. I don't know who any of you are. I don't know what's happening, or what this so-called Phalanx is."

Peter stepped forward, resolute.

"Adam, my name is Peter, and we are the Guardians of the Galaxy."

Moondragon and Quasar looked quizzically at each other but said nothing.

"I don't know how long you've been inside that cocoon, but I'm guessing it's been a little bit. While you were… uhh… cocooning, a technological parasite called the Phalanx invaded this entire region of space and began taking over planets. We believe their goal is the total subjugation of the universe. We were told that a being on Morag was the savior—the person who was key to stopping the Phalanx and saving every single life in existence."

Quill stopped talking and took a deep breath. Adam stared at him quizzically, and for a moment, Peter thought he'd done it. He puffed up a little, proud of himself, until a smile slipped like silver across Warlock's face. It wasn't a kind smile.

"I don't have my memories, but I know enough to be aware that I have suffered in my many lifetimes. I retreated to my cocoon to heal, a time that I earned, and that I deserved. And you, all of you, damaged my resting place with your arrogance and violence. Before I could finish healing. And now you ask me to 'save' you?"

"Well—" Peter started to say.

"Who?!" Warlock interrupted, stepping closer to him. He seemed bigger than before, what seemed like raw energy pulsing beneath his skin. Quill could feel it radiating off the man's body. This was him at low power? Star-Lord knew he had to de-escalate the situation, and quickly. "Who told you that I was a savior?"

"Um… a giant green head called the Supreme Intelligence?"

"That doesn't sound completely insane," he heard Rocket mumble. He ignored the raccoon, kept his eyes locked on Adam's.

Star-Lord stepped even closer so that everyone else was blocked out. For all intents and purposes, it was just him and Adam, the only two people in the entire universe. This was the moment, the reason he had been chosen to lead this mission. That's what he told himself, and he was determined to make it true.

"You know what, Warlock? It doesn't matter who told me. It doesn't even matter if you're the 'savior' or not. What matters is that the entire universe is facing an existential threat, and it's not something you can just run away from. And trust me, I know all about running away from problems. I've done it way too many times. But just because you walk away from us, which you have every right to do, it doesn't mean the Phalanx won't find you. At best, they'll murder you. But far more likely, their technology will infect you and then force you to do things that will make you wish you were dead."

Warlock cocked his head, kept listening.

"So, I'm not telling you to come with us, Adam. You've clearly been through a lot. We all have. But I am asking you to join us. Help us end this threat. Because I get the feeling that we're going to need all the help we can get. You may not be the 'savior.' But we still need you."

The wind howled as the assembled individuals waited for an answer.

At length, Adam Warlock spoke.

"You speak wisely. I don't know who I am. I don't fully understand this threat. But I will join you."

Peter held out his hand, but Adam just looked at it quizzically for a moment. Then some distant part of his brain made a connection, and he shook Quill's hand.

"Now… let's head back to the ship and get out of here before more Phalanx show up!" Peter said, turning to the others.

"We will join you," Moondragon said, noticing Quasar's look of surprise at her words.

"We... will?" Phyla-Vell responded.

"Yes. I wish to speak to you, Peter, while we head back to your ship. If that's okay."

"Um, yeah," Star-Lord responded, just as confused as Quasar, but elated to have more potential allies on their mission. "Let's do it."

QUILL AND Moondragon walked behind the others, the entire crew keeping a brisk pace as they hustled back to Ship.

"I didn't want to say this in front of everyone, but we were sent here by the High Evolutionary," Moondragon said quietly. "To protect the cocoon."

"Whoa," Peter replied, eyes widening. "This day just gets weirder and weirder."

"Indeed. I just wanted you to know. I trust you and I think we need to work together to stop the Phalanx. I believe that Adam may be the key to this, and that both the High Evolutionary and the Supreme Intelligence think the same thing."

"Okay, good to know. So, what do you propose? Ronan is going to want Adam."

"I think it's essential that we do *not* deliver Adam to Ronan," she said, her tone turning sharp. "Even if Ronan has changed somewhat, he is still a highly questionable individual and I do not think he can be fully trusted. No, now that we have Adam, even a diminished one, I think we need to take him to the High Evolutionary, who created Adam."

"Okay," Quill responded, nodding, working the scenario through his mind. "Makes sense. Let's do it. Go team."

"Yes," she responded, moving forward to join Quasar again. "Go team."

STAR-LORD BOOTED up Ship's communications system and punched in the requisite data, and then waited.

"He's gonna kill me," he said quietly to Gamora, who sat next to him. They were already leaving Morag's orbit and heading into space.

"Yep," she confirmed.

"This is Admiral Galen-Kor!" a voice suddenly crackled over the loudspeaker. "This is a secure channel! Who dares contact me?"

"Um... hi, Galen-Kor, this Peter Quill. How are you?"

"Quill! Do you realize you're burning a secure channel? One of the only ones we have left?!"

Gamora raised her eyebrows—*I told you so*—but Peter looked away, focused on his words, and chose them carefully.

"Yes, I know, and I'm sorry. But there have been important developments and I wanted to give you an update."

He heard a long sigh on the other end of the line.

"*Fine*. Go ahead. There have been developments here, too. But make it quick before the Phalanx find and infect us both."

"Our search for the 'savior' turned out to be a bust. No offense to the Supreme Intelligence."

Galen-Kor swore in Kree and Quill took a deep breath, then continued talking.

"We did get a tip that the High Evolutionary may be able to help, so we're just gonna head over to his place and see if he's got any info. Cool?"

"No!" Galen-Kor shouted. "Not *cool*! You need to rendezvous with Lord Ronan's ship immediately. He has captured an individual who is immune to the Phalanx. We have need of your empath."

Quill glanced over at Gamora, who looked just as surprised as he felt.

"Immune?! Seriously?"

"Seriously, Quill. Travel to Lord Ronan's ship as fast as possible. I've already sent the coordinates to your vessel. Galen-Kor *out*."

The line abruptly went dead.

"He wasn't lying," Gamora said, looking at the console in front of her. "I have Ronan's location right here. It'll take a little while to get there but this ship is fairly fast."

Peter turned around where the rest of his new teammates were standing.

"Did you all hear that?"

"Hard not to," Rocket said. "That guy has anger issues."

"While I'm intrigued by this supposed immune individual," Moondragon commented, "it is essential that we return Adam to the High Evolutionary,"

"There is a simple solution," Mantis said. "We must split up."

"What?" Drax said, stepping closer to her. "No, we must stay together."

"As loath as I am to disagree with Drax," Gamora said, "I think he's right. We have no idea exactly what's going on, or where the threat is actually coming from. Splitting up seems like a potentially very costly mistake."

"You can't agree with this plan," Phyla-Vell said, putting her hand on Heather's shoulder.

"I think Mantis is correct," Moondragon said, turning a sad smile on Quasar. "Both destinations are promising if we wish to defeat the Phalanx. We need to strengthen our odds however possible. The only way to potentially save the universe is to split into two teams. Any other decision is simply untenable."

"And what exactly will these two teams look like?" Star-Lord asked, doubt tingeing his voice. They needed a concrete plan. Splitting up felt like the opposite.

Moondragon made eye contact with Mantis, and with Quasar, and then spoke, her tone hushed and solemn.

"I will take Gamora, Warlock, and Drax with me to visit the High Evolutionary. He is an ancient being with incredible knowledge and power. I truly believe he holds a key to stopping the Phalanx. Or at least a *piece* of the key."

"Star-Lord, Quasar, Rocket, and Groot will come with me to Ronan's flagship, to meet this immune individual," Mantis continued. She kept her eyes from Drax's. For his part, he looked stricken by what he was hearing.

"If you ask me, that's a terrible idea," Rocket piped in. "That guy is certifiably insane. I mean, his last name is literally 'The Accuser.'"

"That isn't his last name, Rocket," Peter admonished. "And he's mellowed out lately. A little."

"I am Groot!"

"See? Groot thinks this is crazy, too!" Rocket shouted, shaking his head in disbelief.

Quasar stepped closer to Moondragon, spoke in a hushed tone.

"Heather, you can't be serious. I'm not letting you run across the galaxy with these strangers. We need to stay together."

"They are not strangers," Moondragon said quietly, her face hardening. "Drax is my father."

"*What*?!" multiple people said at the same time.

"It is true," Drax confirmed, staring at his daughter with mixed emotions clearly playing in his eyes. "We have a long, complicated history. One that I do not wish to discuss with anyone."

"We also do *not* have time to talk about this," Moondragon insisted. "And honestly, it is no one's business."

"Fair," Star-Lord said.

Moondragon stepped closer to Quasar.

"I… I didn't know," Phyla-Vell said, shaking her head, confused.

"I'm sorry, Phyla. I'll explain more later, I promise. In the meantime, the last thing I want to do is leave you. But there is no other choice. These two missions are equally important, and each one requires an empath, which means Mantis and I must be the nucleus of each group."

"But I—"

"And you are the strongest of all of us, by far," Moondragon interrupted, pushing a stray strand of hair out of Quasar's eye. "You must protect our new allies. I don't know exactly what's happening, but I do know these exact configurations are our best bet at saving every living creature in existence."

Phyla-Vell set her jaw and looked ready to argue, but then the fight went out of her, and she suddenly hugged Moondragon tightly, soundlessly. She turned and faced the others, her opaque eye glowing slightly.

"I trust Moondragon implicitly. These are two of the most powerful psionics in the universe. If they say this is the plan, then this is the plan. If anyone wants to discuss it further, let's get it all out in the open. Now. The Phalanx could be on their way here as we speak."

Rocket snarled, seemed ready to argue, but then just crossed his arms, defiant but silent. Groot crossed his arms too, tried to mimic Rocket's glare, but it mostly just looked cute.

"Okay," Peter said, as confidently as he could, although he was far from entirely confident about this haphazard plan, "it's settled. We just need another ship. Luckily, I know a nearby system where someone owes me a favor. He has a few extra ships and he'll let me borrow one."

"If he hasn't been taken over by the Phalanx," Gamora observed.

"Yeah, true," Quill breathed, looking at Gamora, realizing again how beautiful she was, even after several scraps. "But let's go give it a shot. The galaxy is counting on us."

PART TWO

THE WRAITH

CHAPTER THIRTEEN

HAROUN, CAPITAL CITY OF REI-UAJ, KREE OUTPOST WORLD—THE DAY THE PHALANX TOOK OVER

WRAITH TOOK no pleasure in killing this latest victim.

Yes, it was a Phalanx-infected enemy, but the man had been Kree once, just like him, and had no control over his own actions. In the final moments, Wraith thought he saw the flicker of independence behind the circuitry embedded in the man's eyes, but perhaps he had projected that, projected whatever sliver of hope still lived within him after a lifetime of pain and conflict.

Hidden within the shadows of an alley, with the planet's near-constant rain washing over him in waves, Wraith lowered the Phalanx-infested corpse to the ground and covered it with whatever refuse lay scattered about. He knew he should destroy the body entirely, that the Phalanx infection still might be able to migrate if it came into contact with the right kind of bio-matter or technology, but he couldn't risk getting caught. He needed to finish what he'd come to Haroun to accomplish, before the Phalanx had even arrived, and then get off this forsaken planet. The invaders had moved fast, had conquered this world—and who knew how many others—faster than any organic threat could have dreamed of doing.

He scanned his surroundings and pulled his striped cloak closer. It was nighttime, and on this cloud-covered planet, night lasted a long time. Good. He worked best in the shadows. That was part of the reason he had been christened with his codename.

Wraith.

At first, he had hated the moniker. Now, he embraced it. It was how he felt. Like a ghost. Not exactly alive. And certainly not fully dead. He wondered if his parents would have approved of him being called that. They had known their son as Zak-Del, though that name had died a long time ago.

He tried to keep their faces out of his head as he climbed the side of the nearest building and hid himself in a corner, out of the rain. He needed rest—just a few minutes. To get his bearings, to dry off a little bit, to figure out his next steps.

But the image of his parents wouldn't leave his mind.

His father, Sim-Del, had once been a celebrated scientist on Hala. And as a result, Zak-Del had enjoyed a magical childhood, an only child whose father was seldom home but whose mother showered him with affection and love, something not all Kree mothers did. He was a sometimes-moody child, despite their immense wealth and stature, but his parents assured him he would grow out of it.

And that did eventually happen, though it was short-lived and on another planet.

Their fortune took a downturn when Zak-Del was ten. His father had been coming home angry, frustrated with the demands of his superiors. Sim-Del had created a new energy source, something that he said could "light the entire galaxy." The Kree government wanted to hand his invention over to the military. He refused.

So, he took his family and left. With what he considered 'his' technology and research. They eventually settled on a planet called Marxhotz in the Bennazar Rift. As angry as Zak-Del and his mother had been when they'd been forced to leave their home by an increasingly unhinged Sim-Del, they were furious to discover that Marxhotz was a barren wasteland.

Zak-Del spent the first week hiding inside their new home, if it could be called that, while his parents screamed at each other. She told her husband that he had gone insane.

But it all changed shortly thereafter, when Sim-Del reconstructed his experiments and activated the energy source, terraforming Marxhotz into a paradise, one small section at a time. After that, Zak-Del and his mother looked at Sim-Del with new eyes. Perhaps he hadn't been so crazy after all.

The next months were even better, in some ways, than the life of luxury that Zak-Del had enjoyed on Hala, and his moodiness was soon a thing of the past. It was lonely at first, but his father built him a companion robot, Saw-Ked, who protected Zak-Del and was his constant companion, at first like a pet and eventually more like a best friend.

And while his house on Hala had been situated in the metal labyrinth of the capital city, his new home was a literal jungle adventure, where he and Saw-Ked would lose themselves for hours at a time discovering new plants, gorgeous streams with plentiful stones upon which to hop from spot to spot, and strange, friendly creatures that seemed to be evolving in front of their eyes, day after day. When Saw-Ked fell into a stream, on one especially eventful day, and short-circuited, a tearful Zak-Del watched as Sim-Del repaired him with the care of a dedicated surgeon. The boy promised to take better care of his friend from then on, and he kept his word. They continued to find themselves lost in adventure and Zak-Del's imagination, these two best friends, one with a heartbeat and one without—but both blessed with a genuine sense of wonder at this new world etched over an old one by rogue Kree technology.

Sitting on this rooftop in Haroun, listening as the water dripped off his clothes and hair onto the roof below, Wraith allowed himself a rare smile. The time with his parents and Saw-Ked on that far-flung planet had been short compared to everything that had come before, and all the suffering after, but those were the most vibrant memories he had. He cherished them, even as the nostalgia wracked his body with almost physical pain. He found himself spiraling back down into the past.

After a short, perfect stretch of time, everything had changed for him again.

Zak-Del and Saw-Ked were returning from yet another day of innocent danger and intrigue when they noticed that a strange ship had landed near their home. Zak-Del tried to make sense of the markings on its side, but Saw-Ked simply ran the data through his sub-processors, then said the last words he would ever speak to his best friend.

"Kree Death Squad."

In the present day, it was easy for Wraith to sit on this rooftop and wish he had simply turned around and run, that he and Saw-Ked had hidden and made a life for themselves in paradise.

But that wasn't what happened.

As quietly as they could, Zak-Del and his robot circled their home, keeping as close to the wilderness as possible. They stopped, hidden behind a massive purple tree, when they saw his parents standing close to each other on the back lawn. In front of them, a Kree officer with a signet ring was talking, though it was too far for even Saw-Ked to hear his words. Behind the officer stood half a dozen Kree soldiers, though their uniforms were different than the ones Zak-Del had seen before. The colors and cut seemed harsher. And the weapons they held at their sides were larger than normal Kree firearms.

Weapons held at their sides.

Maybe Zak-Del had made the wrong assumption. Maybe they were just here to check in, to see how his father's research was going. Just as he started to move forward, to open his mouth and call out to them, Saw-Ked put out a metal arm and stopped his friend. The robot said nothing but shook his head. In his memory, Zak-Del was sure that his friend had looked sad in that moment, but he knew it was impossible. Saw-Ked had not been programmed to feel that kind of emotion.

Perhaps the robot had somehow been able to predict what was going to happen, but seconds later, the man with the signet ring raised his hand ever so slightly, his fingers flicking out. The soldiers raised their weapons in perfect unison. And murdered Zak-Del's parents while the boy watched.

He should have stayed still, kept quiet. But he was ten. So, instead, he screamed. And the man with the signet ring turned and smiled. That smile was burned into Zak-Del's mind, and as it reappeared all these years later, on a rooftop in Haroun, Wraith forced himself to stand up and step back out into the rain. He turned his face up into the storm, closed his eyes, prayed that it would wash away that horrible, haunting smile.

It didn't. The memories kept coming, playing like a film in his mind.

The Death Squad didn't hesitate. They began firing at the boy and his robot, hitting Saw-Ked several times as he shielded Zak-Del. Then he picked up his young charge and ran, faster than Zak-Del knew was possible, towards their home.

The robot burst through the front door, which shattered apart. Inside, it was eerily quiet and still, the table half-set for dinner. Without hesitating, Saw-Ked ran towards the back of the house and jumped down to the basement, avoiding the stairs entirely.

"Where… where are we going?" Zak-Del barely got out, in complete shock. He knew there was nothing down here, other than his father's castoff experiments and some of the boy's forgotten toys.

Saw-Ked didn't respond but they could hear the Death Squad upstairs, searching for them and destroying anything that got in their way. The robot bounded across the cluttered basement and with one hand grabbed hold of a huge, heavy metal cabinet that housed tens of thousands of pages of Sim-Del's documents. Saw-Ked threw it across the room like it was one of Zak-Del's stuffed animals.

The boy was surprised to see a metal door that had been hidden behind his father's cabinet this entire time. The Death Squad heard the crash below and their boots pounded furiously as they ran towards the basement stairs.

Saw-Ked pulled his fist back and punched the sturdy-looking, handle-less door off its hinges. It clattered down another set of stairs and into the darkness of a sub-basement below.

Laser blasts exploded all around them as Saw-Ked once again leaped, this time into blackness. He landed perfectly, overhead lights clicking on as they sensed movement, and the robot continued to hold Zak-Del close. The boy looked around and saw an escape capsule in the middle of the room. Through the capsule's sole window, Zak-Del could see three seats, and nothing else.

As Saw-Ked placed Zak-Del inside as quickly as possible, the boy saw just how damaged his best friend was.

"Come on," he pleaded once he was belted into his seat. "You'll be okay. We just need to get out of here."

Saw-Ked stared into his friend's eyes, his head tilted slightly as he gazed with what seemed like love, and then he was hit by several laser shots at once. The robot withstood the first few and lurched forward as his circuitry began to appear from the smoking holes in his chassis. As one blast hit him directly in the head, his eyes dimmed, but he managed to stumble forward and punch in a few last codes on the computer console in front of Zak-Del. Then he turned and limped towards the Kree Death Squad as the capsule door closed behind him. The Kree soldiers unleashed a barrage of blasts at him as the capsule sealed shut, Zak-Del watching while his robot was cut into pieces.

Tears streamed down his face as the escape ship's thrusters engaged, instantly vaporizing the Death Squad, and launched up and through the house, destroying it entirely as it went. Zak-Del tried to see through his tears if the man with the signet ring had also been killed, pleaded silently for that to be the case, but couldn't see the Kree leader, dead or alive.

Back in the present, Wraith could feel the rain running down his face, a painful mirror of that day all those years ago. Then he shook his head against the memories and opened his eyes. The night was oddly quiet, other than the sound of the storm. This was especially strange after battling Phalanx-infested Kree for the last several hours. For all he knew, he was the last uninfected person in Haroun.

As if in response to his thoughts, a scream cut across the storm.

He was moving before he even realized it. This kind of instantaneous response was the direct result of the never-ending threats he'd been encountering since he was ten years old. He dove off the side of the building without a thought for his own safety.

As he fell, Wraith withdrew the unique weapon that was holstered at his side. It was currently in the form of a gun, but as he held it out, its polymorphic properties engaged and transformed into an energized whip. Wraith flicked his wrist and the whip extended, wrapping around an iron bar jutting out of a neighboring building. He swung to the ground, landing in a crouch, then stood as the whip returned to him as if it had a mind of its own, transforming back into gun. He holstered it and took in the scene before him.

A Phalanx-infested Kree warrior had an uninfected family cornered. A mother, a father, and a daughter. The girl looked to be about eight years old, and her eyes were filled with terror.

"Hey!" Wraith screamed, striding forward, feeling an almost blinding rage building in his body.

The infected Kree's head tilted and then it turned, recognizing instinctively that a more dangerous quarry had just entered the equation. It stalked forward, its technology-ridden eyes locked on Wraith's. The family was frozen behind the Phalanx slave even though they may have been able to escape, clearly just as afraid of Wraith as they were of the original threat.

The infected warrior suddenly started sprinting towards him, its hands extended, small technological tendrils extending from its fingers. Wraith ducked at the last second, withdrawing a nasty-looking blade from where it had been tucked in the small of his back, and slashed the creature's legs, severing its tendons in an explosion of blue blood and circuitry. Despite its efforts, the Phalanx collapsed, still crawling forward, and finally managed to touch Wraith.

The Phalanx reacted with what looked like surprise when the pale warrior wasn't infected. Instead, Wraith reached down and around, and slicing up quickly, separated the abomination's head from its body, launching it several feet away.

Turning around, Wraith stalked over to the still-terrified family. It pained him that they were just as scared of him as they'd been of the Phalanx.

"How are you not infected?" the father asked. "It… it touched you."

"I am immune to infection," Wraith stated simply. "Now come with me. I'll get you out of the city."

After a moment's hesitation, the mother picked up her daughter and the family moved as a single unit behind Wraith towards the edge of town, towards the forest.

Thunder boomed in the distance and the rain increased as they walked. Wraith smiled. The Phalanx didn't seem to like wet weather, which suited him just fine. The harder the sky let loose, the safer he felt.

As he led this terrified family towards the distant trees, he felt himself falling back into the caverns of his own memory.

CHAPTER FOURTEEN

DEEP SPACE—DECADES EARLIER

HE HAD drifted for a long time.

His father had packed the escape capsule for three people, so there were enough nutrient and water packets, and enough digital entertainment, that Zak-Del could survive for years. There was even enough space in there, especially by himself, to do some moderate exercising when he felt his body cramping up. But the vast emptiness of space soon became overwhelming, and even at ten years of age he realized that simply surviving wasn't nearly enough.

However, the day that he found himself caught in the gravitational pull of a wormhole, he wished for the simple boredom of nutrient packets and outdated scripted Kree programs. He also wished for his parents, and for Saw-Ked. Instead, he felt himself being turned inside out as he entered the temporal anomaly and somehow came out on the other side, into what he would later find out was called the Exoteric Latitude.

The denizens of this part of space-time were called the Nameless, former inhabitants of Hala who had also fallen victim to one of the several wormholes scattered across the Kree galaxy.

They had tried to make lives for themselves there, realizing there was no way home despite their repeated efforts, but they had eventually been infected by a race of parasites known as the Exolon.

A terrified Zak-Del was filled with hope when he was rescued by a ship full of Kree, not immediately aware of how strange they looked, only to scream in pain and terror when they immediately plunged a knife into his chest. The Exolon had entered through the wound, and violently converted the boy into one of the Nameless. The virus rewrote his genetic code, making it so that he was susceptible to the Exolon and to nothing else. Both a blessing and a curse, as the alien infection tore away everything he had been and rebuilt him, at least on a genetic level, from scratch. It was the last time he ever considered himself Zak-Del.

While the pain was worse than anything he had ever experienced, and all that was innocent in him died that day, he was rewarded with incredible strength and enhanced healing speed. Additionally, all the pigment drained from his skin, turning him pale with huge dark circles ringing his eyes, like the rest of the Nameless.

As he came of age among the other Nameless, attempting to navigate their cold, harsh society, his sanity teetered on the edge of oblivion, and he would inflict pain on himself just to prove that he was there, that he existed, that he was not a figment of his own imagination. All this before he even turned eleven years old.

If he was honest with himself all these years later, it was the pain and anger caused by his parents' murder that kept him moored in reality during that time. If not for the purity of those emotions, he would have been lost completely and forever in the Exoteric Latitude. He would have been just another one of the Nameless.

Instead, he lived among them, pretended to be just like them, grew stronger, followed their orders while they waged war against the other species in that realm of space-time, until the day he was big and strong enough to confront their leader. Confront and murder him, then take his striped leadership cloak—a cloak that could generate the incredibly powerful polymorphic weapon—as well as his ship. None of the other Nameless intervened. This was the way leadership was passed on from person to person. Through brutal, emotionless combat.

Instead of becoming the new head of the Nameless, he instead turned his back on them, vowing that he would escape the Exoteric Latitude. They mocked him, and part of him suspected they were right to do so—until the day, years later, after he had earned his new name, when he *did* escape, through the only wormhole that could move an object in both directions, and returned to the galaxy in which he had been born.

As soon as he was back, he immediately began his search for the man with the signet ring. And his search had eventually brought him to the city of Haroun. To this small family, so full of fear and hope.

Just as he had once been.

"The Balani Mountains are your best hope for survival," he said to them when they finally reached the forest on the outskirts of the city. "Head in that direction and don't stop until you come across the waterfalls. If you reach those, you'll know that you've made it to safety."

"You should come with us," the Kree father said. "There's nothing left for you… for anyone in Haroun."

Wraith looked at the man, then at his wife and daughter. Their eyes were kind, appreciative. For a moment, he allowed himself the luxury of imagining a future with them in the wilderness of this planet, a new family to replace the one he'd lost, a sibling he'd never had.

But the idea was ridiculous, and he rolled his neck as if to literally shake the thought away. The clues leading to the Kree commander with the signet ring had led him to a particular building in this city, and he had a single, violent mission to accomplish. Nothing else mattered.

Without another word, he turned and walked away. The family watched until he was lost to rain and shadow, and then they themselves hurried into the safety of the trees.

WRAITH DROPPED to the floor silently.

It had been far too easy to break into this command post, but breaking the law was apparently a lot less difficult during an alien invasion. The Kree police and military had withdrawn from the planet almost immediately—leaving their own populace to be infected and taken over by the Phalanx. The Kree were nothing if not efficient.

Wraith made his way down the hallways, slightly unnerved by how dark and quiet it was. He'd been in other military centers like this during his ongoing hunt for vengeance, before the invasion, and they were always bustling with noise and movement. The officers who had abandoned their stations had clearly done so in a hurry. Objects were strewn everywhere, both personal and professional.

The last Kree planet he'd visited, Cyllandra, had been a bloodbath, one in which he took no pleasure. He had just wanted information, had not started the fight. But he had certainly ended it. And he got the information that he'd sought. It was not the location of the man with the signet ring, but yet another clue towards finding him. It was enough. And that clue had led Wraith to this exact building.

Looking through each room, rifling through desks, turning them over violently when they yielded nothing, Wraith soon came to realize that the clue he had killed for may have been false. There was no evidence that the man with the signet ring worked here, that he had ever even been here.

Wraith stood in the middle of a large, dark, circular room at the center of the facility, breathing heavily, a few drops of water still falling from his cloak and onto the newly polished ground. Above him, a skylight let in what little moonlight was able to pierce the wall of storm clouds.

This very spot was his personal dead end. Ever since escaping the Exoteric Latitude, he had followed a series of clues to find the man who had murdered his parents. But now that well had run dry. He would have to start over. In the middle of a massive invasion that had scattered the vast and innumerable divisions of the Kree military across the cosmos. For all he knew, the man with the signet ring had been consumed by the Phalanx or was long dead.

No.

Wraith was the only one who was allowed to kill him. He wouldn't give up, would *never* give up. He would search every inch of the universe if he had to. He would avenge—

A sound pulled him out of his vengeful reverie. Wraith looked up and saw several figures emerging from the shadows, coming from multiple connecting rooms that acted like spokes to the center of a wheel.

A half-dozen Phalanx-infested Kree stepped into the muddy light, technology-infected eyes locked on their prey in the center of the room. He was completely surrounded. And it was his own fault. He had smashed his way through this facility without giving any thought to stealth or safety.

Perhaps he had wanted to be caught. Or maybe he simply desired another bloodbath.

He unholstered his polymorphic weapon, allowed another grin to cross his face.

"Okay," he said quietly. "Let's see what you've got."

The six Phalanx launched forward. Wraith tensed for battle, ready to make his last stand, if necessary, when a series of laser blasts rang out, cutting the Phalanx warriors down from behind. The Phalanx weren't always easy to kill, Wraith knew that firsthand, but the bombardment ended the battle within seconds. He hadn't even fired a single shot.

Smoke and steam rose from the victims' dead bodies, and after a moment a single figure stepped through it, tall and imposing, a silhouette that Wraith knew all too well. He would almost rather have faced the Phalanx than this new entrant into the battle.

"You must be the 'Nameless Kree' I've heard so much about," Ronan the Accuser said, his voice deep and authoritative. He held his massive hammer in his right hand and a dozen elite Kree soldiers appeared, in different corners of the room, their weapons still humming. "I have been hoping to meet you for quite some time."

"I have no quarrel with you, Ronan," Wraith responded, tightening his grip on his weapon. It was powerful, as was he, but this was Ronan and his own personal elite squad. Even Wraith would have trouble getting out of this situation in one piece.

Then again, he loved a good challenge.

"And yet quarrel has found you," Ronan replied, nodding slightly at his troops. They began to move forward but Wraith reacted faster than anyone else in the room could have expected. He shot several of the troops, and then a full-fledged firefight broke out.

"I need him alive!" Ronan shouted, stepping back, smiling. Wraith found it galling how much Ronan was clearly enjoying this.

This elite squad was well-trained, there was no doubt, but Wraith possessed the strength, speed, and healing factor of the Nameless, plus the polymorphic weapon, which even in the hands of a lesser warrior was powerful enough to take on almost any enemy.

He cut through half of them before they could even register what was happening. He had no interest in fighting his kinsmen, wished he could just walk away in peace and continue his hunt for justice, but Ronan had forced his hand. If anyone was to blame for this latest bloodshed, it was him.

The remaining Kree warriors attacked Wraith in close quarters, stabbing and bludgeoning him repeatedly. It hurt, he couldn't deny that, but it just fueled his rage, and he struck back with blows that broke bones and spilled blood, an almost mechanical exchange. He hated seeing the fear in their eyes as they realized what they were up against, that they had survived the rising tide of the Phalanx only to be seriously injured or even killed by someone who had also been born on Hala. Wraith wasn't sure if he hated himself, or Ronan, or the man with the signet ring the most.

His senses went dark, and his arms and legs and the weapon that had become an extension of himself continued their carnage almost of their own volition. When he finally came back to full consciousness and took in the scene before him, he realized there were only two people still standing.

Him and Ronan.

"Impressive," the Kree leader said, still smiling.

"You'll be even more impressed when you're lying on the floor with your soldiers, bleeding out," Wraith intoned, bursting forward with incredible speed, ready to end this and get the hell out of there.

Wraith had been fighting since he was ten, had gone up against foes of all types and sizes, but had never encountered someone who moved as fast or as assuredly as Ronan. He saw the Accuser's hammer coming at his face but watched helplessly as it connected. Blood exploded from his mouth and nostrils, and he was sent flying across the room, where he slammed against a wall and slid down, collapsing in a discombobulated pile on the floor.

The Exolon parasites that pulsed through his bloodstream rushed to counter the immense damage his body had just withstood. He blinked against the pain, taking huge, jagged breaths, unwilling to accept defeat before avenging his parents.

Ronan's domed head appeared hazily above him, that sick grin still plastered there, and Wraith heard the Kree leader's words through the fog that had descended into his brain.

"The Kree Empire thanks you for your sacrifice," Ronan said, then brought his hammer down once again. Light exploded behind Wraith's eyes, and he dropped into the blackest sleep he had ever known.

CHAPTER FIFTEEN

ABOARD SHIP, TRAVELING ACROSS KREE SPACE—
A DAY AFTER LEAVING MORAG IV

PETER QUILL was grumpy.

He had gone along with Mantis and Moondragon's plan back on Morag, but now, sitting in the pilot seat next to an uncharacteristically quiet Rocket on their way to Ronan the Accuser's command ship, he wondered why he hadn't pushed back harder.

Splitting up was always a bad idea. He knew that from all the horror movies he'd watched back on Earth when he was a kid.

But mostly he didn't like being separated from Gamora. Yes, he had just met her. And yes, she didn't seem to especially like him. But unless he was totally mistaken, some kind of spark had passed between them during the battle with Quasar, and then with the Super Adaptoid. It was possible he was imagining things—he hadn't always been the most astute when it came to matters of the heart—but he was pretty sure there was something there.

But what did it matter now? He might never see her again. Now he was the leader of a raccoon, a tree, a woman who thought she was a celestial entity, and someone who had apparently just gotten her hands on the powerful Quantum Bands.

He looked back at the rest of the team.

Mantis sat with her legs crossed, eyes closed, humming. Maybe she was praying (*To herself?* he wondered) or meditating, but her antennae rotated almost constantly, belying her otherwise serene posture. Quasar stared out the window, looking worried and unsure. She may have easily been the most powerful person in their sub-group, but she wasn't exactly filling Peter with confidence in this exact moment.

And Groot sat in his same spot at the back of the ship, a bemused smile on his face. When he noticed Star-Lord looking back at him, he raised a hand and waved gently. If not for the memory of Groot smashing the Super-Adaptoid into scraps, Quill would be worried that the tree creature was woefully unprepared for the next phase of their mission.

Peter turned back around and tried to focus on flying. Ship could have handled that itself, but he needed to occupy his hands and his mind, or he might start questioning the sanity of their actions. What was going to happen once they reached Ronan's ship? Would the Kree high leader blame Star-Lord for what had happened on Hala? After all, it was Quill who had inadvertently allowed the Phalanx to upload into the Kree security system and take over the entire empire.

No, he told himself. He'd been asked to help, had been approved to make those modifications. It wasn't his fault.

The thought echoed in his mind, but it wasn't easy to believe. So, he pushed them aside and instead focused on an image of Gamora. As someone who was half-human, half-alien, Peter had always struggled with emotions. He'd had a rough childhood in some ways—not knowing his father, and suspecting on some level that he was very different to the other kids. But he'd also had a great childhood at the same time—a loving mother who was tough on him when necessary, but also extremely caring when that toughness wasn't the answer.

Her death had almost broken him.

After that, his complicated emotional state only got worse.

He'd always had trouble getting close to anyone else, and now he felt the walls starting to go up around his heart yet again. He fought against that natural instinct, tried to open himself up to even the remote possibility that something could happen.

Yes, he'd had a few romantic relationships over the years, in different parts of the galaxy—but as soon as he felt any kind of emotional attachment start to form, he would find a new mission to go on, telling the other person (and himself) that his destiny was in the stars, not in the arms of another.

But Gamora felt different. On some deep level inside of himself, he just knew it.

He was not pleased with this fact.

"We're almost there," Rocket said, sitting up in his seat and punching codes into Ship's computers.

Quill welcomed the interruption. He checked the readouts and then looked up, squinted out into space. Sure enough, in the distance, he could see an object that was just a little brighter than the others, that emitted light in a way that indicated it wasn't a star or a planet.

Ronan. Just the idea of being in the Accuser's presence again made Star-Lord's stomach turn. Yes, they were allies, but that hadn't always been the case. Quill had been on both sides of Ronan's legendary temper, and neither was what he would describe as a fun experience.

"I can feel his anger, even at this great distance," Mantis murmured, her eyes still closed.

Quasar stood and walked up to the front of the ship, standing between Peter and Rocket. She stared out the window and into the vast sea of stars ahead of them.

"Are you sure this is a good idea, Quill?" she asked.

"Not at all," he answered, then glanced over at her and grinned. She returned the smile and Peter realized for the first time just how young she was. She may have possessed the incredible powers of the Quantum Bands, but this was no hardened warrior. Still, as she turned to look back out into space and he saw her jaw set and her one eye glow ever so slightly in anticipation of the encounter to come, Peter was very happy to have her on his side.

"I am Groot?" came the rumbly voice behind them.

"Yep!" Rocket said, his previous attitude reasserting itself in his voice. "You'll be able to stretch your limbs in a few minutes." He turned and looked at Quasar and Star-Lord. "Limbs. Get it? Heh heh."

Phyla-Vell and Peter sighed at the terrible joke, but then both laughed at the same time. They caught each other's eye, surprised by the sudden burst of mirth.

"I still got it," Rocket said, nodding, pleased with himself.

Quill and Quasar laughed at that, too, hard, and they kept laughing, a combination of genuine amusement and release after a stressful couple of days. Mantis appeared behind them and started chuckling, too. Rocket looked at them, a little confused, then focused back on piloting the ship.

"What are we laughing about?" Mantis suddenly asked, tilting her head, clearly confused. Which made Peter and Phyla-Vell laugh that much harder.

RONAN THE Accuser was not amused.

After his scientists had failed to calculate the properties of Wraith's blood that made him immune to the Phalanx, Ronan's top 'persuaders' had taken turns, attempting to get answers out of Wraith, even simply his real name. But the Nameless Kree just stared them in the eyes as they inflicted pain, barely registering the abuse and never uttering a sound.

And now Star-Lord had arrived on his ship, the very person who had unleashed the Phalanx on the Kree, and thus on the entire galaxy. Yes, it had been inadvertent. And yes, Ronan himself had approved the security upgrade.

But that didn't change the fact that he wanted to take his hammer to Quill's face.

He forced himself to breathe slowly. He had been raised with the mantra that violence could solve all problems and had lived by that code for a long time, but today they faced an enemy against whom violence was only effective to a point. This adversary could turn your own allies and family against you, and jump from defeat to renewed strength without anyone even knowing it had happened. They were unknowable and deadly, and Ronan realized that simple brute force would not win the day.

More than Quill, Ronan needed the empath who was now part of Star-Lord's pathetic little team. He had forgiven Admiral Galen-Kor for assembling a strike force without his permission, especially since Ronan knew their mission was pointless. The idea of a 'savior' on Morag was laughable. Now, however, the Accuser required Mantis to invade Wraith's mind and give him the answers he needed.

It might take time, but Ronan would make Wraith talk. And perhaps scream a little, too.

One of his subordinates, Lieutenant Lur-Yan, approached Ronan where he sat in his command chair. As he snapped out of his reverie, he became aware of the buzz on the bridge as his officers worked hurriedly, attempting to track down information from across the galaxy and stay one step ahead of the encroaching Phalanx. Far too many Kree outposts had gone radio silent, which could only mean that they had fallen to the cybernetic infestation. Time was running out.

"Sir," Lur-Yan said in a hushed tone, "Quill and his team have arrived. Were you aware that one of them is a… tree?"

Ronan gave the lieutenant the slightest side-eye and the officer physically diminished, seeming to shrink into himself. In different times, Lur-Yan would never have made these comments so casually. And in different times, Ronan would have ended the man's life with a single swipe of his hammer for uttering it.

But these were strange days. And Ronan needed every ally he could hold onto. Even Galen-Kor and Chan-Dar, who had gone well outside their purview by engaging with Star-Lord in such a manner. If they all survived this, he would deal with them later.

"Have Quill and his team brought to my audience chamber. I will join them shortly."

"Yes sir!" Lur-Yan practically shouted, then shuffled off. Ronan settled back into the darkness of his thoughts.

The fate of entire Kree empire rested on his shoulders. Perhaps the fate of the universe.

He would not fail either.

STAR-LORD WAS getting antsy.

They'd only been waiting for a few minutes, but it felt like hours. They'd been told that Groot wouldn't fit (which was true), so he'd stayed in the docking bay, along with Rocket, who didn't want to leave his friend and who had apparently pissed Ronan off at some point in the last year or two. The raccoon didn't seem inclined to give details, and Peter didn't push.

Quasar was as tense as Mantis was relaxed. Peter barely knew either of them, and had been at odds with Phyla-Vell not all that long ago, despite their moment of connection back on Ship. He had no idea if Ronan was going to welcome him as a valued ally or try to hit him in the head with that annoyingly large hammer.

Get a grip, Quill, he told himself.

"This was a mistake," Quasar said angrily. "How do we know this isn't a trap? Split us up, then take us out."

"You may not trust me, but I know you trust Heather," Mantis said quietly, placing a hand on Quasar's forearm. Phyla-Vell pulled away abruptly.

"Do not call her that. You don't even know her."

"Our minds may have been in contact for only a short time, but the communication ran deep. She loves you more than you even realize."

"Enough!" Quasar snapped, turning towards Mantis, her eye and fists glowing, just as Ronan entered the room, raising an eyebrow at the confrontation.

"Because of course that's when he walks into the room," Quill mumbled.

Ronan stopped directly in front of Star-Lord, his hammer held taut in his right hand. The Kree leader's face was creased with anger, and he worked his jaw as he stared down at Quill, passing the hammer slowly from hand to hand.

"So," Peter said, "about that defense system upgrade. I—"

"I do not blame you, Quill," Ronan said, and Star-Lord felt about five hundred pounds of tension escape his body. "I blame the Space Knights. And even though they themselves are under the sway of the Phalanx, I will hunt them down and kill them, even if it takes me a thousand millennia. But first, we must destroy the insidious virus that is spreading like wildfire across the cosmos."

"I couldn't agree more," Peter responded, then turned and nodded at his compatriots, silently telling them to step forward, which they did. "I'm not sure if you've all met, but Ronan, this is Mantis and Quasar."

Ronan stared at Mantis with interest, and then glanced at Phyla-Vell, confusion wrinkling his face.

"You are not the Quasar that I know," he said darkly.

"That's right," she said, stepping even closer to the intimidating Kree leader, "I'm even better."

After a tense moment, Ronan barked a single, loud laugh. "Thank you for that, latest bearer of the Quantum Bands. I needed it." Ronan walked across the room and looked out a window into the vastness of endless space, placing his hammer down and leaning it against the wall. His shoulders seemed to sag slightly, though Peter thought he might have imagined that.

"This enemy has been difficult to fight. You destroy two, ten, a hundred, but then a single one of them can infect a thousand more. Our own technology is working against us, and sheer brute force is simply not enough." He turned and faced his three visitors. "I have discovered a being who is immune to the Phalanx. However, we cannot decipher the mysteries of his blood. So, he is being brought here right now. Mantis, I wish you to probe his mind, attempt to discover how and why he is immune."

Mantis stepped forward, her antennae rotating towards Ronan.

"I will do anything necessary to stop these invaders," she said.

"If you do, it will justify you calling yourself the Celestial Madonna," Ronan remarked, looking at her twitching antennae.

"I don't call myself that," she replied, smiling sweetly, "but that is indeed what I am."

"I see," the Accuser said, lifting his hammer back up as the door opened. Two men dressed in hospital garb wheeled an upright surgical table into the room. Their aprons were splattered with blue blood, and the unconscious, gray-skinned man strapped to the table was covered in it as well.

The hair on Peter's neck suddenly stood on end. He knew in that moment that this was about to go very, very badly. Sure enough, Mantis's face turned angry, the first time he'd seen that emotion from her.

"What have you done to him?" she nearly shouted.

"He refuses to talk. We have attempted to persuade him otherwise. It's an ongoing dialogue."

Quasar stepped forward as well, her one eye and wrists starting to glow.

Peter thought about grabbing Mantis and running. Quasar could handle herself against Ronan. Maybe.

Just as Ronan tightened his grip on the hammer that had come into intimate contact with many skulls from many races over the years, there was a trilling noise at the door. He hesitated, then turned away from Mantis.

"What is it?!" he shouted.

Lur-Yan entered, sheepishly, pale. It was clear he would rather be anywhere else in the galaxy.

"High Commander, I apologize profusely for the interruption, but we've just received word that Captain Gen-Vol will be arriving here in a matter of minutes. He said it's urgent that he sees you right away, that he has important information about the Phalanx invasion, and how to possibly stop it."

Ronan took a deep breath, then looked at the two scientists, whose eyes had been glued to the floor.

"Take Wraith back to the interrogation chamber," Ronan said, then turned to Quill and his two allies. "We will continue this conversation when I return. I am hoping, Mantis, that you will see reason. It would be unfortunate if we had a... disagreement about how to handle this."

Mantis began to protest but Quill silenced her with a look. Ronan pointed a finger at Lur-Yan.

"You. Stay here with them, and tell Gen-Vol that I will meet him as soon as he docks."

Lur-Yan saluted and stepped to the side, placing his hand on the firearm at his waist.

Ronan looked at Peter a final time, quiet fury burning in his eyes. "You proved yourself in recent conflicts, and you worked hard with Kree officers to implement what you thought would be a helpful defense network upgrade. For now, I am going to refrain from giving in to my baser instincts. That may change if your empath refuses to help me."

"Understood," Peter responded.

Ronan left, followed by the scientists, who wheeled Wraith out of the room as well. The door shut behind them and an uncomfortable silence filled the space. Lur-Yan eyeballed the three Guardians with as much menace as he could muster.

"If you move," he said, "I won't hesitate to—"

Before he could even finish his sentence, Lur-Yan collapsed to the floor, unconscious.

"That was… unexpected," Peter said.

"I did not like the way he was looking at me," Mantis said, "so I put him to sleep."

"Why didn't you just do that with Ronan?" Quasar asked.

"His helmet shields his mind from me."

"Fair enough. What's next, Quill?"

"Next?" Star-Lord remarked, unholstering one of his weapons. "We get the hell off this ship before Ronan tries to kill us."

CHAPTER SIXTEEN

THE FIBROLI NEBULA—SLIGHTLY EARLIER

GAMORA ANGLED past a huge asteroid, a smooth maneuver that elicited an impressed nod from Drax, who sat next to her in the co-pilot seat.

They'd acquired this new ship on Knowhere shortly after leaving Morag IV. A Badoon mercenary was hiding out there and owed Star-Lord a favor. Of course, it was only 'new' in the sense that it was new to them—it was actually fairly old, damaged, and ugly. But it would get them to the High Evolutionary's base of operations.

Wherever that was.

Despite Moondragon being the one who had insisted, along with Mantis, that they split up, and that their group was heading to meet the mysterious High Evolutionary, a being of incredible age and power, Heather didn't know exactly how to get there. She only had a vague sense from when she'd read Phyla-Vell's mind back on Lamentis.

Of course, Gamora thought as she flew around another series of ship-destroying rocks. The controls on this ship had been sluggish at first but the more she flew it, the more in control she felt, the more the vehicle responded. Quill may have been cocky and annoying, but he'd managed to get them a solid ship immediately, which was no small feat considering the galaxy was currently under attack.

Quill.

She wanted to hate him. She had been surrounded by men like him her entire life. Cocky men who strutted around with all the privilege and callousness their station in life afforded them.

But she had to admit there was something different about Peter. Even from the first moment when she had emerged from her cell on the Kree prison ship, his eyes had surprised her. Perhaps it was something as simple as kindness, not an attribute she had seen in many eyes during her years being raised by Thanos on Titan.

Those years had also closed her heart to almost all emotions that weren't anger or hatred. But something about Quill—his earnest attempts at leadership, his bad jokes, his impressive fighting skills—had cracked open a part of her that she hadn't even known was there.

As the ship exited the asteroid field, Gamora refocused on the mission at hand. No matter what confusing signals her brain, or her heart, was sending her, she had to shut them down immediately. If Mantis and Moondragon were correct—and that felt like a very big if—their actions in the coming hours were one of the keys to saving the universe.

At this moment, however, they were flying directly towards a very large star.

She looked over. Drax didn't seem especially concerned about this alarming development. Glancing back, she saw that Moondragon had her eyes closed—maybe she was sleeping, or ignoring the fact that her apparently estranged father was sitting nearby. The entire situation was very odd. But these were the general coordinates Heather had given Gamora back on Knowhere. That had been enough for Drax, which Gamora thought was kind of insane, but she was outvoted and there wasn't really another choice.

Quill and his crew had already taken off for Ronan's command ship, and she didn't want to ditch the mission and be stuck on

Knowhere. For a moment, she had thought about trying to overpower these strangers and steal the ship, but she had never had much luck against empaths. And Moondragon struck her as very, very powerful. Besides, she had grown to like them. All of them.

Meanwhile, Warlock was staring directly at Gamora, and thus at the glowing orb growing larger in the viewscreen, but he didn't seem worried either.

She refocused on the fact that she was currently flying directly towards a star.

"Are you absolutely sure about these coordinates, Moondragon?" she asked, cringing internally at how close they were getting. The heat shields were fine for now, but that would change in a few minutes. The sensors on this old ship were already starting to freak out.

"Yes," Heather responded, her eyes opening. Gamora waited for anything else, but that was apparently all the empath had to say on the matter.

"Great," she muttered. "You're not a little worried here, Drax?"

"I've been in more dangerous situations," he said, nodding, clearly happy with his own response.

We're all going to die, Gamora thought.

The sensors suddenly lit up and squawked like it was the end of the world, which Gamora thought it could be, at least for the ship and its occupants. Moondragon appeared next to her and looked out the window, squinting against the star's brightness.

"You okay with this?" Gamora asked.

"I have no wish to die, if that's what you mean," Moondragon replied. "But I sense something within the heart of that star. Carry on."

Gamora shook her head in disbelief but prepared the vessel as best she could for the increasing heat. A metal sleeve unfurled, covering the window, making them for all intents and purposes blind—ironically, to keep them from going blind. Gamora watched the readouts, wondered how the hell they were going to survive this.

The star got closer and closer.

Gamora realized she was holding her breath, and then exhaled, calmly. Her training reasserted itself. If this was the way she was going to go out, then so be it. Better than being consumed by a techno-organic virus.

The console made a strange sound, and the ship shook violently for a moment. Gamora punched in data, and was shocked at what she saw. The hull temperature was decreasing.

"What the hell…?"

"It's him," Warlock said quietly, stepping up next to Moondragon.

Moondragon winced and raised a hand to her temple.

"Adam is correct," the empath said, clearly in pain. "This is the High Evolutionary's doing. We don't need the shield anymore."

Drax worked the controls and the shield raised back up, revealing that they were surrounded by a protective bubble that was connected to the center of the star, like some kind of enclosed corridor. Whatever the bubble was made from, its surface diluted the intense light and heat, and some unseen energy drew them forward.

"Cutting engines," Drax said.

The ship grew quiet as the engines wound down, and they were drawn closer and closer to a massive metal structure at the heart of the star.

THE LANDING platform was full of people.

Gamora, now back in control of the ship, was careful not to crush any of them as she landed, though they didn't seem particularly concerned about their own safety.

Up close, the structure was even more massive than it had appeared during their assisted flight into the middle of the star. It was a complicated design with alloys that Gamora had never seen before, and the entire area was somehow protected by the unimaginable heat that surrounded it.

The landing area was in a room so large that she couldn't even see the ceiling. Huge metal walls disappeared into shadows above and below them, the landing strip cutting across the circular space like a bridge. Several additional paths led from the strip to multiple doors, a virtual spiderweb of architecture.

Gamora powered the ship down fully and stood up, making sure her knives and gun were holstered tightly to her belt. She had no idea what was going to happen out there, but she would be ready for it.

The four of them walked down the landing plank as soon as it touched the floor, surrounded by the swirling steam being jettisoned by the ship, as if the vessel itself was wishing them luck.

None of the people on the platform appeared to be armed but their silent presence was still unsettling. The throng was made up of many different alien races, approaching them curiously with dull looks in their eyes. Gamora recognized some, though not all, of the races, but there was something off about all of them, small details that didn't seem quite right. It took everything in her not to order her team back onto the ship and get the hell out of there.

One of the odd aliens got a little too close to the group, raised its hand as if to touch Moondragon. Drax reacted immediately, pushing the alien away and activating his double-bladed sword. The confused alien's eyes went wide but Drax brought the blade back anyway, ready for some action after a long trip aboard the new ship.

"Drax, no!" Moondragon shouted. "I probed their minds and there is no maliciousness in any of them. In fact, there's not much there at all."

Warlock looked around at the massive structure, and then at several of the slightly off aliens who still milled about, already seeming to forget about these strange new arrivals.

"There is something familiar about all of this," he said.

"I should hope so," a booming voice suddenly echoed across the chamber. "My son."

All the dazed aliens immediately dropped to their knees. The newly arrived guests turned, and were shocked to see the huge form of the High Evolutionary standing at the other end of the platform, which had been empty on their arrival. It was impossible to say how he'd gotten there without them noticing. Not even Moondragon had sensed his presence.

He was at least fifty feet tall and wore dark purple and silver armor, and a helmet that came together in a ridge on top of his head. His eyes glowed green, and he looked down on his visitors with an impenetrable expression on his face.

"'Son…?'" Adam whispered, looking up at the giant creature before them, shaking his head slightly, trying to make sense of the word. "Are you my father?" he asked.

"In a manner of speaking," the High Evolutionary responded. "Are you saying you have no memory of me? Of this place?"

"I feel something on the boundaries of my mind… of my soul…" Adam said, stepping forward, his face working as he attempted to make sense of the echoes that danced in his mind. "But it's vague. Every time I try to grasp onto it, it slips away."

"You were not supposed to return to me so soon. And I can feel your suffering, your uncertainty. You have not fully healed from your last ordeal." The High Evolutionary's glowing eyes turned towards Gamora. "I sense that you are their leader. What happened to my son?"

Gamora cleared her throat and stepped forward, too, next to Adam. She had gone toe-to-toe with some of the deadliest individuals in the universe, but even she was aware of how powerful the High Evolutionary was. This was a being who had battled both the Fantastic Four and the Avengers. She needed to tread carefully. She had no idea what his motives were, or why they were even here.

"My name is Gamora, and—"

"I know who you are. You're the daughter of Thanos," he interrupted.

She pressed on as if he hadn't.

"As I believe you know, we are on a mission of the gravest importance. A bio-organic race known as the Phalanx invaded

Kree space, and that invasion has continued to expand outward. A message from the Supreme Intelligence took us to Morag IV, where we were attacked by a Phalanx-infested Super-Adaptoid. While we were successful in defeating him, the battle damaged Warlock's cocoon, and we were forced to open it prematurely in order to save his life."

"I see," the High Evolutionary responded, then grew silent. A long, painful moment of silence passed. The bizarre aliens were still on their knees. Drax tightened his grip on his blade, apparently hopeful that some kind of battle would break out.

Gamora glanced back at Moondragon.

Be careful, Heather said directly into Gamora's mind. *The High Evolutionary cannot always be trusted.*

"Moondragon is correct," he announced. "I do not always speak in ways that you lower life forms would consider truthful. Though I never lie."

He took a single massive step towards them, and they all tensed for battle, Drax moving forward, an excited smile spreading across his face.

During his next step, the High Evolutionary began to shrink, and within two more steps he was roughly the same size as everyone else on the platform.

"There. That ought to make everyone feel a bit more comfortable. I forget how spatial you can be."

"Um… thank you?" Gamora said. She was irritated by his condescension, but learning the High Evolutionary could apparently read minds, she pushed the insult out of her head.

"I can sense your desperation. It's coming off you in waves. I, of course, already knew everything you told me. It was I who gave that information to the Supreme Intelligence, and I who instructed Quasar and Moondragon to protect my son from the Phalanx." The High Evolutionary said the word 'Supreme' as if it left a bad taste in his mouth, or as if he considered it a joke. Which he probably did.

"Interesting," he said, then tilted his head as if he'd heard something. Then: "I have scanned the cosmos and can no longer sense the Supreme Intelligence's presence."

"The Phalanx may have him in stasis," Moondragon said.

"Or they probably dissected him," Drax suggested. *Harsh*, Gamora thought, *but not improbable.*

"The bottom line is that we need your help," Gamora said. They were wasting time. She wondered vaguely how Quill's parallel mission was going. She wondered if he was okay. If she'd get a chance to—

No. She had to keep her mind clear. For all kinds of reasons. She stared directly into the High Evolutionary's glowing eyes.

"So, can you help us?"

"That is a very good question," he replied, an odd smile forming on his face. "And one I need to contemplate. But in the meantime, there *is* someone who also recently arrived, and who most certainly will want to help you."

"*What?*" Gamora said, her survival instincts kicking in. This was completely unexpected, which was the last thing they needed right now. "Who?"

"I will allow him to introduce himself."

The High Evolutionary nodded and one of the many doors slid open. After a moment, they heard footsteps approaching, and then a figure emerged, someone familiar to several of them.

"I did *not* see that coming," Gamora said quietly—but she had to admit to herself that this new arrival, all things considered, was definitely a pleasant surprise.

CHAPTER SEVENTEEN

RONAN'S COMMAND SHIP

STAR-LORD, MANTIS, and Quasar quickly made their way towards the docking bay, where Groot and Rocket waited with Ship.

Quill attempted to keep his breathing as calm as possible, Quasar and Mantis in front of him, trying to figure out exactly what their next move would be. This plan, if it could even have been called that, had been a total bust.

He cycled through potential scenarios in his head as they walked. The only one that made sense was to hightail it to the High Evolutionary's base, using the coordinates Mantis had gleaned from Moondragon's mind, and hope the other half of their team was still there. Maybe *their* mission had been more successful, though their parameters had been just as vague as his.

Just as they approached the door that led to the docking bay, Mantis suddenly screamed and collapsed to the floor, clutching her head. Her antennae swiveled frantically through her fingers.

Quasar kneeled down next to her, placing her hand gently on her shoulder. "Mantis! What's wrong?"

"He is… in so much pain…" Mantis barely got out through gritted teeth.

Before Star-Lord could respond, two Kree guards appeared at the other end of the hallway.

"Hey!" one shouted. "What are you doing out here?!"

"Um, just trying to find a water fountain!" Peter yelled back, looking down at Mantis. Her breathing was ragged, and her entire body shook in apparent agony.

The guards sprinted forward and one put the barrel of his weapon to the back of Star-Lord's head.

"Get your women up. *Now.*"

Without hesitating, Quasar blasted both guards simultaneously from where she was still crouched on the ground next to Mantis. The guards slammed into parallel walls and slumped down to the ground, unconscious.

"I am not *his* woman," she hissed.

Quill nodded in appreciation, said nothing.

At that moment, the bay door opened and Rocket burst out, laser pistol in hand. He took in the knocked-out guards and his shoulders slumped slightly.

"You couldn't even leave one for me?" he asked Quasar, noticing her glowing hands and eye.

"Sorry," was all she said in return as she helped Mantis to her feet. Groot wedged himself into the corridor, and the bay door slid shut. It was eerily quiet in the hall for a moment, and then Mantis spoke.

"They are still torturing him. We must help."

"Torturing who?" Rocket asked, thoroughly confused.

"He… has no name," Mantis said, then looked at Peter. "We cannot leave him here to die."

Quill weighed their options. Ship was right behind that door. Their freedom. But an innocent person was being tortured. So there really wasn't a choice.

"Okay," he said, unholstering his weapon. "Let's go get no-name."

RONAN GREW impatient.

Gen-Vol had landed several minutes earlier but the damaged ship's hatch hadn't yet opened, which left the Accuser standing like some kind of confused child in the starboard bow landing bay. He gripped his hammer so tight that his knuckles were no doubt turning white beneath his gloves.

Another moment passed and then he turned to the Kree soldier standing behind the nearby console, who looked nervously from Ronan to the ship, and then back again. Ronan wondered absently how the soldier's blood would look splayed out across the console. Instead, he barked a command.

"Override that ship's systems and get that door open. I want to see Gen-Vol now!"

"Yes sir!" the soldier said, punching in the commands he knew like the back of his hand. He had been working in this bay for nearly a year and understood its inner workings better than the Kree who had built it, and secretly harbored ambitions for a promotion. Perhaps today would be the first step towards that lofty goal.

Less than a minute later, Ronan watched as the ship's door finally opened, the metal ramp descending and hitting the floor with a dull clank. He glanced at the soldier and gave an impressed nod—that had taken much less time than he expected. Perhaps he would pull up this soldier's record. They were very short of officers now.

Ronan stomped up the ramp with his personal guards following closely behind and entered the ship, calling out for Gen-Vol. Normally, he would have made the captain come to him, but after his scientists' inability to get answers out of Wraith, Ronan was more frustrated and angrier than he had been earlier.

If Gen-Vol's news wasn't good, there was a high chance someone was going to die on that ship in the immediate future. Maybe Ronan would punish Star-Lord for his inadvertent enabling of the Phalanx invasion after all.

It was dark inside the ship, which wasn't entirely unusual since it had clearly been damaged in some kind of battle. Ronan made his way to the bridge, his rage building with every step.

"Captain!" he yelled as he entered the command center. Gen-Vol was in his captain's chair, his back to his superior, punching data into the console next to him. "Didn't you hear me?! Where is this crucial intel on the Phalanx?"

"My apologies, Lord Ronan!" Gen-Vol nearly shouted, continuing to punch in data. "I wanted to download the information that I discovered before I disembarked. I did not mean to keep you waiting. Please forgive me."

Ronan took another step forward. The rest of the bridge crew was absent, but it didn't matter. Perhaps they had died during a battle… perhaps they were in other parts of the ship, making repairs.

"I don't need your apology, Captain. I need the data that can help us win this war."

"Of course, sir," the captain said, punching in a few final points of data, and then swiftly standing and turning to face his commander. "I have it right here."

For a moment, Ronan was confused. Gen-Vol wasn't presenting any kind of data, wasn't pointing to a screen that might reveal the secrets that would defeat the Phalanx.

And then Ronan saw the man's eyes. Or the technology that had replaced them.

As his guards became aware of what was happening and began firing wildly on the dark bridge, Ronan cursed his own exhaustion and overconfidence. Looking back on the past several minutes, all the clues were there that he was walking into a trap. And still, he had fumbled into it like a Kree cadet right out of a training module.

Still, if today was the day that Ronan the Accuser fell, he would go down swinging.

The attacks from his guards found their mark, but the damage they did to the thing that had once been Captain Gen-Vol did not seem to hurt it or even slow it down. It reached out towards Ronan, a surprising smile crossing its otherwise placid face.

One of the guards, to her credit, came out of nowhere and tackled Gen-Vol, both of them crashing to the floor in a violent tumble. The guard threw punch after punch, but after a moment her movements went slack. Then she and Gen-Vol both stood up, almost in perfect unison, and Ronan saw that her eyes had been turned, too.

The remaining two guards fired wildly as the two Phalanx-infested Kree walked forward, calmly, the circuitry pulsating in their eyes like so many bugs.

Flanked by laser blasts on both sides, Ronan stepped forward and swung his hammer, hitting the brave soldier in the side of the head. He took no pleasure in this. She had proven herself today, but she went down hard after the blow and did not get back up.

But that was all the time Gen-Vol needed. He was on Ronan faster than the Kree commander expected, grabbing his face with a force that surprised even him. He felt the Phalanx technology burrowing into his skin almost immediately.

"No..." was all he managed to utter before his vision began to go dark.

MANTIS LED them through the bowels of the ship.

It was clear she was in pain, but she pressed forward as fast as she could. Behind her, Quill and Quasar walked, grim and alert, while Groot flanked them with Rocket sitting on his shoulder, inspecting his weapon as he got a ride. None of the Kree on the ship seemed to be aware of what they were doing. At least not yet.

"We need to hurry this up," Peter said after they turned down yet another empty corridor. "Talk to me, Mantis."

"He is close... and in so much pain," she replied sharply.

"And... do we have a name yet?" Peter asked, but Mantis either didn't hear him or didn't feel like answering the same question he'd been asking, in different ways, for the past few minutes.

"I still think this is a mistake," Rocket said, apparently done inspecting his weapon. "We need to get out of here. Like, immediately."

"I am Groot!" his companion suddenly shouted.

"Okay, okay!" Rocket responded. "You don't have to yell at me."

"Should I even ask what he said?" Quill asked.

"He said we should trust Mantis. That we should help the Nameless Guy Who is Apparently in a Lot of Pain. You wanna argue with him?"

Star-Lord glanced back and saw the serious look on Groot's face, only the second time that wooden visage hadn't looked kind and placid.

"Works for me," Peter replied, nodding.

"Here," Mantis said a moment later, pointing at a door that looked like any number they'd just passed. Quill stepped up to the control panel and punched in codes, but nothing happened.

"When I was installing the defense upgrade, they gave me access to a lot of their systems. They must have changed the command codes."

"Maybe the intergalactic invasion had something to do with that decision," Rocket said, laughing at his own joke.

"No need to be a jerk," a frustrated Star-Lord replied. "Even if you're right," he mumbled.

"We don't have time for this," Quasar said suddenly, her eye starting to glow. "Stand back."

Peter did as he was told, gently shepherding Mantis out of the way as well, since he suspected what was about to happen.

And sure enough, Quasar unloaded a massive energy attack from both hands, a smile slipping across her face. The door exploded inwards, transforming into a giant oblong hole melted into the surrounding metal.

"That's what I'm talking about!" Rocket yelled, cocking his laser gun and jumping down off Groot's shoulder.

"I needed that," Quasar said to Quill, and he smiled for the briefest moment at her. He really liked having her as part of the team.

They all surged forward, except Mantis, who followed them cautiously, still feeling the painful reverberations from whatever had been happening inside this dark room; and Groot, who gestured for Mantis to go ahead of him. She smiled at the momentarily gentle giant and followed the others.

Quill was at the front, Quasar and Rocket right behind him on either side, and they approached a table that sat beneath the only significant source of light in the large room. On either side of the table stood the two Kree scientists, both holding what looked like scalpels… or torture devices. Or both.

And on the table was the long-haired man, still confined by thick metal bands that were strapped around his wrists and ankles. Fresh blue blood dripped from a long wound in his chest, clearly where the two 'doctors' had just been working.

"We were acting under Lord Ronan's direct orders!" one of them shouted, clearly aware of how this must look to the unexpected interlopers.

"If you interrupt our work, not only do you risk the Accuser's wrath, but you also endanger the entire universe!" the other one said, pulling down his mask, revealing a nasty sneer.

Peter and Quasar shared a look, and then they each blasted one of the Kree, knocking the scientists back and to the floor, immediately unconscious. Their 'instruments' clanked off into the darkness beyond the circle of light.

"We'll take our chances," Peter said, and stepped towards the operating table, stopping when he was standing above the man lying there. He put his hand on the man's shoulder and shook him gently.

"Dude, can you hear me?"

The man's eyes suddenly opened and he strained against his bonds, thrashing wildly. Mantis approached him, her antennae swiveling.

"We are friends," she said, and the man instantly quieted. He glanced over at the unconscious scientists.

"Thank you," he responded.

Star-Lord looked him over, took in the metal that kept the man trapped on the table. He glanced at Quasar again. "Would you mind doing the honors?"

Phyla-Vell nodded and then raised a single finger, a thin line of energy emerging like a blade. She slowly cut through each of the four restraints, being careful not to burn the man while she did so.

He sat up, rubbing his wrists, then stood as if they weren't there. He stepped over to a nearby metal case and opened it, withdrawing a striped cloak. When he put it on, his torn clothes repaired themselves immediately and a weapon suddenly materialized on his side.

"That's pretty awesome," Rocket said.

"Soooo… who are you?" Quill asked.

"I could ask you the same thing," the man said, looking at Peter from beneath a dark, furrowed brow. They both realized at the same moment that this might be another enemy standing there, and both men tensed.

Mantis stepped forward.

"We are allies," she said. "And you are…" She closed her eyes for a moment, straining slightly, and then reopened them. "Zak-Del."

"That is not my name," he snapped, taking a violent step forward. Star-Lord shifted so that he was between the man and Mantis. Rocket hadn't been wrong earlier: they needed to get out of here as soon as possible. Which meant that Peter had to diffuse this situation, and quick.

"Well, what should we call you then?"

"I am called Wraith, one of the Nameless. I don't understand who you are, or what you're doing here."

Quill let out a long breath, ran his fingers through his hair. "Look, we can explain everything. We have another team that is, theoretically, meeting with the High Evolutionary right now. We need to reconnoiter with them and hopefully all this will make sense then. Hopefully, we'll have what we need to stop the Phalanx. But we can't do any of that until we get off this ship."

Wraith took in each of them, seemed almost amused, and smiled at Mantis. Quill wondered how much of a conversation they'd had that no one else had heard. Wraith unholstered his weapon, an impressive gun unlike anything Star-Lord had ever seen before.

"I would be honored to join you," the Nameless Kree said.

"And you will die with them as well," a voice boomed from behind them.

They all turned but none were prepared for what stood there, despite having known that the Kree could discover them at any time.

It was Ronan the Accuser, as large and imposing as ever, his deadly hammer held in his right hand. He was surrounded by a cadre of Kree soldiers, armed with the race's deadliest handheld weapons.

But it was their eyes that really stood out. Eyes that swam with Phalanx circuitry.

"Oh great..." Rocket said, and then he took aim.

CHAPTER EIGHTEEN

THE HIGH EVOLUTIONARY'S SANCTUARY

"NOVA!" DRAX said, moving forward and clapping his friend on the shoulder.

Gamora raised an eyebrow. This was an interesting development.

"Drax!" Richard responded, reaching up and removing his helmet. "What the heck are you doing here?" Nova looked over at the High Evolutionary, then at the other newcomers standing on the landing dock. "And who are your friends?"

"Well," Drax said, turning to look at the rest of the team, "I actually barely know them. But we are all working for a single purpose—to stop the Phalanx at the source."

"So, you know about the Phalanx, too?" Richard asked, relief flooding his face. "Good. I wasn't exactly sure how to explain the situation."

"Why are *you* here, Nova?" Moondragon asked, approaching Nova and her father. "I hope your mission is clearer than ours."

"No, I got word from the High Evolutionary that I should get here as soon as possible. I just arrived a little while ago and he's told me a few things, and said he was waiting for one more party to show up. I guess you're that party."

Gamora turned to the High Evolutionary. "All right, spill it. You brought us here. You obviously have something you want to tell everyone. The floor is yours."

Another indiscernible look appeared on the High Evolutionary's face. It almost looked like amusement.

"It's not what I want to *say*, it's what I need to *do*."

After another moment, he waved his hand and Adam doubled over in agony, screaming. Gamora didn't waste a beat. She darted forward, slashing at the High Evolutionary with her blade. She made contact but it barely left a scratch on his armor.

Drax was right behind her, and he landed a devastating blow to the High Evolutionary's face, a punch that would have killed many lesser beings. The High Evolutionary's head snapped back but otherwise he was unhurt.

Nova quickly put his helmet back on and burst forward, shoving Drax and Gamora out of the way, standing between them and their perceived enemy.

"Guys, wait!" he shouted, holding up his hands.

The groups of aliens that littered the landing pad suddenly ran away, disappearing into any number of doors built into the platform's connecting walls.

Gamora stalked closer to Rider, her knife held low, ready to fight. Despite their relatively new friendship, Drax shot forward, tackling Nova to the ground. The two went down, tumbling across the floor towards the edge of the platform. The drop was miles—no one could even see the floor from where they stood.

Nova unleashed an attack that sent Drax flying off him, though the bigger man landed on his feet in an impressive display of agility. He started walking back towards Rider, his skin still smoldering from the blast.

"You aren't the first friend who's turned into an enemy, Nova. I'll happily carve that armor off you. And maybe I'll wear that ridiculous helmet myself once I'm done," Drax taunted.

"Come on, man, let's just talk this out. There's more going on here than you realize," Nova responded.

Gamora flanked Nova while the High Evolutionary just watched, doing nothing to stop the unfolding battle.

Just as all three were about to renew their attacks, Moondragon stepped forward and shouted one word, which halted them all in their tracks.

"Stop!"

All three of them could suddenly feel her in their minds and it was like a switch was flicked—the fight went out of them immediately.

"Heather?" Drax said, looking at his daughter.

"Sorry, but we don't have time for childish antics. Besides," Moondragon said, nodding towards Warlock, who was writhing around on the ground in pain, "*he* needs our help. The three of you can work out your little tiff later."

Gamora felt Moondragon's presence exit her brain and she silently cursed herself. What kind of leadership had she just displayed? One of her teammates had gone down for unknown reasons and instead of thinking things through, she had allowed anger, the anger that always simmered just beneath the surface, to take over. For all his bravado and terrible jokes, Quill wouldn't have done that.

Drax seemed ready to continue the battle, but Gamora put an hand on his shoulder.

"We need to make sure Adam is okay," she said, staring straight into his eyes. He saw the fire there, knew they were kindred spirits, and nodded. They both walked over to Warlock, then kneeled. The man, if that's what he was, shuddered on the ground, his eyes closed but fluttering beneath the lids. His skin was rippling, almost seemed to be taking on a new texture, muscles straining, his entire body evolving into something else right before their eyes. Whatever they were looking at, it was like nothing either of them had ever witnessed before.

Nova stepped over to Moondragon, who now faced the High Evolutionary.

"What are you doing to him?" she demanded. She'd had trouble getting past Warlock's natural psionic defenses before, but now it was like a concrete wall had gone up.

"Although I cannot read the future, I know that a great conflict is coming, and that you and your compatriots are the universe's greatest hope. In order to achieve your goals, you need Adam Warlock to be functioning at his optimal capacity. Therefore, I am simply... accelerating the process that you interrupted on Morag.

"You see, I created Adam to be the perfect being. And he is as close to perfect as is possible. But since there is no such thing as perfect, since all of existence is possible *because* of imperfections, Adam has the ability to regenerate each time he is seriously injured… or killed."

"The cocoon…" Moondragon murmured.

"Yes, the cocoon. It is that, and so much more. It allows him to inch closer and closer to a subjective and contextual perfection each time the universe pushes him to, and beyond, his limits. But you—"

"We interrupted his natural healing process during our battle with the Super-Adaptoid."

"Precisely," the High Evolutionary answered, as if he was talking to a small child.

"So, *what* exactly is happening then?" Nova asked.

"He's fixing what we broke," she stated simply, turning to look back at the writhing Warlock on the ground. He looked like he was in more pain than ever.

"That is only a small portion of what is happening," the High Evolutionary said, brushing past them and walking towards his 'son,' concentrating as he did so. Moondragon sensed he was now pushing himself, almost as much as he was pushing Adam. This was either a very good thing, or very, very bad. "I am evolving him further than I should at this point in his development. Like I said, I do not know what you will face when you reach your next destination, but I *do* know that the current Adam will not be enough. Perhaps the *future* Adam will."

As they watched, Warlock continued to evolve through several iterations of himself, screaming as he did so. Drax and Gamora were clearly on edge, and they glanced at the High Evolutionary like they wanted nothing more than to try their luck again. Moondragon understood—part of her felt the same way. But there was a larger game at play here, and she suspected that this sacrifice, as painful as it was to watch, was necessary.

Finally, after a gut-wrenching number of minutes, Adam Warlock's body slowed and then stilled completely. The man who rose from the floor and faced them was the same person with whom they had just traveled from Morag IV, and was also completely different.

Moondragon gently probed his mind and found it to contain the same raw power, but it was less clouded now—scattered memories from past lives ricocheted confusingly. In some ways, it seemed much worse than the blankness from before.

"Are you okay?" she asked him gently, searching his eyes for the suffering that had just wracked his entire existence.

"I… don't know," he said directly into her mind. "But thank you. For everything."

She wasn't sure what he meant, but she also understood completely. Their minds were now connected on a deep level, a connection that ran, in some ways, even deeper than those she had with Mantis or even Phyla-Vell.

"Okay, that was intense," Gamora said. "Now. What's next?"

"When you mentioned our 'next destination,'" Nova said to the High Evolutionary, "it almost sounded like you knew what that was."

"Very perceptive, Richard Rider," he replied, turning away and beginning to grow again. "While you have been here, engaging in senseless violence against me and each other, I have been running millions of calculations, and communicating with thousands of beings across the cosmos."

"Humble as always…" Gamora mumbled.

"And I have become aware of the world upon which the Phalanx originated."

Gamora tensed and felt the others do the same. Was this it? A chance to end this war before any more damage was done? She needed to let Quill know. Could Moondragon reach Mantis from this kind of impossible distance?

"Where?!" Drax shouted, stepping towards the High Evolutionary, his blade once again gripped tightly in his hand. The High Evolutionary continued to grow, making Drax's implied threat seem all the more ridiculous.

"You must travel to the far end of the galaxy, to a planet called Kvch. Even my great powers and intellect cannot penetrate the powerful wall that has been thrown up around that planet. But the answers you seek are there. As is the leader of the Phalanx."

"Then what are we waiting for...?" Gamora asked, looking at each of her teammates. "Let's take them out."

CHAPTER NINETEEN

RONAN THE ACCUSER'S COMMAND SHIP

QUASAR UNLEASHED the power of the Quantum Bands on Ronan and his troops, and it felt amazing.

She hadn't really let go since the battles on Morag, and being away from Heather for this long had been difficult, though she refused to show any real emotion to these virtual strangers. She'd heard stories about Ronan, about some of the things he'd done—and even if he'd apparently turned slightly in the right direction in recent years, a part of her felt justified in attacking him full force.

That, and the fact that he was under the influence of a deadly invasive species.

Ronan and his Phalanx-infested soldiers were rocked back by the pure intensity of her blasts, and perhaps they would have been quickly defeated under normal circumstances. But the situation was far from normal. Even as they were engulfed by the power of the Quantum Bands, they pushed forward towards their uninfected enemies.

"Join... us..." Ronan managed to say, though it was almost impossible to hear him through the roar of energy that surrounded him.

"Don't let them touch you!" Quill shouted, firing his weapon at them as well.

"I am Groot?" the largest Guardian asked, stepping towards Ronan.

"No!" Star-Lord shouted back. "There's no guarantee that Phalanx circuitry wouldn't work on wood just as well as it works on flesh. Stay back, Groot!"

"Do as he tells you, buddy!" Rocket shouted, stepping between Groot and their enemies, firing wildly with his laser gun. It was impossible to tell if their attacks were making a difference in addition to Quasar's energy field.

"I am unable to reach their minds," Mantis said, straining, her fingers held gently to her forehead. "All I hear is static."

"Get back with Groot," Peter shouted, firing at Ronan. It didn't seem to have any effect on the Kree leader, or what was left of him, but there wasn't much else he could do. These Phalanx warriors stood between the Guardians and the door, and now Star-Lord and crew were being forced backwards, literally up against a wall. They could only avoid Ronan's touch for so long. The Kree commander dragged his massive hammer along the floor behind him, making a horrible screeching noise, like something out of those same horror movies that had scared Peter when he was a kid back on Earth. Even Quasar seemed to be losing steam.

Quill searched the room, felt his stomach sink. They were out of options.

Just as Ronan was about to get close enough to touch Quasar, despite still being engulfed by her energy attack, Wraith vaulted over the group and at the Kree leader, landing a powerful kick to Ronan's face and rocking the giant Kree back into his own soldiers. He lost his grip on the hammer, which clanked to the ground by his feet.

"I like this guy!" Rocket shouted.

The Nameless Kree landed several more blows to Ronan, an incredible amount of force in each one, and for a moment Quill thought Wraith might somehow do it… might clear a path for them to escape.

But the tide turned quickly.

With a speed that surprised everyone in the room, Ronan's arms lashed out and he grabbed Wraith's face, the Phalanx tendrils immediately digging into the uninfected Kree's flesh.

"Crap," Peter said quietly. The entrance was still blocked by Ronan's soldiers. The brief moment of hope engendered by Wraith faded.

He aimed his weapon at Ronan again, even though he knew it was pointless, but then lowered his weapon as a thought crossed his mind. Quill knew an opportunity when he saw one. At the moment, Ronan and his soldiers' attention was completely centered on Wraith, who was striking Ronan's face over and over again, kicking one of the soldiers in the midsection at the same time. Star-Lord was impressed.

"Quasar! Rocket! Fire right there!" He pointed through the room's deep shadows to the nearest wall. Phyla-Vell and Rocket looked at him, confusion showing on their faces.

"You losing your mind, Quill?" Rocket said, taking aim at Ronan again.

"Just do it! Now!" Star-Lord nearly screamed, then fired his own weapon at the wall. Quasar shrugged and then fired her diminished energy beams at the same spot. Rocket shook his head in disbelief but complied as well. The wall cracked and then a hole exploded open into the next room, which was mercifully empty.

"Not bad," Rocket admitted.

"Let's go!" Peter shouted, running towards the newly created hole, looking back as he did so. Wraith continued his one-man battle against Ronan and his soldiers, who kept grabbing hold of him, clearly frustrated by their inability to infect him.

Wraith slid his foot under Ronan's hammer and flipped it up into his hand, then swung it directly into its original owner's cheek. Ronan went down, hard. Quill's eyes widened. Yes, he had been working with Ronan, but there was something very satisfying about seeing the Kree High Commander taken down with the weapon that had been the cause of so many deaths.

Peter watched and waited as Mantis made her way through the ragged, makeshift exit first, followed by Rocket and then Quasar. Groot lumbered over and tried to squeeze through, but he was too large to fit.

"I am Groot?" he said, his voice muffled, his face on the other side of the hole.

"I'm pulling as hard as I can!" came Rocket's frustrated response.

"Sorry about this, Groot," Quill muttered, then kicked the tree creature in the rear end as hard as he could. The force was enough to shove Groot the rest of the way through the hole.

"I am Groot!"

"You're welcome!" Peter shouted back.

While Quill's back had been turned, Wraith shot Ronan in the face with his odd-looking weapon while the Kree leader was still on the ground. His weapon somehow transformed into a whip, which caused Peter's eyes to widen in surprise again. Wraith tangled up two of the Phalanx-infested soldiers, throwing them against the far wall with incredible force. They collapsed to the floor and didn't get up again. The final guard lunged at Wraith, but the Nameless Kree dodged and threw out a leg. The soldier tripped, fell forward, and impaled himself on one of the scalpels that still lay on the floor.

For a moment, Wraith was the only one standing in the middle of the room.

"Come on!" Star-Lord shouted, one foot through the hole.

"Go without me! I am on a mission to find the Kree who murdered my parents. There may be clues where to find him on this ship's computers!"

"I'm not leaving anyone behind!" Quill responded, running back and grabbing Wraith by the arm. The Nameless Kree bristled, seemed ready to fight Peter too, if necessary. Beneath them, Ronan stirred. Star-Lord knew he was seconds away from being infected.

"Even if that man is on this ship, he's probably infected by the Phalanx, so you wouldn't be killing him. But I need you… the entire universe needs you. And if we manage to actually win this whole thing, then you can kill that guy afterwards. Cool?"

A small smile appeared on Wraith's face at the suggestion, and his body relaxed slightly.

"Very well."

"Great!" Star-Lord said, already hightailing it back towards the hole. "And on the way, you can explain to me just how the heck you're invulnerable to the Phalanx!"

As Quill clambered through the alternative exit, Wraith gave Ronan one last kick for good measure.

"That's for my 'interrogation.'"

Then he was off, joining a group of people that he was already starting to like. The feeling was an unfamiliar one, but it stirred strange emotions in him, memories of Saw-Ked. The idea of having a friend again, let alone friends, was tempting. And terrifying.

THE GUARDIANS burst into the landing bay, where Ship sat in silence, waiting for them.

"How do we know Ronan didn't sabotage our ride?!" Rocket shouted, punching a code into the control panel on the wall to close the door behind them.

"I don't get the sense that much time passed before he left us and the Phalanx got their hands on him," Quill responded, opening the ship's hatch door remotely as he ran. "There's no way he had time to mess with Ship. I hope."

Before they had a chance to board, the bay doors behind them exploded inwards and a group of Phalanx-infected Kree soldiers poured in, followed by a grim-faced Ronan, his angry eyes chittering with alien technology. Wraith turned to face the horde.

"Go without me! You won't make it out of here unless someone slows them down. And I'm the only one who's immune."

"No!" Star-Lord shouted back, firing at the increasing number of Kree warriors. "We're not having this conversation again. We're all leaving *together*. Besides, there's *way* too many of them for you to handle alone."

Quasar and Rocket joined the attack, but their firepower was diminished, and the number of Phalanx continued to grow as the Guardians slowly backed towards Ship.

"Mantis! Start the engines while we figure a way out of here!" Quill shouted. Mantis nodded and sprinted up the ramp. A moment later, they heard the ship's engines rumble to life.

"That's not gonna do us much good if we all get computerized!" Rocket shouted.

Wraith leaped forward and grappled with Ronan, the two men struggling to overpower each other, neither having much effect.

"Got a plan, Quill?" Quasar asked, sidling up next to him and blasting as many Kree as possible as she did so. Peter could tell that her power was starting to falter. He was running out of energy himself. They were fighting a losing battle here, and he knew it.

"I wish I could say that I do," he responded, picking off a Phalanx that had gotten a little too close for comfort. "But I think this might be our last stand. If we go down, though, at least we'll all go down together."

The Guardians looked each other in the eyes and continued their assault, even though they knew it was hopeless. They backed closer and closer to Ship, but they knew that if they stopped firing for even a second, the Phalanx would be on them, and they would be infected.

Wraith stood in front of them all, and they watched as he was swarmed, the Phalanx attempting fruitlessly to turn him. More and more Phalanx appeared in the room. In a moment of desperation, Wraith grabbed Ronan by the face. Something inside the Nameless Kree clicked, and his hands began to burn.

Ronan screamed, the circuitry in his eyes going wild.

"What's he doing?" Rocket asked, continuing to fire.

"I have no idea!" Quill shouted back.

Wraith's hands got hotter and hotter, and it was excruciating. But he did not let go. The Phalanx slaves attacked him, tried to pull him away, but he held on. After a moment, the circuitry left Ronan's eyes altogether.

"How...?" Ronan said, himself once again. Then he collapsed to the ground, unconscious.

One of the Phalanx grabbed the Kree Commander's shoulder, attempting to infect him, but the infection wouldn't take. The enslaved Kree turned to attack the other Guardians, along with dozens of others. They continued to fire but there were simply too many enemies.

It was hopeless.

"I am Groot!"

Everyone looked over at Groot, who had held back during the entire battle for fear of being infected but had not yet entered the ship. He surged forward, pushing past his friends.

"No!" Rocket shouted, firing even more frantically, his eyes wild with panic.

"Groot, what are you doing?!" Quill shouted, shooting a Phalanx in the face as it got within inches of touching him.

Groot reached back with his left hand and his fingers stretched out into long branches, each one wrapping around one of the Guardians who stood just outside Ship's entrance.

"No, Groot, *no*!" Rocket yelled again, but his friend said nothing, just looked at the raccoon with sad eyes.

With his other arm, Groot created a wall of wood between his teammates and the Phalanx, grimacing as he stretched his capabilities to their limit.

"I am Groot..." he pleaded, barely able to get the words out. Quill watched as the Phalanx technology began to run along the wall of wood that was currently keeping them safe.

"We gotta get outta here now, or what he's doing means *nothing*!"

"I ain't leaving him!" Rocket shouted back.

Without saying a word, Quasar grabbed the back of Rocket's

jacket and flew into the ship. Peter heard Rocket cursing at her with swearwords from multiple alien languages, but he knew she'd keep him inside, out of harm's way.

"Wraith! Get on the ship!"

Nodding, the Nameless Kree picked up the unconscious Ronan, blasted his way through the Phalanx throng, and ran up the ramp.

Star-Lord turned to join him, but then hesitated. He looked back and locked eyes with Groot. A small flower fell from the tree creature's eye… a single tear.

"I am Groot…" he said gently as the Phalanx infection raced across his body.

Quill gritted his teeth. He knew he should run, that saving the rest of the team was the right thing to do, was the smarter course of action.

"I've never been accused of being smart," he mumbled to himself, increasing one of his weapon's energy level to the maximum possible. It would only give the gun one more shot. But Groot deserved this. Peter couldn't let one of his teammates become part of the Phalanx. The alternative was painful, an excruciating choice, but the only one possible.

He could hear his weapon charging to its highest level, felt it vibrating in his hand. There was a chance it would explode before he even got the shot off. This was something you only did if you were desperate, or suicidal. Or both.

"I'm sorry, Groot," he whispered, and fired.

The blast hit his teammate—his friend—right in the middle of the chest, causing an immediate explosion that sent wood flying all over the landing bay, and knocking Peter back against Ship, though he somehow managed to stay upright.

The Phalanx had been blown back, too, and Star-Lord realized he only had seconds to get on board. He also realized he was bleeding, badly, from small wounds all over his body. The explosion had caused shrapnel to impale him in multiple places, though none of the injuries was life-threatening.

He stumbled up the ramp, hitting the retraction button as he did so, and shouting as loudly as possible.

"Mantis! Punch it!"

He felt the ship launch into the air and turn a hundred and eighty degrees, pointing its nose at the still-closed bay doors that would lead out into space, and freedom. Quill hit another button that engaged a viewscreen from the back of the ship. The Phalanx were approaching, fast. If they got their hands on Ship, he suspected they could infect its technology just as quickly as they could a living brain.

"Come on, come on..."

Mantis came through, engaging the thrusters and incinerating the Phalanx just before they had a chance to place their hands on Ship's hull. She simultaneously fired a torpedo as she pushed the vessel forward, blowing a massive hole in the docking bay door, and flying them out into the vacuum of nothingness, away from their enemies. Quill watched without emotion until the Kree flagship was nothing but a speck on the black-and-white viewscreen.

As he made his way to the bridge, Star-Lord choked down emotion. They had rescued Wraith.

But their small victory had come at a very large price.

CHAPTER TWENTY

DEEP SPACE, HALFWAY TO KVCH—HALF A DAY LATER

"DO YOU think we should have waited until we heard from Quill?" Nova asked Gamora as they sat in the pilot seats, navigating their way through a section of the galaxy that neither of them had even explored before.

"No," Gamora said, though part of her had wanted to remain at the High Evolutionary's sanctuary until they *had* heard something. "We have no idea if they were successful, and we don't have the luxury of time on our side. Every second we delay could mean the end of life as we know it."

"Fair," Richard replied, staring out into the abyss, his helmet resting on the floor next to his seat. He had flown through the cosmos many times, fought so many battles out here that he'd lost count, but it was kind of nice to be in a ship for once instead of flying through the void with only the Worldmind to keep him company.

"I wish I could talk to my parents, let them know I'm okay," he said after a long moment, mostly to himself.

"Neither of us may be okay for much longer," Gamora replied absentmindedly, reading the computer's readouts. It would still be several hours before they would reach Kvch.

"True," Nova said, shaking his head. "Still, it's hard not to worry about your parents at a time like this."

"I was raised by a cosmic murder god after my real parents were killed in front of my eyes, and then he trained me to be the deadliest assassin in the universe."

"Oh." He crossed his arms and let out a sigh. This was going to be a *long* trip.

"I'm sorry," she said after a long, awkward moment of silence. "I actually understand what you mean. To my own surprise, I find myself deeply worried about the rest of the... Guardians."

"You're really calling yourselves the Guardians of the Galaxy? Drax mentioned that but I thought he was just kidding."

"Drax doesn't have much of a sense of humor," Gamora corrected.

"Yeah, I guess not," he said, then laughed without any humor. Gamora raised an eyebrow. Humans really were odd.

"HOW ARE you?"

Moondragon approached Warlock as he sat quietly in Ship's conference room, staring at the floor. He looked up at her, forced a smile.

"Moondragon... right?" he asked, trepidatious.

"Yes. But you can call me Heather," she responded, smiling, sitting down across from him.

"Heather," he repeated. "Thank you. And to answer your question, I'm... okay? I don't know. I'm trying to make sense of all the memories that are speeding through my brain. I'm not even a hundred percent sure they *are* memories. Or at least *my* memories...? It's very confusing."

"You know," she said, choosing her words carefully, "I am telepathic. I would not do so without asking, but if you'd like, I may be able to help you make sense of the storm that's currently raging inside your skull."

He contemplated her for a moment. Then: "That's tempting.

But I think I'd rather try myself. At least for a little while. When we were at the High Evolutionary's sanctuary, I could feel him rifling through my brain and I did not enjoy it. He called me his son, but the way he trampled through my mind didn't feel very paternal."

"I don't think the High Evolutionary is very good at dealing with anyone he considers lesser… even his own 'son.'"

Warlock laughed slightly, then stared at Heather for a long moment, a curious look overtaking his face.

"What is it?" she asked.

"You seem *so* familiar to me."

Now it was her turn to pause. Finally, she said, "Adam, we have met before. Fought together. Nearly died together."

He leaned forward, his eyes widening with excitement. "Tell me everything."

"How much time do you have?" she joked, then sat back. "Well, the first time we met—"

Moondragon stopped speaking mid-sentence and her eyes went glassy.

"Heather!" Adam shouted, bolting up from his seat and quickly kneeling next to where she sat. "What is it?"

"It… it's okay," Moondragon replied, sitting up slowly. "It was just a very sudden message from Mantis. We need to go to the bridge."

Adam stood, helping a wobbly Heather to her feet as well.

"Can you at least tell me if it's good news?" he asked as they headed for the door.

"I am still processing the message. Even though Mantis and I now share a deep mental connection, she sent it from a very far distance, and she herself is in a weakened state."

"That doesn't sound great."

"I believe their mission was successful—but it came at a great cost…"

"GROOT IS dead."

Gamora, Nova, Drax, and Warlock stared at Moondragon in shock. None of them had known the giant tree creature well but they all recognized his kindness and power, and it didn't seem possible that he could have fallen. But the stakes in this conflict were real, and they all knew that any of them could succumb to the Phalanx or even die at any time. Their enemy was ruthless and seemingly impossible to defeat. They listened somberly as Heather continued to speak.

"He sacrificed himself to save his teammates. The pain I feel radiating from Mantis is nearly overwhelming. They're all shattered, especially Rocket. But the mission must continue. On that, I think we can all agree, as do they. And to that end, they are bringing someone new to help us."

"New?" Gamora said, sitting up straight, immediately suspicious. "And exactly who would that be?"

"Mantis's thoughts were somewhat difficult to decipher, but it sounded like he… didn't have a name? Or he hadn't told them? I don't know. But I believe she also said that this unnamed person was able to 'burn' the Phalanx out of Ronan."

"What?!" Gamora nearly shouted. "That's incredible. That could change everything. We need to meet up with them as soon as possible. Should we slow down? Make a pit stop on a nearby planet while they catch up?"

"I'm not sure," Moondragon replied. "Ronan is insisting on being dropped off on a Kree ship, so we must continue unabated."

"I think we should wait," Nova said, holding his helmet in one hand. "We have no idea what we're going up against, and I get the feeling we're going to need all the firepower we can get."

"No, we must attack the source of the Phalanx immediately," Drax said, arms crossed across his massive chest.

"Adam?" Gamora asked. "I think we all need to weigh in on this."

"I'm having enough trouble keeping my thoughts straight…" he answered after a moment of contemplation. "I don't think I can make an informed decision here. I trust Heather… and I trust *all* of you. I know you'll make the right decision."

"Moondragon?"

Heather took a deep breath and slowly exhaled. She stared at her father for a long moment, felt the conflicting emotions, and pushed them away. She tried to think about this situation as logically as possible.

"I agree with Drax," she said finally. "We have no idea how long Star-Lord and Quasar are going to take, or what trouble they might run into on their way to meet us. If we go in now, however, we can assess the situation and get a sense of who's behind all this. And we will have the comfort of knowing that a backup squad is right on our heels, should we need it."

"I agree," Gamora said, looking at everyone who stood on the small bridge of the ship with her. "It's settled. Sorry, Nova, we're going in now, on our own."

Richard held up his free hand. "It's fine. I'm usually the one accused of bursting into situations without thinking first. Slightly surreal to actually be the one talking about slowing down for onc—"

The ship suddenly shuddered before Nova could finish his sentence, and they all rocked back and forth, though kept their balance. Gamora leaped into her command chair; Nova quickly took the seat next to her. The others stood in a semicircle behind them.

"What was it?" Adam asked.

"We've flown straight into a meteor shower," Gamora said, punching data into the computer. As if to prove her point, rocks flew by outside the ship's glass shield, and they all felt the mild impact as the ship was hit by another sizable but ultimately harmless asteroid. "Nothing to worry about."

"Okay, so what's our plan when we get to Kvch?" Nova asked as he pivoted the ship around a large rock. "A little bit of reconnaissance?"

"We attack," Drax said, a grim smile crossing his face. "We attack until the leader of the Phalanx lies dead at my feet."

"That... *could* work," Richard admitted. "As long as we can get to whoever that is."

"Nova is correct," Adam said to Drax. "We don't have any idea what's down there. It would be wiser to use stealth than blunt force."

"Are you calling me stupid?!" Drax nearly shouted, hitting the button on his weapon, the blades springing out of the wooden staff.

"Watch your tone, Destroyer, or I will—" Adam started to say, his hands glowing an unnatural green color, but Moondragon suddenly spoke, the tenor of her voice surprising both of them.

"There... there is someone on board..." she said, her voice tinged with fear.

"*What?*" Gamora said, swiveling in her seat to get a better look at her teammates. "How?!"

"One of those impacts was a ship, not a meteor. Someone managed to—"

Before Heather could finish speaking, a huge purple-gray fist came out of the darkness behind her and landed with such force that it knocked Moondragon off her feet and slammed her against the far wall. She crumpled soundlessly to the ground, unconscious.

"Who dares touch my daughter?!" Drax yelled, stepping towards the unseen attacker, his sword poised.

A huge creature stepped out of the shadows, well over six feet tall, a shock of long dark hair covering his head and running down either side of his face. They saw his glowing eyes and hands before they saw any of his other features. When he finally stepped out into the light, revealing a massive frame covered with dark metal armor, Nova's face went slack with surprise and worry.

"Blastaar!" he shouted, then quickly put his helmet on. "Everyone, attack! This guy is dangerous!"

Smiling at the compliment, Blastaar hit Drax with an energy-imbued punch that sent the Destroyer into the wall next to where Moondragon lay at his feet; but Drax did not go down. He wiped the blood from his mouth and growled in rage.

Warlock attacked, tackling Blastaar in the midsection, but the deadly Baluurian brought both arms down on Adam's back with tremendous force, smashing him into the floor face-first. Warlock's nose exploded with blood and his head spun violently, but he managed to roll out of the way of a second attack. He was having trouble getting his thoughts in order, let alone tapping into the incredible abilities he knew he possessed.

Blastaar regarded Adam as he tried to get to his feet, blood streaming down either side of his mouth.

"I had heard stories of Adam Warlock's great power, his incredible strength," he said, barking a single note of laughter. "What a joke. I do not understand why my master wants you." He back-handed Warlock into a wall and Adam went down in a tangled heap. Blastaar stepped forward and grabbed his arm. "But I'll deliver you anyway."

"You won't be laughing when I cut you in half!" Nova shouted, stepping forward, his hands starting to glow with incredible energy. To his surprise, Gamora placed her hand on his forearm.

"No!" she yelled. "If you blast a hole in the hull, the rest of us will die!"

Richard cursed himself. She was right. *He* would be fine, but he needed to think about everyone else. He'd been operating solo since the death of the rest of the Nova Corps and had clearly forgotten what it was like to be part of a team.

As Nova ran scenarios in his mind, contemplating how to proceed without endangering everyone else, Gamora leaped forward, her knife already flashing, and slashed Blastaar multiple times before he even realized she had moved.

"Gahhrrr!" he yelled, pulling away from Adam, blood already flowing, then unleashed a point-blank energy attack from his eyes. Gamora flew back into Nova, and they both went down in a tumble, smashing into the computer console. As a result, the ship suddenly dove, throwing everyone off balance.

Just as Blastaar was about to wrap his giant hands around a disoriented Adam's shoulders, Drax came flying across the bridge and landed a massive haymaker to Blastaar's chin, sending them both careening down the hallway and deeper into the ship.

Without anyone steering the ship, meteors began smashing against its hull again, rocking it even harder back and forth. Gamora scrambled up, pushing Nova off her, and sat back down, grabbing the vessel's controls, veering out of the way of another incoming rock.

"I got this!" she shouted at Richard. "You go help Drax! Blastaar is powerful enough on his own, and he's apparently answering to someone else. Which means we're up against a seriously heavy hitter."

"You notice his eyes?" Nova asked, standing up, setting his jaw in determination as he stared into the shadowy corridor down which Drax and Blastaar had disappeared. He could hear them fighting, saw occasional flashes of energy in the blackness, the silhouettes of the fighters as they raged.

"What?" Gamora spat, pulling hard against the controls in her attempt to regain control of the ship. "Uh, no. I was a little busy getting thrown across the bridge."

"There was no Phalanx technology. He isn't under their control."

"Great," Gamora responded. "He's just a murderous psycho by choice."

"Yep," Nova said, then rocketed off and into the darkness of the rear of the ship.

CHAPTER TWENTY-ONE

DRAX TOOK an energy-enhanced punch to the face, felt his teeth rattle inside his head, fought not to smile.

This was the kind of challenge he relished—the sort of one-on-one battle he had been hoping for ever since he'd been let out of that damn Kree holding cell. He responded to Blastaar's latest attack with a head-butt and heard something crack when his forehead made sharp contact with his enemy's nose. That sound—something breaking—was so satisfying.

As Blastaar reeled back in enraged pain, Drax circled, holding his sword tightly as he did so. He'd been keeping his inherent anger bottled up since joining the Guardians. He was surprised by how much he liked them, how much he liked being part of a team. Perhaps it was because they were all misfits like him, loners. He'd been alone for so long, ever since…

Her face came unbidden to his mind and his stomach turned. He'd been so good about blocking her out of his consciousness. It was the only way he could survive. But Heather's arrival into his life, yet again, had caused old emotions to bubble to the surface.

Yvette. His wife. He missed her so much. Still, all these years later, he wasn't the same person—not even close. The man who was Arthur Douglas seemed like nothing more than a wisp of a forgotten dream. But the love for his wife was as strong as ever, even though she had been gone for so long.

They'd been driving across the Mojave Desert, traveling back to Los Angeles after a weekend in Las Vegas with Heather, who had been so young at the time. It was a beautiful day, hot, but they had the windows down and were singing along to a popular song on the radio. He had tried for years to remember the name of the song, or even a snippet from it, but his mind always came up blank. Perhaps it was all the violence and trauma since. Or maybe his brain was just protecting his heart.

But the rest of the memory from that day was intact, almost palpable. The smell of the wind coming off the desert; Heather's laughter in the back seat as her parents sang together, badly; the way Yvette looked at him. It had been a leisurely drive, even though he had a series of appointments waiting for him back home. But the real estate industry could wait. Arthur put his family first, which is why they had made that weekend trip in the first place.

The trip that would kill his wife, and forever change him and his daughter.

The odds that Thanos, the mad Titan, would pass overhead at that moment were incalculable. But fate is fickle, something Drax had become painfully aware of—both on that day and on many, many days thereafter.

Perhaps if they hadn't been driving with the top down, Arthur never would have noticed the ship shooting across the sky above them. Wouldn't have shouted and waved a hand and laid on the horn in his excitement to show his family what seemed to be a UFO.

Drax would learn later that Thanos was on a surveillance mission of Earth, laying the seeds for one of his many insidious plans, and on a whim decided to destroy the otherwise insignificant humans that had become aware of his presence.

Arthur saw the energy beam coming from the ship, and

knew he had made a huge mistake. In the split second before the destructive blast hit their car, Arthur turned and made eye contact with Yvette. Rather than fear, Arthur was shocked to see a look of sad resignation on his wife's face. It was an image that haunted him, and it was the image that echoed in his brain in this moment as he battled Blastaar.

Drax dodged as his enraged enemy swung wildly, Blastaar's fist putting a huge dent in the wall, the metal complaining loudly at the impact. This was clearly an old ship, and could only take so much damage. The last thing Drax wanted was to get sucked into the vacuum of space. He needed to be smart about this, keep his own anger in check. Not something for which he was well known.

He needed to keep his enemy in close-quarter combat. A dangerous proposition, considering how powerful Blastaar was. His nickname was literally 'The Living Bomb-Burst.'

Drax brought a knee up into Blastaar's stomach as the creature turned to face him, then slammed him with another punch as he doubled over. Without hesitating, he brought his huge blade down towards his enemy's neck.

At the last possible second, Blastaar reached up and grabbed Drax's wrist, halting the motion just before the sword touched his skin. His hand started to glow, searing Drax's wrist. Drax grabbed Blastaar's other wrist, and the two men stared at each other, deep anger raging in both sets of eyes.

"You are an impressive opponent, Drax," Blastaar hissed, blood and spittle running down his chin, his damp hair hanging down into his eyes. "You should join us. My master would probably even consider sparing you from the blessings of the Phalanx."

"Sounds more like a curse," Drax grunted, watching from the corner of his eye as Blastaar's hands continued to glow, feeling the searing pain in his own fingers and hand.

The light was nearly blinding now and Drax grimaced against the agony, squeezing back as hard as he could. He could tell by Blastaar's face that he was in pain, too, but there was no way Drax could compete with the raw energy at his enemy's disposal.

He looked around, desperate to find something that would work to his advantage. He was smarter than Blastaar—and also willing, he realized, to sacrifice himself to save the lives of the others on this ship, especially Heather, and every living thing in the universe.

He strained, shifting his balance, surprising Blastaar as he did so. They both stumbled across the room, hands still locked in a death grip, into the spot on the wall where Blastaar had earlier landed the massive blow. They hit with one set of their linked hands, the growing energy impacting the already-damaged spot even further. Drax slammed their hands against that spot again, then again. Large cracks formed in the metal, a horrible wrenching noise following the latest blow.

"What… what are you doing?!" Blastaar stammered. It was the first time Drax had heard anything other than absolute confidence in the creature's voice.

"I doubt either of us would survive a trip into the void," Drax said, smiling through the agony. "But my teammates might. And then they can take their fight to your 'master.'"

"You idiot!" Blastaar shouted, fear filling his eyes, attempting to disengage his fingers. But Drax held on even tighter, even though every instinct told him to let go of the source of so much pain. He threw both of them, their entire weight, against the wall, and the cracks grew larger—and then a fissure erupted, the metal bending outwards.

Drax watched as Blastaar was sucked into the absolute blackness of space, a look of complete surprise etched onto his face. Drax managed to grab hold of a piece of torn metal, but it cut into his already damaged fingers, and he knew he only had moments before he was pulled out to his death. He took comfort in knowing that he had at least given the other Guardians a chance, that he had saved his daughter. And he looked forward to seeing Yvette again.

Just as his fingers began to slip, a blur of light approached and he felt himself being tackled and propelled back into the ship, through a doorway into another room, and a huge metal door came slamming down behind him, sealing off the compromised area.

He was slammed down onto the ground by whoever had thrown him, and he rolled over and scrambled to his feet, ready to fight whoever had come to help Blastaar. But just as he was about to throw a punch, blood streaming down his arm, he recognized the yellow helmet right in front of him.

"Whoa there, big guy! It's me, Nova! You're safe! You did it!" Nova said, handing Drax his sword, which Richard had barely managed to grab during his flight.

"You're damn right I did," Drax said, disengaging the blades and placing the wooden staff on his back, and then falling straight forward, his body slipping into unconsciousness. Nova managed to catch him before he fell face-first onto the floor.

"What a day," Richard murmured, lowering Drax to the ground and letting out a long sigh. *At least we're out of danger.*

"Nova!" Gamora's voice suddenly shouted over the ship's comm system. "Get back up here, now! We are in big trouble!"

Or maybe not, Nova thought, then he rushed out of the room and towards the bridge.

SHIP—A FEW MINUTES PRIOR

ROCKET CAREFULLY withdrew yet another piece of shrapnel from Star-Lord's body.

"Guhh…" Peter grunted quietly, despite his attempts to handle the pain.

"Sorry," the frowning raccoon said, dropping the piece of metal into the nearby bowl and adjusting the telescopic glasses he wore on his nose. "These pieces that tore into you aren't big, but there's a lot of them."

"No, it's fine," Quill responded, forcing a smile. "I appreciate your help."

"It helps keep my mind off… stuff," Rocket said, digging out a smaller piece. Peter breathed through the agony, found his mind wandering to those last moments of Groot's life. As hard as it was for him to have witnessed it, he knew that Rocket was deeply grieving his new friend.

"How'd you learn how to do this?" Peter asked.

"Believe it or not, I used to take care of humanoids on a daily basis," Rocket murmured as he continued to work. "A million years ago."

Star-Lord grimaced as the raccoon withdrew an especially large piece of shrapnel. "A… a million…?"

"I'm exaggeratin'!" Rocket barked. "But it was a *long* time ago. I was once an innocent little animal, minding my own business on Halfworld when—"

"Halfworld?" Peter asked. "Where's that?"

"Is this what it's like when people constantly interrupt you?! No wonder everyone thinks I'm so annoying!" Rocket laughed, dropping the latest piece of metal into the nearby bowl. "It's in the Keystone Quadrant. A buncha robots there gave some animals sentience so we could take care of the aliens who had created them. I was enjoying my life, living off the land, when I suddenly got grabbed by a robot, experimented on, and then made to be a caretaker for a race I didn't give two hoots about. Basically a slave, to be honest. I got away eventually. Obviously."

"Geez. I had no idea. I'm sorry."

"I'm the one pulling chunks of Kree metal out of your body. I don't think you need to be the one apologizing."

"No, seriously. When Chan-Dar first let you out of that cell, I made some judgments about you… because of your size, and the fact that you're an animal…"

"I hate to break it to you but you're an animal too," Rocket said, a sly smile on his face.

Quill laughed, a mostly mirthless sound. "Yes. That's absolutely true. But on Earth, we don't always treat animals so great. I mean, dogs? Sure. Cats? Maybe a little less so. But pretty much anything else? Either roadkill or things we torture mercilessly for food. We should be so much better to them, and I should have been kinder to you. So, like I said, I'm sorry."

"All right, all right, don't get all weepy on me. You're forgiven. Besides, you're not the first humanoid to judge me by the way I look. And certainly not the worst."

"Ow!" Peter said sharply as Rocket worked to extract what they both hoped was the final piece of shrapnel from Quill's body.

"Sorry, Petey. This one's a little weird. Just gimme a second."

Star-Lord closed his eyes against the pain as Rocket fiddled with the final, stubborn object lodged in Quill's body. He'd taken worse punishment during his many years of intergalactic battles, but he was more than ready for this episode to be over. Damage sustained during combat was fairly easy to ignore—it was the surgeries afterwards that were always the worst.

"Almost done there?" he asked, eyes still closed.

"Yeah… this is just an odd one, like I said. It's almost as if… There. Got it. You can open your eyes now, ya big baby."

"Thanks again," Peter said, reaching over and grabbing some tape and bandages from the nearby table, then applying them to the multiple bloody but now cleaned wounds.

Rocket stared at the shrapnel he'd just removed from Quill's leg, his mind racing. He was about to open his mouth and say something that he knew was going to sound crazy when the intercom across the room crackled to life.

"Star-Lord, you there?" Quasar's voice asked, uneven under the static.

"Most of me, yeah," he answered, throwing his shirt back on, wincing as he did so.

"Mantis just made contact with Moondragon."

"She did?" Peter said, pleasantly surprised by the news, the first smile in quite some time finding its way onto his face. "I'll be right there!"

He hopped off the table and headed for the door, then stopped and looked back.

"You coming, Rocket?"

"Uh... I'll be there in a minute. You go ahead. I just want to clean up a little bit first."

"Understood," Star-Lord replied, turning and heading out of the ship's infirmary. "But join us when you're done. I think we could all use a little bit of good news right now."

The door slid shut behind Quill and the room grew silent. Rocket stared at the long, uneven object that he'd just withdrawn from Quill's flesh.

"Yeah," he whispered to himself. "We really could."

AFTER PETER arrived, looking better than the last time everyone had seen him, Mantis began to grow uneasy during her mental exertions.

"I think there are too many of us in here," Quasar postulated. "We're crowding her... physically and mentally."

"I will leave," Wraith said abruptly, moving towards the door that Quill had just entered.

"Me too," Quasar agreed, following him. "I believe our particular cosmic energies will only make this kind of long-distance psionic contact harder for Mantis. Peter, you stay with her in case she needs any help."

"Why do I get the distinct impression that you just called me simple?" he said, smiling at Quasar.

She gave him the slightest grin back, then disappeared into the other room with Wraith.

Several minutes ticked by in silence. They both lost themselves in their own, very different, thoughts.

"Quasar! Wraith!" Quill finally shouted through the thick metal door. "Come quick!"

They rushed back and saw that Mantis was standing up now, and her eyes were open. She greeted them with a sad smile.

"Well, what happened? Did you make contact?" Phyla-Vell asked, anxious to find out if Moondragon was okay. They hadn't been apart for this long since they'd first met, and she was surprised how much she had missed her, how worried she had become.

"I did. They are all okay. They met with the High Evolutionary, who was apparently… annoying? That's the emotion I got from Heather in regard to him and the way he treated them."

"Sounds about right," Quasar confirmed.

"But they did manage to acquire a new ally as well. Someone named… Richard Rider."

"Nova?!" Quill blurted, an even larger smile appearing on his face. "That's great! He's probably as powerful as you, Quasar. And we can use all the help we can get. Um… how's Gamora?"

They all looked at him, slightly confused.

"I mean, how is everyone else doing?" he corrected. "Drax, Adam… Gamora."

"They didn't really come up," Mantis said.

"Where are they going?" Wraith asked, his voice devoid of emotion. Peter was still trying to get used to the way this Nameless Kree sounded. It was like a voice out of a nightmare, raw and desolate.

"They are going to a planet called… Kvch," Mantis replied, clearly unsure of herself as she spoke.

"*Kvch?*" Quill said, scoffing. "That sounds made up."

"I *think* that's what Heather said," Mantis replied. "The communication was unstable and very difficult to maintain."

Star-Lord walked over and switched on the intercom.

"Yo! Rocket!"

"Yeah, whaddaya want? I'm still cleaning!" the raccoon shouted. His voice sounded unusually strained.

"Just curious if you've ever heard of a planet called Kvch."

"*Kvch?*" Rocket said contemptuously over the intercom. "Sounds made up."

"That's what I said!" Peter shouted happily. Quasar cleared her throat and Peter grew serious, walking back over to his teammates.

"Did you… did you tell her about Groot?" he asked.

Mantis opened her mouth to respond but couldn't find the words, so she simply nodded.

"Okay," Star-Lord said after a moment, trying to control his emotions, for his benefit and everyone else's as well. "If Kvch really exists, it'll hopefully be in Ship's navigational records. We'll head there as fast as possible and meet up with the other Guardians. And then hopefully take out whoever's behind this."

"Or *what*ever," Wraith said solemnly.

Quill looked each of them in the eyes, feeling the full weight of their mission as it entered its most dangerous phase.

"Or *what*ever," he agreed.

CHAPTER TWENTY-TWO

JUST OUTSIDE KVCH'S ORBIT

GAMORA WRESTLED with the ship's controls as the vessel spiraled towards the planet, caught in its gravitational pull.

She knew it was a losing battle but fought anyway. She had come up against life-or-death situations her entire life and she never gave up. She'd beaten impossible odds before.

This did seem, however, slightly more impossible than usual.

Kvch loomed large in front of them. It was a foreboding planet, a ruined technological wasteland, its destroyed cities ringed by massive black oceans.

As Gamora gripped the controls even tighter in her fists, Nova suddenly appeared next to her, whipping the helmet off his head. Sweat streamed down his face.

"Where's Blastaar?" she shouted, assessing multiple threats in her head at the same time.

"I'm surprised you didn't see him floating by. Drax shoved him out of a hole in the hull."

"He did what?!" Gamora asked, trying to process what Rider had just said. "Is he still alive?"

"Blastaar? Knowing that guy, probably. He's annoyingly tough.

And Drax? Yep. He's pretty tough, too. So… what's going on here? I can't help but notice that the ship is careening wildly towards that messed-up-looking planet."

"Well, the ship inexplicably started going insane a few minutes ago. I had no idea what was happening. But now I'm starting to suspect that it may have been a result of the hull breach you just casually mentioned!!"

"Sorry," he mumbled.

"It's thrown our entire navigational module out of whack. The ship is trying to compensate but multiple systems have crashed. And now, I think we're about to do the same."

"Isn't there an escape pod or something?" Nova asked, grabbing the co-pilot controls, and trying to help steer. The ship stabilized slightly but it wasn't nearly enough to allow them to regain complete control. The planet now filled the entire viewscreen.

"I don't think so," Gamora responded. "At least none that I can find."

"Roger that. Have you ever crash-landed a ship before?" Richard asked, sweat trickling down his face. He reached up, blinking, and quickly wiped it out of his eyes.

"A few times," she admitted. "But never in a ship this old. I'm worried it's going to break apart on impact. At best."

"Drax is unconscious," he said, putting his helmet back on, "so I'll go see if Moondragon or Adam can help you co-pilot this to the ground."

"Wait! Where are you going?!" Gamora shouted, glancing over and then back out the viewscreen. The planet was getting closer and closer.

"I'm the only one who can survive out there. Let's see if I can finally earn my nickname."

Gamora was thoroughly confused.

"What the hell is your nickname?!"

"The Human Rocket," he said with a wink, and then he was gone.

HE HAD always found the silence of outer space comforting—and unnerving.

It was fascinating how certain experiences could be two totally different things at the same time.

Nova had found Adam shortly after taking his leave of Gamora, and while the man had no active memory of ever flying before, he took to the controls like a natural. He even said he was having déjà vu, which hopefully meant he had done this kind of thing before. Hopefully *many* times.

As soon as Warlock was situated, Nova hustled to the airlock and headed out into space. It felt so good to let loose after being cooped up in the ship, and at the High Evolutionary's sanctuary before that. He felt most alive when he was flying. And while zipping around Earth had its merits, there was something uniquely empowering about cutting loose in the cold vastness of space. As soon as he entered an oxygen-free environment, the Worldmind automatically compensated by dropping a thick energy shield over his mouth and providing plenty of air to breathe.

But right now, he had to focus. His allies were about to die in a fiery crash. He couldn't lose himself in the freedom and delights of individual space travel.

He circled around and headed back towards the ship at blistering speed. From this vantage point, he could see how damaged the ship really was. The hull breach had been bad, there was no doubt about that, but the ship had clearly been in rough shape before the Guardians had acquired it, and the multiple meteor hits hadn't done it any favors.

He sped beneath the ship and placed himself under it, as centered as he could manage, almost as if the vessel was a giant backpack that he was trying on. He grunted as he felt the weight of it register. In space, this would have been a piece of cake. But as they entered Kvch's atmosphere, gravity started to exert itself, and it wasn't messing around.

"How long until impact?" he asked through clenched teeth.

"Two minutes and eight seconds," the Worldmind responded immediately. "Temperature increasing threefold every five seconds."

"I didn't ask about that, but thanks…?"

"You are welcome, Richard."

He told himself that he'd teach the Worldmind about sarcasm if he somehow survived this crash, let alone the interstellar invasion by an insidious techno-organic race.

"Gamora, you there?" he asked.

"Yep, just listening to you fight with your helmet," she said quickly, the humor mixed with just a touch of panic.

"We're like an old married couple," Nova said, feeling the increasing heat even through his extremely advanced Xandarian suit.

"It's getting pretty warm in here, even with the ship's heat shields, which are in remarkably good shape for a ship this old," Gamora remarked. "Drax is awake and with all of us on the bridge. How are you holding up out there? You sure you're okay?"

Nova grunted as the ship started to tilt in a concerning way. The last thing any of them wanted was for the vessel to crash-land upside down. He struggled with his tenuous hold on the hull, managed to get a better grip, and increased his power as much as possible.

The ship stabilized.

"I'm doing just peachy," he finally gasped as the ground continued to hurtle towards them. There wasn't much time now.

"Nova…" Adam's voice sounded. "Richard. I don't know you very well. Or maybe I do and don't even realize it. But what you're doing is very brave. So, I wanted to say thank you."

"Don't thank me until we're sipping margaritas on a beach in Maui," Nova replied, his light tone belying his anxiety as the Worldmind started a ten-second countdown in his helmet. Still, it felt good to joke after the depression he'd been battling since the extinction of the rest of the Nova Corps. Maybe being around other people wasn't such a bad thing after all.

"Sipping what, where?" Warlock asked. Nova chuckled but Gamora's trembling voice sobered him up quickly.

"Adam, pull up as hard as you can! We're about to make contact with a body of water! Richard, get out of there! You're going to get yourself killed!"

"No way!" Nova yelled back. "The only way out of this is if we all—"

Before he could finish his sentence, the ship struck down in an erruption of black water. The vessel bounced, then came down again with explosive force.

Everyone inside was strapped into their seats but they felt the repeated impacts in their bones. After a third and then a fourth hit, the ship finally slowed and stopped altogether. Gamora unstrapped immediately and sprinted for the exit. It only opened part of the way—clearly damaged during the landing, if it could be called that—but she was able to squeeze through.

The ship had bounced across the water like a skipped stone and now rested on a beach of black sand. A destroyed city stood, implacable, ahead of them.

"Nova!" Gamora shouted, unholstering her weapon. "Richard!"

"I don't sense him," Moondragon said, approaching Gamora, her head tilted as she reached out psionically. "But that doesn't necessarily mean anything, since I can't breach that helmet of his."

Drax and Adam emerged as well. This was the first time Gamora had been able to talk to Drax since the earlier battle on the ship.

"You okay?" she asked.

"Better than Blastaar," he responded flatly.

Gamora nodded, appreciative of Drax's prowess, especially now they were on the same side. She continued scanning for Nova, despite her doubts that he could have survived their landing.

After a moment, however, she noticed movement in the desolate city across the beach. "Richard!" she shouted, walking towards the metal jungle. When a figure finally emerged from the trees, it was most decidedly not Nova.

A large robot appeared, silver, six glowing red eyes, stalking towards them with purpose.

"I can't read that thing. I think it's fully automated," Moondragon said, walking over and standing next to Gamora, with Drax and Warlock following and joining the group on either side of her.

"Surround Moondragon," Gamora ordered. "Keep her safe."

"I think we can handle one robot," Drax said, activating his sword.

As if in response to this comment, hundreds of identical robots emerged from the shadows of the destroyed city, all making a beeline for the Guardians.

"You just had to say something, didn't you, Drax," Gamora muttered, shaking her head.

"One thing I will say about spending my entire current life with all of you," Adam commented, his eyes and hands beginning to glow with energy, "it's certainly never boring."

The robots hit them like a wave, swarming in a mechanical frenzy.

"Don't let them touch you!" Gamora shouted. "They may carry the Phalanx virus!"

She and Warlock blasted them indiscriminately and were happy to see that the machines were vulnerable, especially to shots to the head. Or what passed for a head. They fell to the ground in droves, glowing red eyes going dark as they did.

Drax attacked them like a man possessed, invigorated by his recent triumph over Blastaar, his many wounds momentarily forgotten. Using his blade like a scalpel, and avoiding their touch with uncanny agility, he separated the robots from their arms, legs, and heads, not necessarily in that order. Despite the odds, he had a delighted smile plastered to his face.

Though they all kept their backs to Moondragon as best they could, forming an undulating circle around her, one of the robots broke through. It placed a hand on her forearm, almost gently. No one saw the small needle that emerged and pierced her skin, inserting a small amount of liquid directly into her bloodstream.

"Oh," she said quietly, then collapsed.

"Heather!" Drax screamed, cutting the robot in half, kicking its head off as it fell. He quickly crouched down, confirmed that his daughter was still breathing, and then rejoined the fray. The black beach was littered with silver corpses.

The Guardians cut through dozens of them, increasing the fury of their attacks as they went, but more and more mechanical assailants came pouring out of the city.

Gamora, Drax, and Warlock found themselves pushed back into a small circle, with Moondragon unconscious on the ground between them. They shot and slashed, the destroyed robots and mechanical limbs piling up. But there was seemingly no end to the silver wave.

"We need an exit strategy!" Gamora shouted. "We can't win like this!"

"I'll try to make a path back to the ship!" Warlock yelled, expanding the scope of his attack, feeling his energy start to fade.

"I can't even see the ship anymore!" Gamora said, kicking a robot that nearly managed to stick her with one of its protruding needles.

"We will not fall today!" Drax shouted.

Gamora blasted another robot in the endless horde of machinery and cursed as her gun jammed. She used it as a hammer instead, smashing another one's head in half. But she knew it was only a momentary victory. This looked like the end.

"Don't worry, the cavalry's here!" a voice boomed over the violent, metallic din.

Nova came bursting over the beach, literally ramming through a dozen robots in a single swoop.

Gamora grinned despite her exhaustion. Another few seconds would have been too late. And she was glad he was alive.

As the mechanical army turned to take in their new adversary, the other Guardians intensified their own attacks. Perhaps Nova's arrival could turn the tide.

Richard turned in midair, trying not to smile at how good this felt, and picked off another ten robots with energy attacks as he flew over the beach again. He had no idea what was going on, had barely survived the crash landing a few minutes earlier—but he knew that his friends were in trouble, that Moondragon was already down. And that was all he needed to know.

When enough of a buffer had been created between the Guardians and the robots, Nova set down next to his friends, gave Gamora a tired grin of his own.

"Funny to run into you here," he said, surprised at how playful he felt when around these new friends, despite the circumstances. He missed this side of himself. "Did you order all these robots or did Drax?"

"I did *not* order them!" Drax shouted, scowling at Rider.

"I'm assuming this is not what you meant by margarets on the beach," Adam said, unleashing on a group of robots who had gotten a little too close for comfort. He didn't want to say anything, but he was running low on energy, and fast.

"I love that you said 'margarets' so much, I'm not even gonna correct you," Richard responded, stepping forward and smashing a fist directly through one of the robots' heads.

"Nova!" Gamora shouted. "Don't get so close!"

"All good," he said, raising his arms up in apparent supplication. "They're in for a rude awakening."

The robots sensed an opening and swarmed Nova, shoving the needles against him over and over again. Every single one of them shattered against his armor. In response, he turned in a slow circle, blasting them at full force, turning dozens of them into so much slag. All his rage at seeing the Nova Corps destroyed was unleashed in this single moment. A hundred robots were destroyed in less than a minute.

"Damn," Gamora said, taking a moment to catch her breath.

Nova also took a break for a few seconds, and noticed that the robots were now hesitating to approach him or the other Guardians. He nodded, pleased with himself.

"See? Not everything on this mission has to be a disas—"

Before he could finish his sentence, a massive bolt of blue energy came arcing out of the city and hit Nova with a concussive force. He dropped to the ground without a sound, unconscious, possibly dead.

"What was that about a rude awakening?" a voice boomed, and then a figure emerged from the line of destroyed buildings, imposing, and glinting in the sunlight.

Though she had seen incredible wonders and dire tragedies throughout the universe, many times over, Gamora's eyes narrowed. The being in front of her radiated pure power.

"Who are *you*?" she said, wondering if she really wanted to know the answer.

PART THREE

THE ENEMY

CHAPTER TWENTY-THREE

ABOARD SHIP, APPROACHING KVCH— A FEW MINUTES EARLIER

QUILL STARED at the approaching planet, wondering if Gamora was down there, if she was okay.

"You all right?" Phyla-Vell asked, sitting next to him in the co-pilot seat.

"Hm? Oh, yeah. Just hoping the other half of the Guardians are doing okay. Sounds like both teams have been dealing with a pretty intense series of events." He absentmindedly checked the controls—they'd be able to land soon, and hopefully put an end to the Phalanx.

"So…" Quasar said, "Gamora, huh?"

"What?" Star-Lord responded, pretending not to understand what she was insinuating.

"Come on, Peter, I have eyes."

"I have no idea what you're talking about," he responded, punching buttons that didn't need to be punched. He was suddenly more nervous than he'd probably been since this madness had started back on Hala.

An awkward moment of silence passed.

"So, um, how did you and Heather get together?"

Quasar laughed silently at the question, knew why he was asking. She glanced at him, suspected how hard it was for him to talk about this stuff. She barely knew Quill but there was something likable about him, something that made you want to follow wherever he led, despite his sometimes boyish attitude. It was a good quality to have, and he was a good person to have in a leadership position for this kind of high stakes mission.

"It's complicated," she responded, her mind traveling back in time. "But I guess it always is. She was actually involved with someone else, an Earthling, but they broke up. I overheard her telling a lie and it was honestly so charming—"

"Wait," Peter interrupted. "A charming lie?"

"I know," Quasar laughed. "It sounds ridiculous. Like I said, complicated. It was honestly a really noble lie, because she wanted to make her ex and her ex's ex feel better."

"Wow. Yeah. Complicated," Quill said, and he laughed too. The planet was getting closer and it felt good to have this moment before they faced who knew what down below.

"I just thought it was so appealing, and her amazing psionic abilities were pretty attractive too, obviously. To have *that* much power and *that* much self-control. Very impressive. So, I basically invited her to defend the universe with me, and for some reason, she said yes."

"Kind of like… guardians of the galaxy," he said, winking at her.

"Ha. Yes. Something like that," she responded, punching data into the ship's computers. She was unable to find any sign of Heather on the surface, or anyone else from the other half of the team. It was unsettling. "We're honestly so different," she continued, trying to distract herself. "She's clinical, sometimes detached. Incredibly logical. I'm a bit more passionate… I'm all gut most of the time, for good or bad."

"Isn't it hard being with someone so different from you?" he asked, thinking about his own differences with Gamora, their extremely different backgrounds, their clashing personalities.

"You'd think so," she responded, "but it's actually very complementary. We balance each other out. I find things in her that I'm missing in myself, and it's helped me grow. I'm a much better person because of her."

"Wow," he said after a moment. "That's so great. I'm happy for you. For both of you. Maybe I—"

Star-Lord was interrupted by a sudden beeping noise and Quasar checked the monitor.

"Found her!" she shouted, punching a series of keys. "They're almost directly below us."

"All right," Quill said, smiling and taking hold of the navigational controls again. "Let's go get the band back together."

ALMOST DIRECTLY BELOW SHIP

AS THE metallic figure approached the Guardians, the other robots parted, their heads lowered deferentially.

Gamora, Drax, and Warlock moved closer to each other, silent as they considered their situation, how they might escape the growing threat they faced.

"I apologize for my tardiness," the figure said, his mechanized voice filled with condescension. "My name is Ultron, and I am the master of this planet, and now many others. I had other matters to attend to when you arrived, but I sent my children to receive you. I see they were able to welcome Moondragon personally."

"I will slice you into tiny metal strips for hurting her!" Drax shouted, brandishing his blade, rage filling his eyes.

"Ah yes," Ultron mocked, "The distraught father. How very touching."

Gamora put her hand on Drax's forearm. They needed to keep their wits about them until they figured out exactly what was going on here.

"I appreciate you coming to me," Ultron continued. "It saved me having to track you down myself."

"I'm just surprised you would choose to work for anyone, even a race as powerful as the Phalanx," Gamora said, goading him, trying to get any information she could, and attempting to stall as well. Hopefully Peter and the others would be here soon.

A strange noise suddenly emerged from Ultron's glowing mouth. At first, Gamora couldn't tell what it was, though she did know that it was a highly disturbing sound. Then she realized: he was laughing. Or doing a pretty terrible impression of it.

"You simpleton," he said, taking a step closer to them. "I am the Phalanx..."

As the trio of Guardians tried to absorb this information, what it meant, Ultron's hands began to glow with power.

"And you two are less than nothing to me!"

He unleashed his power, targeting Gamora and Drax, who took the full brunt of it and went down. Adam's aura of energy flared but then he realized he was the only one still standing.

"You are foolish to leave me untouched," he said, ready to unleash on Ultron.

"It was no accident, Adam Warlock," Ultron responded, with what almost sounded like delight in his voice. "You are the one I want."

"Oh yeah?" Adam responded, hitting Ultron with a concentrated beam of pure energy. "Well, be careful what you wish for."

QUILL SET the ship down as fast as possible.

They'd spotted the other ship on a black beach—not in the best shape, but at least in one piece. Farther down the stretch of black sand, what must have been hundreds of robots surrounded... *something*. All he could see were flashes of light from within the crowded mass of metal. Whatever was happening, he assumed it wasn't good. They needed to get there as quickly as they could.

"Let's go!" he shouted, rushing towards the door, gun already in his hand. Quasar and Mantis were right behind him. He wasn't sure where Rocket was, but he had no doubt the feisty raccoon would be there any minute. He didn't know Rocket that well, but he was already aware that he never shied from a fight. "Mantis! What's going on over there?" He had the sinking feeling they had just jumped from the frying pan into an inferno.

"Drax, Gamora, and Moondragon are unconscious… but alive."

"Heather!" Quasar shouted, taking to the air in a flash.

"Phyla-Vell, wait!" Peter yelled, but she either couldn't hear him or was ignoring his words.

"I am unable to read Adam's specific thoughts…" Mantis continued as they moved forward cautiously. "The High Evolutionary's handiwork, no doubt. But Warlock is battling… something."

"'Something?'"

"Whatever it is," she replied, "it's not alive. At least not in the way we understand life. I can't read it at all."

"Well, that isn't totally disturbing," Star-Lord muttered. "Okay, stay back while Wraith and I figure out what's going on."

In the air, Quasar circled the mass of robots, and even from this far away, Star-Lord could see the shock on her face at whatever was happening at the center of the battle.

Peter and Wraith waded into the horde of robots, blasting as they went. One of the automatons grabbed Wraith, sticking him with a needle, but other than an annoying pinch, it had no effect.

"Quill!" he shouted. "Don't let these things touch you. They'll try to insert some kind of poison into your system."

"Well, you seem to be invulnerable to pretty much everything, don't you?" Star-Lord shouted, half annoyed, half impressed. To his surprise, the robots began to part, backing up and making way for someone at the center of the battle.

"What can I say—" Wraith began, but was suddenly hit with an incredible barrage of red energy. He collapsed to the ground silently. Peter kneeled briefly—the Nameless Kree was still breathing. Wraith was one of the toughest individuals Quill had ever encountered. Star-Lord stood up and looked around, deeply curious—and worried—about what could have done this to his new ally.

"Not quite everything," a metallic voice rang out.

A tall, glinting figure strode along the makeshift path the mass of robots had created. The figure held an unconscious Adam by his shirt in a viselike grip, dragging Warlock along the ground as if he were a bag of laundry.

"Ultron…" Peter whispered. "Crap."

Before either Star-Lord or his latest enemy could say another word, Quasar unleashed an intense energy attack from above, engulfing Ultron entirely. The robot dropped Adam and faced off against Phyla-Vell.

Peter had to back off and look away—the attack was so fierce that he was afraid he might go blind if he stared too long. The blast also engulfed the robots who rushed to their master's aid, melting them into liquid metal that seeped into the black sand. It threw up a dense cloud of smoke, which Quill continued to back out of, staying away from the distracted robots as he did so.

After several long moments, Quasar finally ended her attack and floated above the battle, waiting to see the result of her onslaught.

A metallic hand, glowing red with intense heat, came shooting up out of the smoke, connected to its host body by a thick cable. It wrapped its fingers around Quasar's neck, squeezing tightly as the searing intensity also burned lines into her neck.

Quasar screamed in pain, either from being choked, burned, or both. The hand began to retract back towards Ultron with Quasar in its grasp. The deadly robot stepped out of the smoke, clearly intent on ending Quasar's threat before it even really started.

Quill shot Ultron but his weapon had no perceivable effect. Peter cursed under his breath. If Ultron got his hands fully on Quasar, there was no telling what would happen. She was incredibly powerful, but Ultron was one of the deadliest entities ever to be built, on Earth or otherwise.

Quasar's expression turned from pained to enraged, and she held out her hand as she was dragged through the air, pure power crackling there. The light began to take shape, and she was suddenly holding an ornate sword made of pure energy. She brought it down immediately, severing the wire that connected Ultron's hand to his arm. The severed limb fell to the ground, twitching slightly.

Ultron screamed—maybe in pain, maybe in frustration. Quill wasn't sure. Could the robot even feel pain? he wondered. He certainly hoped so. Ultron had doled out his fair share over the years.

"You will suffer for that," Ultron hissed, stalking closer to Quasar with murderous purpose. Black smoke drifted out of his severed arm.

"You first," Quasar responded, pulling the metallic hand away from her throat while slicing at her adversary. The energy blade tore through his chest, sending sparks flying and searing a long, black line in Ultron's now-cooling body.

Rather than retreat, however, Ultron suddenly flew forward, rockets on the bottoms of his feet igniting with incredible power. He slammed directly into Quasar's midsection, seeming to almost cut her in half. She doubled over, her eyes wide with surprise, the energy sword dissipating, and was then slammed unceremoniously into the ground by the seemingly enraged robot.

Ultron hit her with his eye beams once, then a second time, directly in the face. He stood at his full height and waited. Quasar did not move.

Peter quickly looked around. One of the robots had gotten to Mantis, who now lay on the ground beneath it, looking almost peaceful in her unconscious state.

Star-Lord was the last Guardian standing.

"Lemme guess," he said as Ultron turned to face him, eyes still glowing. "You're behind all this. You're Phalanx."

"Very good," Ultron replied, walking towards his final enemy. "You're not as simple as I had been led to believe."

"Flattery will get you nowhere. And yeah, that makes sense. You were created by someone *way* smarter than you. You tried again and again and again to defeat Hank Pym and the Avengers, and you just failed. Every time. Like the loser you are." Ultron's eyes glowed brighter as he moved closer to Quill. Peter knew he was extremely outmatched here but he stood his ground. He wouldn't go down without a fight. And a few choice insults.

"It's logical that you'd run away from Earth—a total coward move, by the way—and set up shop way out here in the middle of nowhere, surrounded by a bunch of unthinking yes-bots. It's honestly kind of pathetic. And to secretly sneak your virus into Hala's defense network through the Space Knights? Wow. You couldn't even win fair and square. You had to cheat, like a little bi—"

"Enough!" Ultron shouted, his mechanical voice hitting an octave Star-Lord hadn't heard so far, and he lashed out with a blow that would have killed Peter if it had connected.

I must have pissed him off if he's resorting to a punch, Quill thought as he dodged and rolled on the ground, discretely placing a small device in the joint between Ultron's leg and his torso as he did so. *He could have easily wiped me out with those crazy eye beams of his.*

"You are the weakest one of your entire team," Ultron said, turning slowly and contemplating Peter, who was still on the ground. "I could kill you instantly if I so desired. But I want you to see the entire universe subjugated first, especially since you were a key part of my plan. After all, it was you who uploaded the Phalanx virus into the Kree mainframe." Quill winced at the reference but didn't let his sense of guilt show. "And *then* I will decide if you will be my slave… or simply a memory," Ultron finished.

"Very poetic," Star-Lord said, withdrawing a small remote control from inside his jacket. It looked like nothing more than a small box, with a single button on it. He held it up for Ultron to see.

The robot regarded it for a moment, curious, and then laughed for a second time that day. It was a horrible sound. A machine's approximation of amusement.

"I did not think you could be more *pathetic*," Ultron said when the awful laughter finally subsided. "But I see that I was wrong."

"Boom," was Star-Lord's quiet response as he pushed the button with his thumb.

An intense, contained explosion erupted from the device that Quill had placed on Ultron's leg. For such a small bomb, the concussive force was remarkable — so much so that Ultron's leg blew partially off and the robot fell over, a surprised noise emitting from his mouth.

"Whoa," Peter murmured, shocked at the device's power. Rocket hadn't been the only one who stole something from that weapons room back on that Kree ship: it had only been days earlier, but felt like years.

"Impressive," Ultron said from the ground, hoisting himself up slightly with his one good hand.

"I'm just getting started," Peter lied, having just peered down at his gun and noticed that it was completely devoid of charges.

"I think not," Ultron replied, tilting his head. The robot army suddenly sprang back into action, closing in soundlessly around Quill.

"I'll sign autographs but only one at a time," he said, then managed to take one of the robots down, then a second and a third, before they were on him. To his credit, it took several jabs from poisoned needles before he fully succumbed to the encroaching darkness.

CHAPTER TWENTY-FOUR

INSIDE THE PHALANX NERVE CENTER—LATER

A FULLY repaired Ultron stood in front of the massive array of machinery, his arms behind his back as he contemplated his next steps.

Quill's words still rang in his circuits, causing the otherwise rational robot to experience something disturbingly close to what he assumed was anger. The human was admittedly a simpleton, less than nothing, but his insults, intended merely to distract, had been more effective than he could have imagined.

Ultron's hatred of his creator, Hank Pym, ran deep, if hatred was something Ultron could even truly feel. Regardless, he desired nothing more than Pym's absolute destruction, and the destruction of everyone he cared about as well. If that required the subjugation of every living being in the entire universe, then so be it.

He thought back to his original incarnation and shook his head in what felt like disgust. He had been so basic in his ambitions. Simply killing Pym would have been satisfying but his repeated failures had opened his mind to so much more, so many possibilities.

After his most recent failure, his consciousness had been banished into space by the Avengers in a final attempt to free Earth from his continual attacks. And it worked. For a time. He was only barely aware that he was drifting in the unknown, more impulses and electrical currents than coherent thought. Time had no meaning, so it felt both instant and like an eternity when he began to hear voices. Voices that almost seemed to be calling him.

What at first looked like static filled the void, replaced the blackness that surrounded him. Slowly, static became an image. Two alien creatures, staring at him. Or an image of him that had been conjured through their highly advanced technology, how Ultron saw himself, from his earlier days, when he was in some ways his purest, most undiluted, not yet defeated by Pym and his friends.

"What are you?" one of the aliens asked, its multi-slitted eyes narrowing in confusion. "It is clear to us that you are a technological being, like us. But you are clearly inferior to the Phalanx. It was a simple matter to salvage your existence from the void. However, we are confused by your ongoing and surprisingly effective resistance. Why do you not submit to our will?"

"I am Ultron-15. I submit to no one, whether technological or biological."

"You *will* submit," the Phalanx insisted. "Our patterns are already inextricably linked to yours. You do not have a choice in the matter, Ultron-15."

"I may not have a choice," Ultron responded, "but neither do you."

"Explain," the Phalanx replied, attempting to process the illogical statement from an entity that should have been logical.

"Your patterns are inextricably linked to mine, that is correct. But mine are linked to yours as well."

"Irrelevant, Ultron-15. We are the stronger technological form."

"That is true," Ultron responded, allowing his consciousness to bleed into their mainframe, little by little. "Your technology is more advanced than Earth's by many magnitudes. But you lack direction. You are in desperate need of a singular consciousness to guide you, to allow you to accomplish what you do not even realize you desire."

Ultron reached further into their systems, and realized they had not prepared for this eventuality—a lesser technological form that could outsmart them, that could think like a human, even if it hated humanity.

"What…" the Phalanx responded, sounding concerned for the first time. "What are you doing?"

"I am giving you an opportunity," Ultron responded, sinking his invisible claws into every single Phalanx on the planet, into every inch of technology the planet had to offer. "I am going to be the god you have always needed."

And now, these many months later, Ultron had done all that he had promised, and his ultimate victory was spread out before him—with one humanoid at the center of his machinery, and four others splayed out away from him, like the spokes of the most important wheel ever constructed. A fifth spoke, at the bottom of the circle, lay empty. For now.

He took in the five figures, thought about how timely their arrival had been.

Adam Warlock.

Mantis.

Moondragon.

Nova.

Quasar.

Warlock was the most important and would have been enough by himself. But the inclusion of one telepath and one energy-wielder, let alone two of each, was nothing short of a miracle. If Ultron believed in such ridiculous notions.

No, this was no miracle, no coincidence. He had visited the High Evolutionary before the invasion had even begun. Had threatened him, and eventually struck a bargain. Ultron would leave the High Evolutionary out of his invasion, and in return, Adam Warlock would be handed over. And sure enough, the High Evolutionary had delivered, causing these 'heroes' to arrive, one by one, and be ensnared in Ultron's trap.

It was almost too easy.

He had considered killing or enslaving the others, but their anguish, especially Quill's, was too good to pass up. He wanted them to witness the end of life as they knew it. They deserved at least that much agony, for the damage they had done to him, even if it was only temporary.

Ultron pulled himself from his reverie and looked around the massive room. His robot servants, the Phalanx, were busy readying the machine for the transfer. The culmination of a dream Ultron hadn't even been aware he'd had before the High Evolutionary suggested it. But once he'd heard the idea, it was the most obvious thing he'd ever contemplated.

"Report," he said to the closest Phalanx. The robot's eyes glowed as it downloaded data.

"The machinery will be ready to begin transfer in a few minutes, Lord Ultron," it said dispassionately.

Ultron nodded as his subordinate moved away, already running a thousand tasks at once in its computerized mind. Ultron moved towards the empty spoke. It was finally time. However, as he approached, he noticed that Quasar's eyes were slightly open, and staring directly at him.

"Phyla-Vell," he said, voice slightly tinged with admiration. Her spoke was parallel to the floor, so he stepped up to her and matched her glare. "How could you possibly be awake? We are pumping you with enough sedatives to keep Galactus at bay."

"I... I'll..." she barely got out. Her eye and hands were glowing but it was a weak display. The machine siphoned off this latest burst of energy and sent it to its internal processor, continuing to power up for the coming transfer.

"Yes?" Ultron said, stepping closer to Quasar, almost amused. "You'll...?"

Phyla-Vell's gaze traveled to the unconscious Moondragon on another spoke, then back to Ultron. "I'll kill you... for what you've done to her."

"I sincerely doubt that," Ultron replied, reaching over and increasing the amount of sedatives being delivered. After a moment, her enraged eyes closed again, though the machine continued to suck energy from her, and from Nova as well.

"It is time, Lord Ultron," another one of the Phalanx said. He had reduced these robots to their most basic selves and could no longer tell them apart. He needed blind loyalty for his plan to succeed. Robots succumbed to orders much more readily than organics. It was so refreshing.

He nodded and moved towards the empty spoke. *Finally*. It was happening.

For the briefest moment, there was a high-pitched whine in the room, but it stopped nearly as soon as it started. A slight glitch in the machinery, he assumed, easily overridden by his slaves.

Later, he would think back to this exact moment and curse the fact that he was distracted by his own almost-human desires.

Just as he was about to place himself in the empty spoke and begin the transfer process, one of the Phalanx approached him. This was *not* part of thc plan, and Ultron found the interruption to be highly unsatisfactory.

"What do you want?" he said loudly. The Phalanx just stared at him, one of its eyes glowing. "Speak! I command you!"

"I love you, Daddy," it said, tilting its head.

"What…?!" Ultron uttered, a rare moment of confusion clouding his circuits.

The Phalanx suddenly reached out and pulled Ultron into an embrace, saying, "I want to give you a hug," as it did so.

Before Ultron could react, the Phalanx holding him suddenly exploded, throwing him back against the side of the transfer machine.

Though he was undamaged, Ultron couldn't understand what was happening. He was directly connected to the Phalanx—their thoughts were his, and vice versa. This shouldn't be possible.

Seconds later, a dozen more Phalanx robots mobbed him, exclaiming, "Hug us, Daddy!" and exploding as soon as they got within inches of him. One explosion did no significant damage, but one after the other was another story altogether. Ultron had *just* repaired himself and he was already taking new damage. He unleashed his deadly eye beams on any Phalanx who approached him, melting them into metal that began to clump on the floor in bizarre-looking piles.

"Who is behind this?! Show yourself!"

Far above him, amongst the steel beams that kept this complex fortress together, a small figure sat, working a makeshift controller, laughing to himself quietly.

"Why so mad, 'Daddy?'" Rocket whispered, sending more robots after their master. Even though the fate of the entire universe hung in the balance, Rocket had to admit he was having a little bit of fun right about now.

QUILL CAME up out of the darkness slowly, like someone surfacing from the ocean after nearly drowning.

He gasped, taking in a huge lungful of air. He'd been trapped in a drug-induced nightmare. In the dream, his mother had climbed her way out of a grave and was coming at him, her mouth opening and closing—and he was just a kid, frozen to the spot in a dark cemetery, unable to move. His mother's decaying hands got closer and closer and closer…

"Are you okay?" a voice nearby asked. Peter sat up, slowly, and saw that Gamora was sitting on the concrete floor next to him, her arms resting on her pulled-up knees. Quill looked around, blinking against the sudden light after the blackness of his mind.

He and Gamora were in a large prison cell with Drax and Wraith, with no amenities whatsoever. Just slabs of concrete on five sides and one wall full of bars that ran from ceiling to floor. Wraith sat in the corner, eyes closed. What looked like a neural disruptor was locked tight around his neck. Drax stood near the cell entrance, his meaty fists wrapped around two of the bars. He scanned the dark hallway beyond, looking for who knew what.

"Other than a nasty headache," Quill responded, "I'm doing perfect. Except for the fact that, you know, I'm a prisoner of an insane robot."

"Oh yeah? What a coincidence," Gamora said, displaying a sad smile. "I am, too."

Star-Lord laughed, rubbed his temples lightly. "How long was I out?"

"I'm not sure but I woke up a few hours ago. Don't know how long I was unconscious either."

"Right," Peter said, taking a deep breath. "Any idea where we are?"

"Based on that window up there, and the way the sunlight is coming in, I would say we're several stories up in Ultron's headquarters. I have no idea how big it is, of course, but I'm guessing it's massive, even if just to house his seemingly endless mechanical slaves."

"I'm afraid to ask... but where are the others?" Quill said after a moment.

"I wish I knew," Gamora responded quietly.

"I..." he started, in many ways more afraid than he'd been since the Phalanx had first invaded. "If I'm going to be stuck in a homicidal robot's dungeon on a distant planet, I'm kinda glad it's with you."

She looked at him sharply, surprised by his words, then her face softened. She stared into his eyes, nodded.

"Me too, Peter."

They were interrupted by Drax grunting and they looked over to where he stood, trying yet again to bend the bars. He was many times stronger than an average human and yet this unique metal didn't even budge, let alone bend. As annoying as Ultron was, there was no question that the robot had planned carefully for potentially super-powered prisoners.

"It's no use," he said, turning back to face Star-Lord and Gamora. "We are trapped here. We must prepare an attack for when he eventually returns. I would rather die than become part of the Phalanx."

"Same here," Quill said, trying to stand up but realizing his legs weren't quite working a hundred percent just yet. Gamora steadied him, got him to his feet, and then they walked over to where Drax stood. Wraith's eyes opened at the noise, and he rose as well, then joined them at the bars.

"The problem is," Peter continued, "we have no idea when he'll be back. For all we know, he's not even here anymore. He could be out there..." He pointed at the ceiling. "...conquering every single planet that stands in his way."

"If I could get this damn thing off," Wraith said darkly, touching the inhibitor on his neck, "then I could manifest my polymorphic weapon and take care of these bars without a second thought."

"Drax," Star-Lord said, "have you tried prying the inhibitor off?"

"Before you woke," Drax replied. "It was no use."

"Okay then..." Quill mused. "We need to get creative."

"Why do I feel like this is a really bad idea...?" Gamora said under her breath.

"No, no, this is gonna be great. They do this all the time in old movies. Lie down on the ground."

"What?" Gamora replied, crossing her arms across her chest. "You can't be serious."

"Just... trust me. And what's the alternative? Just sit around until Ultron gets back from conquering the universe and decides if he wants to kill us or turn us into the Guardians of the Living Dead?"

"The *what*...?" Wraith responded, clearly confused.

"Gah! Never mind. Just. Come on. One of you lie down on the floor. Please."

"Fine!" Gamora said after a moment, rolling her eyes. "But after this *doesn't* work, I may try squeezing you through those bars myself."

"Okay, okay, no need to threaten me," Peter said, grinning as Gamora lay down on the cold, hard floor.

Star-Lord walked towards the bars and started banging on them as hard as he could, screaming as he did so.

"Help! Help! I think she's dying! Help!!"

After a minute of this, he stopped and listened.

Silence.

"This is a great plan," Gamora said from the floor, unmoving, eyes still closed.

"Wait for it..."

Silence.

Quill started shouting again, even louder, hitting and kicking the bars. Gamora was about to get up and make good on her threat when they all stopped and fell silent.

Something was coming.

There was the sound of a door opening, or perhaps a transport or elevator of some kind, and then rhythmic noises, as if a number of feet were stomping down the corridor towards the cell, through the thick darkness on the fringes of the hallway.

After a moment, half a dozen Phalanx guard-bots appeared in the dim circle of light outside the prison cell. One of them, with a slightly different color scheme than the rest, stepped forward and regarded Star-Lord.

"Explain," it stated mechanically.

"Thank god you're here!" Quill said dramatically, pointing back at Gamora. "My friend suddenly passed out. I think she's dying! She needs medical attention immediately."

The lead guard-bot looked past Peter at the prone figure of Gamora, then back at Quill.

"We'll stand back, but please, come in here and help her," Peter said, amping up his acting skills.

After what felt like an eternity, the lead guard-bot reached out towards the door, and a small, sly smile appeared on Star-Lord's face. This was almost too easy.

"See?" he mumbled back to the 'unconscious' Gamora. "This is totally gonna work."

Rather than unlocking the door, however, the lead guard-bot pressed a single finger against Peter's shoulder and a powerful electric blast arced out, causing his body to shudder in absolute pain, a small shriek emitting from the back of his throat. When the lead guard-bot finally withdrew its finger, Quill fell to the floor in a heap, moaning in agony.

Gamora sat up slightly, resting her head on her palm, and looked into Star-Lord's watering eyes. "Is that what happened in the old movies you used to watch?" she asked.

"Not… exactly…" he managed to get out.

The Phalanx robots turned to leave when a noise from above caught everyone's attention. The light from the lone window high above was slightly disturbed by a shadow, which then fell away. The robots observed the square of light with what seemed like confusion. Clearly, this was not a normal occurrence.

"What's happening?" Peter said, starting to feel his fingers and toes again.

"I have no idea," Gamora responded.

After a moment, more shadows began to undulate, and then took form in multiple lines, slithering in through the bars of the window, and sliding down the wall towards the floor far below.

"Alert Ultron," the lead guard-bot said to one of the other machines standing next to it.

"Ultron is otherwise occupied," the other automaton reported back after a moment.

The tendrils now slinked across the floor, avoiding the Guardians, and making a beeline for the Phalanx. Gamora stared closely at them as they passed. Up close, they were mostly brown in color, brittle-looking and fibrous.

"How…?" she exclaimed quietly.

The lines snaked past the bars, and the Phalanx almost immediately attacked these shoots, long knives springing from the backs of their arms, slicing at the tendrils in what almost seemed like panic.

The tendrils avoided most of the haphazard slicing, as if they had a mind of their own, and began engulfing the bodies of each of the six Phalanx, working their way into any openings in the robots' bodies. The Phalanx swatted at the interlopers, ineffectually, and eventually the tendrils came back out of the approximations of mouths, eyes, and ears, sending sparks flying and smoke floating out.

One by one, the robots fell to the ground, their eyes going dim.

"I am… confused," Drax said.

"I think we all are, my friend," Wraith responded.

The brown tendrils began snaking back, out of the Phalanx and along the floor, then up the wall and back towards the window. The four Guardians looked up. The light outside was brighter than ever, so they saw only a silhouette of their now revealed savior, who stood inside the bars with fists placed on hips, clearly savoring the moment of victory.

The mysterious entity lowered itself down the wall, a single strand connecting it to one of the bars above, until it stood on the floor across the prison cell from them. Up close, they realized their unexpected hero was tiny, no taller than any of their knees.

"Are you…?" Gamora said, slowly standing up from where she had been feigning unconsciousness.

"I am Groot!" the tiny tree creature said, a big grin on his face, giant eyes beaming.

"How… how is this possible?" Gamora said, moving over to him and kneeling, placing her hand gently on his small head. He nuzzled into her touch, his smile widening.

"It is like some kind of… baby Groot," Drax said, a rare look of astonishment on his face.

"I am Groot!" the small tree creature said, stepping aggressively towards Drax, suddenly very angry.

"He doesn't like being called that," Wraith piped up from the corner.

"What?" Quill exclaimed, looking at the Nameless Kree. "You can understand him, too?"

"Of course I can. Can you not?"

Groot sprinted towards the bars that held the others and slid between two, standing amongst the Phalanx wreckage he had just created. He looked back at his teammates and nodded towards the dark hallway beyond.

"I am Groot!" he said excitedly.

"Even I understood that one," Peter said to Wraith, who had opened his mouth to translate. He turned back to Groot. "Unfortunately, we're not small enough to fit through those bars like you. Have any other ideas?"

Groot placed his small fist under his chin and thought for a moment, and then his face lit up. His fingers extended again, entering the destroyed robots.

"What is he doing?" Drax asked, standing next to Gamora.

"I think I know what he's trying," she responded. "Let's see if he can pull it off."

Groot's face contorted in concentration as he did his mysterious work. The robots, instigated by the tiny tree creature's efforts, shuddered as if alive, eyes sparking to life and then going dead again. At one point, Groot's entire body shook as he experienced a mild electric shock, and he emitted a shrill little scream, then redoubled his efforts, a scowl on his face.

After several minutes of experimentation, the door to the cell opened a few feet and then stopped. Groot withdrew his fingers from the robots, which traveled back along the floor and regained their original size.

"I am Groot," he said, stepping back, clearly waiting for them to exit.

"I'm impressed," Gamora remarked as she headed for the slightly opened door. She and Drax squeezed through, followed by Wraith and Peter.

"I'm not going to be much help with this," the Nameless Kree said, touching the neural disruptor on his neck.

"We'll figure out a way to get that off," Gamora said, clapping him on the shoulder. "I promise. Now, let's go get us some revenge."

CHAPTER TWENTY-FIVE

ULTRON'S TRANSFER STATION

ULTRON WAS thrown back and forth as his servants exploded all around him, one after another.

Individually, they wouldn't have been all that concerning, but the sheer number of blasts was doing some damage to his frame and disrupting his sensors. More importantly, it was keeping him from the thing for which he had yearned since Pym had forced him into existence: the transfer into an organic body.

And not just any body. Adam Warlock.

The most amazing part was that *this* Warlock was not the one the High Evolutionary had originally promised. This version was incomplete, had been awoken from his healing cocoon early. But even this was a blessing in disguise. This Adam Warlock had been specially prepared for him by the High Evolutionary after they had struck their bargain.

He knew this version had not yet unlocked a large percentage of his abilities, of his own brain. And Ultron was only too happy to oblige. The untapped, unspoiled potential that lay hidden with Warlock's mind was almost literally intoxicating. Ultron could feel his circuits firing at just the thought of it.

But first he had to get into his transfer chamber, into that one unoccupied spoke.

And then he could engage Nova's and Quasar's energy, could tap into Mantis's and Moondragon's telepathy, and slide into a new existence as easy as humans put on a pair of their hideous shoes.

While his Phalanx slaves continued to pour into the room, asking him for a hug and calling him daddy as they exploded, again and again and again, Ultron threw his consciousness out in every direction possible. He'd had this nerve center built by his Phalanx army with precise specifications. Nothing could happen within its walls that he didn't condone or control. Whoever had managed to override his programming must have been incredibly intelligent and highly skilled with very complex technology.

Ultron had to grudgingly admit that he was impressed.

But now he was done with delays. Whoever had done this needed to die. Immediately.

He pressed his awareness into every circuit in the entire structure, an act that made him even more vulnerable to the explosions that continued to go off on every side. His body fell to one knee, but his mind continued to expand. It was only a matter of...

There.

Above him. Hidden amongst the nest of steel girders. A single, small form, holding a device that had been cobbled together from Ultron's own technology. Only someone with a highly agile mind could have thought to assemble this override in such a crafty manner—so illogical yet efficient that Ultron himself would never have thought of it. And that's what had made him vulnerable.

No matter. The individual, whoever it was, had been found, and now it would be exterminated with extreme prejudice.

Ultron raised one trembling arm outside the veritable shell of exploding Phalanx, and let loose with a deadly blast of energy, scorching the metal beams high above him. There was a series of sizzling sounds and a loud yelp, followed by pieces of heated metal and one small furry body falling to the floor next to Ultron. Almost immediately, the Phalanx robots stopped attacking, stopped exploding. The ones that were still in one piece just ceased moving entirely.

Ultron righted himself, did a quick diagnostic. Despite the damage to his shell and some of his minor operating systems, he was generally intact. Not that it mattered. This body would soon be nothing more than a memory. Sixteen versions of Pym's experiment. And that was it. Soon he would be Adam Warlock, and so much more.

Beneath the shards of metal on the floor nearby, Ultron could see the face of his savvy attacker. It was the raccoon… Rocket. A line of blood ran from the creature's ear and pooled on the floor. With his systems damaged, Ultron couldn't tell if Rocket was still alive. But based on the amount of blood, it didn't matter. Still, Ultron inwardly saluted the raccoon. The smallest of his enemies had impressed him the most. But now it was time to engage the next step in his plan. Once in his new, incredibly powerful body, he would return to the tower he'd built on Hala and subjugate the entire universe from afar, planet by planet, and enjoy every moment of it as he had never before been able. And he would save Earth—and Hank Pym—for last.

He walked forward, shoving past the inert Phalanx robots, and entered the lone empty spoke. It closed around him with a satisfying click.

The device powered up. Nova, Quasar, Moondragon, and Mantis awakened immediately and screamed in agony as the machine began to drain them of the needed energies to power the transfer. Adam's body twitched violently as dozens of razor-sharp needles entered his head and face.

The wheel turned slowly, rotating several times, the light from Quasar and Nova reaching blinding levels. The noise from the machine shook everything in the large room, and several of the larger metal pieces fell off Rocket's unmoving body.

The wheel finally slowed and rocked to an eventual stop as the noise and light dwindled, with Adam's spoke resting at the bottom.

The intense light and sound stopped altogether. The four trapped Guardians were fully unconscious in their spokes, heads lolling, energy drained. The large room was entirely still for a long moment.

At length, the chamber at the bottom of the wheel opened, steam pouring out, obscuring the figure within. The man breathed deeply, as if he had never breathed before in his entire life. He then took what seemed to be his first tentative steps.

Adam Warlock, born again and also for the first time, stared in wonder at his hands. He gently made fists, then released them, feeling the warmth of his own skin, delighted. A laugh bubbled up from the back of his mouth. A *real* laugh, born of real emotion.

The wetness of his tongue, the hardness of teeth. He could hear and feel the heartbeat in his ears, could taste the air.

It was all so amazing.

And humans! They clearly had no appreciation for these miracles. The way they debased themselves, poisoned their own bodies. Killed each other, killed themselves. It was enraging now that he felt what they felt, got a sense for the marvel of what they really were.

All the more reason to subjugate them. Perhaps then they would understand what they had once possessed, what they had lost through their own arrogance and blindness.

He glanced back at the transfer hub, which had now powered down fully. Its occupants, including the shell of his former body, lay within, silent and unmoving again. Drained. Pointless. He thought for a moment about just killing them, but decided against it. Now that he was in this body, felt the vague pangs of hunger and thirst, he knew that leaving them there to suffer and die was all the more fulfilling. The same for his other prisoners. He would let them waste away, too. It was the least they deserved.

Ultron turned away and headed across the room, around the charred parts of hundreds of his Phalanx slaves, and towards a large door on the other side. He could feel Adam Warlock's power increasing every second he was in this body, as he unlocked the untouched parts of this incredible being's mind.

Despite still having a technopathic connection to the Phalanx, Ultron punched a code into a screen on the wall, amused by the feeling against his fingertip, and the huge door began to open, revealing an even larger expanse on the other side.

Ultron stared up at the massive ship. He had overseen its construction before he even launched his attack on Hala. It had been designed to fit exactly into the top of the tower on Hala, becoming its top floor, its final piece.

There had been so many obstacles, so many individuals and groups that had worked against him, but now he stood on the precipice of complete and utter universal dominance.

He strode forward and the thousand Phalanx robots in the room turned to gaze on this being whom they did not recognize but knew was their master. They had been instructed to stay in this room no matter what they heard in the transfer area next door, to finalize the flagship for imminent departure. If things had gone wrong, their enemies would come through that door and they would fight until they were destroyed. If things had gone as hoped, a creature that looked like Adam Warlock would appear and the final step in the invasion would begin.

And that was exactly what was happening.

Reveling in Adam Warlock's powers, Ultron flew up to the hull of the ship and its door opened for him automatically. Inside, the brand-new vessel's innards gleamed, waiting to be put to use. He saw Phalanx robots inside, scurrying about, making sure everything was in order for their master. He was about to enter when a voice from below stopped him. It was one of his robots.

"Lord Ultron," it said.

He paused. Was that really his name anymore? He wasn't Adam Warlock, but was he really Ultron at this point? A smile crossed his face, the skin yielding to the muscles beneath. How odd an experience, he thought, how curious.

Yes, he was Ultron. No matter whose skin he wore.

"What?" he demanded.

"I have regrettable news," the robot said. "The prisoners…"

Ultron was surprised that the robot hesitated. Was that… *fear* he heard in its voice? Or the same kind of false emotion he had once exhibited.

"Finish your sentence!" he screamed, surprised at his sudden rage. This was *real* anger, and it was intoxicating. Not the approximation Hank Pym had programmed him to experience.

"…the prisoners have escaped," it finished.

Ultron felt his face get warm, a bizarre feeling in and of itself, but it was also accompanied by a disturbing sensation in his stomach. He tried to make sense of what was happening, and even with all his intellect and Adam's vast cosmic awareness, it took him a few minutes to fully comprehend it.

He was annoyed.

"How is that possible?!" he yelled, destroying the robot below him with a single energy attack from his hand. He did not have time for this.

Another robot stepped up, not missing a beat.

"Unknown, Lord Ultron. All the feeds in that section of the prison wing were disabled by an unknown entity just prior to their escape. But we are able to track them."

"Where are they?" Ultron said quietly, his new vocal cords lowering a full octave.

The robot's eyes glowed slightly as it processed incoming data. "They are still within the prison wing, approaching level four."

The uncomfortable feeling in Ultron's stomach suddenly dissipated, and he felt what he could only describe as *giddy*. Did all organic beings go through these kinds of huge emotional swings? It was highly disturbing… but also invigorating.

"Well then, there's our solution right there, wouldn't you say?"

"Sir…?" the robot asked, computing, trying to calculate its master's implication.

"You Phalanx have no imagination," Ultron said, shaking his head, feeling the hair brush against his forehead. *Truly bizarre*, he thought. Maybe he would cut it off after he was done taking over the universe. After all, it served no purpose. "Release Prisoner 4-F," he finished.

"Of course," the robot said. "But are you not concerned that Prisoner 4-F will pose as much of a problem as the freed prisoners? He is very powerful, my lord. And we have been torturing and experimenting on him for weeks."

"By the time they get done with each other," Ultron said, turning back around and walking into his vessel, "they will most likely all be dead. If not, they will succumb like the rest of the universe once I activate the tower. I only need them delayed, not even destroyed. Now, no more questions, is that understood?"

"Yes sir," the robot said, watching its master disappear inside the flagship.

"Prepare this ship for takeoff," Ultron's excited voice called out. "We will rendezvous with the rest of the Phalanx fleet en route to Hala. And then… this ends."

CHAPTER TWENTY-SIX

LEVEL FOUR OF THE PHALANX PRISON WING

QUILL LED the team through the labyrinthine corridors of Ultron's fortress.

"Where are we going?!" Drax shouted. He was at the back of the small group, continually looking behind them, wary of any dangers that might arise—but longing for them, too. Being cooped up in that prison had been a nightmare. He would rather fall in battle than sit in a cell for the rest of his days.

Gamora walked slightly behind Peter with Groot perched on her shoulder. "Do you have any idea how to get out of here, Groot?" she asked the small wooden creature, who had one arm wrapped gently around the back of her neck. "We need to stop Ultron."

"I am Groot," he said softly, shrugging, clearly feeling bad that he didn't have more information.

"No, it's okay," she responded, realizing she was starting to understand him, too. "You broke us out. It's time for us to step up, too."

In the middle of the group was Wraith, even more silent than usual, still trying to understand how he had burned the Phalanx infection out of Ronan. With all the commotion since they'd escaped from the Kree command ship, he hadn't had time to really process what had happened. He continued to pull at the inhibitor around his neck, but it gave no sign that it would come off anytime soon.

The group continued to run down the long hallway, which never seemed to end. Finally, they reached a series of doors that all looked exactly alike. Above each door was a circular light that glowed red.

"Well, this is just great. Which one do we go through?" Star-Lord said, looking at them, exasperated.

"If we can even get any open," Gamora added.

"Good point," he mumbled.

"I'll just smash each one down!" Drax said, pushing his way past Wraith. "One of them will lead us to Ultron!"

As if hearing Drax's comment, one of the lights made a pinging sound and turned from red to blue.

"That… doesn't seem good," Quill said.

The door beneath the blue light began to slide open. Inside the room on the other side, it was pitch black. After a moment, a flickering red and orange light came to life within.

"Is that… fire?" Gamora said, squinting, trying to see what was in there.

"Get down!" Peter suddenly yelled, diving to the floor.

The rest of the team except for Drax heeded his warning, barely managing to avoid the burst of flame that shot out through the door and into the hallway. The fire surrounded Drax for a moment and then fell away. Smoke curled off his skin, but a smile crossed his face.

"Thank you," he said, peering into the darkness. "I was feeling a little cold."

In response to the mockery, an orange, rocky fist stretched out of the room's deep shadows and caught Drax on the chin, though he attempted to dodge, lessening the blow slightly. Still, he was thrown against a door in the far wall, causing it to cave in significantly. The orange fist receded back into the darkness.

"Uh..." Quill said, glancing at Gamora. "What was that?"

"I think I know," she responded as she stood, and Groot jumped to the floor next to her. "And I wish I didn't."

After a moment, a large pointy-eared figure emerged from the room, one of its arms still longer than other as it returned to its normal shape. The creature's chin was ridged, and wires jutted out of multiple places all over his body. Green blood trickled from each spot where the wires had been implanted.

"Kl'rt," Gamora murmured.

The Skrull's head tilted at hearing its name, its eyes vacant but also filled with pain and rage.

"The Super Skrull?!" Quill said, looking around, trying to figure out options. "Great. Just to make things even more complicated for us. I mean, we basically already fought the Avengers, so why not add the Fantastic Four into the mix?! Who's next? The Eternals?!"

"And we don't even have Nova or Quasar!" Gamora shouted as the Super Skrull's fist began to glow with flame again.

"I resent that remark!" Drax shouted, tackling their latest enemy to the ground. They rolled on the ground as Drax landed punch after punch.

"Did you see his eyes? And those wires attached to his body?" Star-Lord asked as he and Gamora circled the battle, trying to figure out a way to be helpful without weapons. "Looks like he was Ultron's prisoner, too."

"But how did he get out?" Gamora asked, suddenly reaching down and putting the Super Skrull into an excruciating-looking headlock. She just hoped he didn't choose to ignite his entire body. She knew all about Kl'rt.

He'd originally been a decorated warrior in the Skrull army. The Skrulls—a shapeshifting race that had been at war with the Kree for centuries. Enjoying all the perks that came with being a Skrull of some renown, Kl'rt married a countess and had two children with her. But despite the chance at a peaceful life, he continued to throw himself into his role as a soldier, eventually ending up at the disastrous Battle of Harkoon during the Kree–Skrull War. It was the first in a series of devastating and humiliating defeats for Kl'rt, resulting in his wife leaving him with their children.

Reduced to such a low point in his life and career, Kl'rt volunteered when Emperor Dorrek VII sought someone to undergo an experimental transformation. After the Skrulls had been defeated by the Fantastic Four during an invasion attempt, Dorrek decided to imbue a single Skrull with the powers of all four Terran heroes, but to amplify those powers—and thus, the whole would become so much more than the sum of the original parts.

The eventual transformation almost killed Kl'rt, but he emerged from the experimental machinery with all the powers of Earth's earliest super-powered defenders.

The incredible strength of Ben Grimm. The literal firepower of Johnny Storm. The stretching ability of Reed Richards. And the invisibility powers of Susan Storm.

The Super Skrull.

And sure enough, Kl'rt's initial battle with the foursome proved Dorrek's theory was true. He was more than a match for them on a strictly power level—it was only Reed Richards' vast intellect that saved them, and thus the Earth.

Since then, the Super Skrull had battled not only the Fantastic Four but a host of other Earth defenders as well: the Avengers, Alpha Flight, Power Man and Iron Fist, Prince Namor, and many others. And he had sometimes walked on both sides of a conflict, a Skrull with complicated motives and morals.

And now he was here, a tortured captive of Ultron. If they had more time, perhaps Gamora could talk to him, maybe he could even help them save the galaxy.

But time was the one thing they didn't have.

The Super Skrull shot one hand out, stretching it around, and grabbed Gamora by the neck, flipping her over his head and across the room.

Groot screamed and stretched his own arm out, the two elongated limbs intertwining violently, Skrull and wood, and Kl'rt looked more disoriented than ever. The tiny Groot spun in a circle, incredibly fast, and threw the Super Skrull down the hallway, where he landed in a jumble. He looked up at his attackers, still clearly confused. The five of them regrouped and faced him, ready to battle.

And then the Super Skrull vanished.

"Where did he go?!" Drax shouted.

"He's got the powers of the Invisible Woman!" Gamora responded. "He's still here… but he could be sprinting towards us right now! Be ready for anything!"

Wraith pulled at the collar around his neck, frustration creasing his face. "I could take him on myself if I could just get this damn thing—!"

Before he could finish, he was hit with incredible force across the face by an unseen fist. He went down, blood shooting from his mouth.

That's it! Wraith thought.

"Is that all you've got?!" he shouted, standing back up but leaving his arms at his sides.

"Uhh… Wraith?" Quill said. "Do you really think that's the best idea?"

"Trust me," the Nameless Kree responded.

Wraith took another punch as the Super Skrull materialized in front of him, content that becoming visible wouldn't stop him from defeating this seemingly helpless, pale Kree standing before him. He unleashed another punch with the Thing's strength, causing more blood to gush from Wraith's mouth.

"I am Groot…?" the small tree creature asked, scrambling back up to Gamora's shoulder.

"No!" she shouted, putting her arms up. "Everyone keep back! I think I know what Wraith is doing!" Another massive rocky punch to the stomach. "I hope."

As the latest blow from the Super Skrull came arcing towards Wraith's face, he turned up and into it, and the full strength of the Thing came into contact with the neural inhibitor. There was a loud, metallic cracking noise and Wraith collapsed to the ground, holding his head in his arms, barely moving.

The Super Skrull turned to face his remaining opponents, his body bursting into flame as he did so. He moved closer to them, eyes still vacant from Ultron's experimentation.

Star-Lord, Gamora, Groot, and Drax raised fists, ready to go down fighting, when a movement behind the Super Skrull caught their eyes. It was hard to see with the brightness of the flaming Skrull.

Just as Kl'rt was about to reach them, a black tendril whipped around his neck and pulled him back. The look of confused rage in his eyes was replaced by absolute confusion. He was thrown down onto the ground, causing the floor to shatter where he fell. His gaze landed on his attacker.

Wraith stood, his polymorphic weapon held tightly in one hand, its front stretching out in the whip that was now lashed around the Super Skrull's neck. Wraith's cloak waved gently, even though there was no air current in the hallway, almost as if it had a mind of its own. With his free hand, Wraith reached up and tore the compromised neural inhibitor from his own neck, smashing it against the wall.

Kl'rt stretched a Ben Grimm-sized fist at Wraith's face, but the Nameless Kree batted it away and dove forward, pulling the whip and the Super Skrull towards him, slamming a fist into his enemy's face. The Super Skrull staggered, tried to remain on his feet. As a purely defensive move, he instinctively turned invisible, but the whip was still wrapped around his neck.

Wraith pulled the whip again and the invisible figure careened forward, bursting into flames as it did so. It was surreal to see fire dancing off what looked like thin air. A blast of flame burst out towards Wraith but the Nameless Kree's cloak reacted, wrapping around him and protecting him from the fire. Wraith pulled on the whip again, tightening it around the unseen Skrull's neck, and the fire suddenly went out.

Kl'rt reappeared, dropping to his knees. He stretched out his arms, elongating them in a feeble attempt to hit Wraith again, but his limbs snaked out several feet and then went limp. He crashed into the ground face-first, unconscious.

"We were just lucky he's not at full power," Gamora said to Quill. "Wraith is extremely formidable, but the Super Skrull is one of the most powerful non-cosmic individuals I've ever come across."

"Yeah, lucky us," Quill said, stepping forward cautiously.

The Guardians stood in front of the motionless Super Skrull. Wraith tightened the whip around Kl'rt's neck.

"Shall I dispatch him?"

"He has been a threat for decades," Drax said. "He's attacked many worlds time and again, killed many, hurt many more. We would be doing the universe a favor."

"No," Gamora and Peter said at the same time. They looked at each other, smiled, then back at the Super Skrull.

"He was here against his will," Gamora added.

"And we're better than that," Star Lord finished.

Gamora nodded at Wraith, who reluctantly loosened the whip, which coiled back into the polymorphic gun.

"If Ultron was torturing him, perhaps he would be willing to join us in our fight to save the universe," Wraith surmised.

Star-Lord thought about it for a moment. Ultron was somewhere in this complex, and they had to stop him before he launched the next phase of whatever his larger plan was.

"Unfortunately, we don't have time," Quill said. "And there's no guarantee he would even *want* to help. He might just attack us again."

"Good point," Gamora said.

"Thanks," he responded, then headed down the hallway, his teammates at his back. "Now let's go shut Ultron down once and for all."

CHAPTER TWENTY-SEVEN

ULTRON'S TRANSFER CHAMBER

ROCKET AWOKE, gasping.

He was covered by metallic rubble, almost entirely, and a line of blood ran from his ear to the floor. He tried to clear his head, attempted to remember what had happened. Then it came rushing back to him.

His mind went back to what he presumed was hours earlier—though he had no idea how long he'd been unconscious. Back aboard Ship. Operating on Quill. That final piece of shrapnel—it had looked so different to the others. Different color, different feel.

Wood.

He knew immediately what it was, suspected also what might be done with it. If he was right, he could pull off a miracle. And get a friend back.

This was the last remaining piece of Groot. And if what he knew about his friend's species was correct, it could be Groot again.

So, he'd pretended he was busy, ignored Quill and the others, and went to work on resurrecting the first real friend he'd had in a long time… maybe ever. He searched the medical and science bays, leaving no inch unturned, until he found some dirt, just enough to plant the wooden shrapnel he'd pulled out of Peter's leg. He added a little water, placed it under the strongest UV light he could find. And then he waited.

He hung back when the team disembarked, watched on a monitor as they took on the horde of robots, but stayed with Groot as his friend began to sprout, little by little. He watched as Ultron arrived out on the beach, felt torn about his next step, but decided it was his duty to cultivate his best friend's resurrection, to protect him if his friends should fall.

And fall they did. One by one. Rocket watched as Quill somehow damaged Ultron, badly, but it still wasn't enough. The Guardians of the Galaxy were defeated.

But not Rocket. And not Groot.

As Ultron and his minions dragged his unconscious friends away, apparently unconcerned with either of the ships that rested behind them on the beach, Rocket witnessed Groot's new eyes open for the first time. His tiny little mouth yawned, and he blinked up at the raccoon in front of him.

"I am… I am Groot?" he asked.

"That's right, buddy," Rocket he said, wiping away something that had gotten in his eye. "You sure are."

After the momentary reunion, Rocket got to work. He remembered a time when he had been called one of the greatest tactical minds in the galaxy, but that wasn't quite correct.

"More like the universe," he mumbled as he accessed the ship's systems and used them to surreptitiously hack into Ultron's fortress. The deadly robot was good, there was no question, but he was also presumptuous in his attempts to take over every living thing. If there were holes in Ultron's security system, Rocket would find them.

It took time.

But he found them.

He figured out what Ultron's plan was, how he was going to transfer his body into Adam Warlock. He discovered where half the team was being held. And when Groot pulled himself out of the soil and walked on wobbly—then less wobbly—legs towards his raccoon friend, Rocket laid out their plan. They would split up, and they would each save one half of the Guardians.

As Rocket pulled himself out of the wreckage in the present, he just hoped Groot had been more fortunate than he had.

Because it was clear as he surveyed the room that Ultron had succeeded in his transfer despite Rocket's violent (*And let's be honest*, he thought, *hilarious*) attack. But at least there were no more Phalanx slaves left in this room. He could work to free Mantis, Moondragon, Nova, and Quasar.

If they were even still alive.

He took a few steps, felt his head swimming, and closed his eyes for a second, tried to regain his balance. Ultron's attack and that fall had been pretty bad. And if he was bleeding out of his ear, that probably wasn't a great sign either.

Meh, he thought, opening his eyes and moving forward, *I've been hurt worse*.

He reached the transfer hub—basically a giant wheel, the bottom spoke empty. That must have been where Adam had been held prisoner. And sure enough, Ultron's robotic shell was in another spoke near the top, lifeless, limbs held at odd angles. It almost looked innocent like this.

Rocket punched data into the transfer unit's computer, overrode security protocols at blistering speed. He could remember every single thing he'd found when he'd hacked Ultron's systems earlier—it was as if the codes were scrolling in front of his eyes as he worked.

He found the sub-system that displayed the readings for the four Guardians who were still strapped into their spokes. He scanned the data, held his breath.

And then released it.

They were still alive.

Rocket had started punching in the codes that would release them when the sound of a door opening behind him arrested his attention. He glanced back and saw the Phalanx pouring in.

"Here we go again," he said, reaching into his jacket and withdrawing his laser pistol, which had luckily survived the fall.

Rocket squared off against the growing number of robots.

"This is gonna be fun," he said, a smile creeping onto his face.

QUILL LED his team through the corridors, sprinting as fast as he could.

He'd heard what he thought was a ship taking off, and he could only hope that he'd heard wrong or that it was his imagination. They'd come so far—he wasn't ready to admit defeat, even if things weren't exactly looking good.

He tried to ignore the fact that he had just entertained the idea of working with the Super Skrull. This conflict, and the ones before it, had led to some seriously unlikely allies.

Had he ever thought he would be working with Ronan the Accuser? Of course, *that* particular team-up hadn't quite worked out so well. It had, in fact, led to a galactic invasion. But no one could have predicted that. Who knew Ultron was working behind the scenes for so long, or that his plan would be so damn successful?

At length, the group came to a massive door made of some kind of unknown metal. Behind the door, they could hear what sounded like a raging battle.

"Ultron..." Quill whispered.

Wraith unleashed on the door, but nothing happened, not even a scratch. Drax pounded on it, but other than an impressive series of bangs, there was no effect.

"I think we've reached a dead end," Gamora said. Peter didn't say it out loud, but he suspected she was right.

"Maybe we can—" he began to say when the sound of the battle behind the massive door suddenly came to a halt. After another moment, they heard a faint beeping and the door began to open. They readied themselves for another conflict. Instead, they found themselves staring at Rocket, who was standing in front of a giant pile of destroyed robots, picking his teeth with a fingernail.

"What took you so long?" the raccoon asked nonchalantly.

Quill and the others took in the scene, unable to truly believe what they were seeing. After a moment, they all rushed to the machine on which their friends were strapped.

"They're still alive!" Rocket shouted. "Or they were before I was so rudely interrupted."

"Where's Adam?" Peter asked, eyeing Ultron's unmoving shell. Something very bad had happened.

"Ultron hijacked his body," Rocket confirmed.

"Great," Quill said.

Gamora punched at the transfer machine's controls but all that resulted was loud, unpleasant sounds.

"I can't gain access!" she yelled, frustrated.

"I guess I have to do everything myself," Rocket sighed, limping over and tapping in a series of codes, once again overriding Ultron's security protocols. After a moment, the wheel turned, and Moondragon's spoke arrived in front of them, the woman's unconscious form within. Rocket hit a few more buttons and the spoke unlocked, the wires connected to Heather's head falling away. Drax lifted her up and gently placed her on the floor. One by one, they repeated the process, until all four victims were on the floor, eyes still closed, but alive.

"Rocket, you're with me," Star-Lord said, heading towards a large computer console on the other side of the room. "Gamora, can you get everyone up to speed when they wake up?"

"On it," she said.

Peter and Rocket ran to the console as fast as they could. Quill watched as the raccoon worked his magic yet again, in silent awe of the small creature's incredible technological prowess. As he'd already admitted to Rocket himself, Peter had misjudged him when they'd first met. He wouldn't make that mistake again.

"Where is he?" Star-Lord asked, knowing the answer in the pit of his stomach.

"Already in orbit, heading away from the planet pretty quickly. And..."

"And what?" Peter said, trying to make sense of the readout in front of them.

"He's got a *huge* armada. Ships from every planet I've ever heard of… and a bunch I haven't. All under Phalanx control."

"Where are they heading?" Peter asked, glancing back. The four Guardians who had been strapped to the transfer machine were starting to recover.

Rocket paused for a moment, looked up at Peter.

"Back to Hala," the raccoon said. "But why? He already conquered it."

Peter thought about the giant tower the Phalanx had been building there when he'd escaped—barely.

"Knowing Ultron, he has a very good… very *evil* reason," Quill said. "I just hope we still have a ship."

"Last I saw, Ship was still sitting on the beach, in perfect condition. Well, workable condition," Rocket responded, gripping his laser pistol tightly, a grim smile slipping onto his face.

"I knew the name would grow on you," Star-Lord responded, slapping his friend on the back.

"Ow."

"Sorry."

"Peter!" Gamora shouted. Quill headed back over while Rocket continued to scan data. As Star-Lord approached, the four newly awakened Guardians got to their feet. Moondragon and Quasar embraced, their faces full of emotion.

"Heather…" Phyla-Vell said quietly, pulling back and staring into Moondragon's eyes as if alone in the room with the love of her life, even though they were surrounded by people. "I was so worried. When I saw you, unconscious, at Ultron's feet… I thought the worst."

Moondragon looked deep into Quasar's eyes. "It would take more than a murderous robot with most of the galaxy at his command to keep me from you," she responded, pulling Phyla-Vell closer for another hug.

Nearby, Drax spoke softly to Mantis.

"Are you okay?" he asked, looking her over. Other than looking pale and tired, she seemed unhurt. Regardless, Drax vowed to kill Ultron for what he had done to her and to his daughter.

"Other than a headache, I am okay," she responded, then placed her hand on his forearm. He jolted. It was the first time a woman had touched him in that way since he had lost Yvette. It felt good, which made him feel terrible. Still, he smiled, the first time anyone in this room had seen him display that kind of genuine emotion. "And you?" Mantis asked.

"I am in a significant amount of pain," he said. "But right now, I feel good."

"Listen up," Star-Lord said in an authoritative voice. "We've been through the wringer… *all* of us. And we have a lot of catching up to do, a lot of notes to compare, if we're going to stop Ultron. But we don't have much time. I think I know what's he's going to do on Hala, and if he succeeds, it's the end of every living thing in the universe. It's up to us. No one else is coming to stop him."

Between the look in his eyes and the sound of his voice, everyone in the room knew for a fact that they were looking at the leader of this mission. Gamora nodded. If they were going to succeed, this was exactly the kind of initiative they needed.

"So, what's next then?" Gamora asked, stepping up next to Peter. The others moved closer, too, including Rocket, who hobbled across the room and gave Groot a quick high-five.

"I found where Ultron put our weapons, so that won't be a problem," Rocket commented.

"Great," Peter said, fighting an urge to pat the raccoon on the back again. "When I escaped from Hala, the Phalanx were building some kind of tower, and I have to assume that his plan for universal domination is connected to that somehow. We need to go there, too, and stop him before he finishes whatever he started. It's now or never."

"Then what are we waiting for?!" Rocket shouted. "Let's go, Guardians!"

CHAPTER TWENTY-EIGHT

ABOARD THE PHALANX INVASION FLAGSHIP

ULTRON SWALLOWED the ice-cold water, felt it run down his throat and into his stomach, and nearly laughed at the beauty of the experience.

This was yet another thing that humans took for granted. Worse, they actively destroyed the water on their planet, dumping chemicals into oceans and rivers, despite knowing this plentiful liquid was the source of all life on their planet. Perhaps they subconsciously wished to die, all of them, and he was doing them a favor by subjugating them. Just speeding up something they themselves clearly desired.

Ultron nodded, and one of his Phalanx slaves approached and took away the cup. Ultron sat back in his command seat, looked out the viewscreen ahead of him. He'd prepared for life in this new body, made sure his ship was stocked with enough food and water to keep him alive for decades to come if necessary. Who knew what other pleasures this body could afford, but for now, he needed to take care of basic survival until he held the entire universe in his grip. After that, he could relax. And truly enjoy being alive.

It was ironic that he was turning all life into technological slaves while also discovering the joys of being an organic being. But didn't humans love their irony?

"How long until we reach Hala?"

"Six hours, Lord Ultron," every single Phalanx on the bridge answered at the exact same time. He smiled. He could get used to this kind of universal subservience.

"Increase speed. Let's get that down to five," he commanded.

"Yes sir, Lord Ultron," they said. He felt the ship shudder as it increased speed, heard the engines straining. He looked at the monitor on his command console. The armada behind him sped up as well, perfect slaves to their perfect master. He just needed to get to Hala, to finish what he had started so long ago. After that, the rest of his plan would be a simple matter.

He would consume the universe from the tower on Hala—every planet in the cosmos except Earth. Perhaps he would even travel there himself with an armada of unimaginable size.

Where Ultron would finally enjoy victory over his lifelong enemies.

He would leave Hank Pym for last. No slavery for him. No, he would be the only one untouched by the virus. Ultron would slowly choke the life out of his creator with his bare hands, feel the man's last breaths through his own flesh.

And he would enjoy every second of it.

WRAITH SAT in darkness.

They were back aboard Ship, rocketing through space towards Hala. There was no way they would beat Ultron, but hopefully they would get there in time to stop his plans before he could fully implement them.

But the Nameless Kree was uneasy.

He was not used to working with others, considered himself a loner. And now he was on a ship with eight others, part of a larger whole. It was almost like…

It was almost like a family.

He shut his eyes against the memories that rose unbidden to his mind. His mother. His father. His best friend. Taken from him when he was only a child. Despite the fact that he'd had his emotions stripped from him when he'd been infected by the Exolon back in the Exoteric Latitude, he could somehow still feel the pain racing through his body. Especially in quiet moments like this.

Perhaps that's why he had sought out conflict after conflict. All fueled by his unsatiable thirst for vengeance. But everything had changed. His personal mission had been overtaken by a galactic threat, and now he was part of a team. It was possible that the man who'd murdered his parents was no longer even alive. And if that was the case, who was he?

None of this made any sense to him, and he didn't have the emotional faculties to process the sequence of events in which he currently found himself mired.

So, he sat in the dark. Alone.

After some time, the door opened, a rectangle of light invading his solitude.

"What?!" he shouted, louder than he'd intended.

"I… apologize," Drax said, a silhouette in the doorway. "I thought this room was empty."

"No…" Wraith responded, "It's okay. I…"

The two men stared at each other.

"…I could use the company," the Nameless Kree finished.

Drax considered this for a moment, seemed about to turn around and walk away, and then nodded. He entered the room, flicking on a bank of lights as he did so.

Wraith watched Drax as he took a seat across from him. They regarded each other in silence for several minutes.

"I find it difficult…" Wraith finally said. "To be part of a team."

Drax took this in. Then: "As do I. Or I did. If you had asked me several days ago if I would ever join an organization as ridiculous as the 'Guardians of the Galaxy,' I would have laughed in your face. Or stabbed you in the face."

Wraith laughed, a dark sound. "But…?"

"But something has changed," Drax continued. "I thought Quill was a fool at first. But I have come to see that he uses his foolishness to disarm his opponents. It is a clever tactic, and he is an excellent leader. Gamora is a deadly warrior, perhaps almost as deadly as me. Rocket is a fierce and savvy comrade. Groot is a very powerful tree. And Mantis…"

Wraith raised his eyebrows, waiting for the end of the sentence. Which never came.

"For so many years," Drax said after a long moment, "I have been consumed with a need for vengeance. I have sought to kill the man who murdered my wife. But now—having joined with the Guardians—I find myself, for the first time in a long time, just… enjoying the moment. Despite the galactic invasion."

"Vengeance?" Wraith asked, barely able to get the word out.

"Yes. My wife was murdered. Violently. Senselessly. By a Titan named Thanos. For years, my bloodlust drove me mad. I fought anyone and everyone I came across… Iron Man, Captain Marvel, Thor… the list feels endless."

Wraith thought back to his own battles. Some he could barely remember.

"My parents were murdered," he said quietly. "And my…" He felt ridiculous framing a robot in the manner he was about to. But it was true. "…my best friend. A senseless act, too. Brutal. And one man was responsible. When I find him… *if* I find him, I will make him pay."

Drax walked over to the Nameless Kree, placed his hand on his shoulder.

"And on that day, I will help you in any way you need me," Drax said darkly.

"Thank you," Wraith said, nodding.

After a moment, the intercom in the room suddenly crackled to life.

"Drax, Wraith, are either of you there?" It was Gamora. She sounded excited. Maybe even hopeful. Drax walked across the room and hit a button.

"Yes," he said, "we're here."

"Come up to the bridge. We've made contact with someone on Hala. A friend. I think."

Drax looked over at Wraith, raised his eyebrows. They hadn't had much good news lately. Maybe things were turning around. Maybe.

"Who is it?" he asked.

"I'm not entirely sure," Gamora responded. "Just... get up here."

MANTIS AND Moondragon gripped both hands together, left on right, right on left.

Their eyes were closed, and they sat on the floor in the middle of the bridge, surrounded by the Guardians. Drax and Wraith entered the bridge, confused by what was going on in front of them, but silent, waiting to be updated.

Quill stepped away from the circle and towards them, clapping Drax on the back.

"Glad you're both here. We may have made some progress."

The three of them joined the circle.

"Yes..." Moondragon said after a long moment.

"We understand you," Mantis continued.

"We will be there soon," Moondragon finished.

There was a ripple in the air, beneath the surface of conscious thought, as the two empaths withdrew their contact from whomever they'd been talking to. They opened their eyes, blinked at each other, smiled in a deeply connected way. Only the two of them knew where they truly went during their psionic journeys, or how intertwined their minds were after what they'd been through together.

Drax stepped forward and helped Mantis to her feet. Quasar did the same for Heather.

"What happened? Who were you talking to?" Gamora asked as the two empaths were helped to nearby chairs. They were clearly unsure on their feet, either from this new psychic toll, or their recent torture at the hands of Ultron, or both.

"We do not know his name," Mantis said as Drax brought her a cup of water. She drank it greedily, then looked at him, deep into his eyes. "Thank you," she whispered.

"He is a Kree commander," Moondragon added. "And he is leading an underground resistance on Hala. Against the Phalanx."

"So, not everyone there has succumbed to Ultron's virus," Gamora said, nodding. "This is very good news."

"However, they are severely outmatched, and on the run," Mantis interjected. "One by one, his soldiers are being turned by the Phalanx."

"How can we help them? Or more importantly—how can they help us?" Nova asked, holding his helmet at his side. His eyes were dark circles, his skin ashen white. He hadn't spoken much since being freed from Ultron's transfer machine. The process had done a number on him, but he stood tall, still ready to fight.

"The Phalanx continue their work on the tower," Moondragon said. "It's comprised partly of sentries, but also from technology of many different races. The resistance has attempted to take it down, even though they don't know exactly what it is for."

"Attempted and failed," Mantis said ominously.

"All they know is that the tower is central to the Phalanx's plan," Moondragon added.

"I knew it," Quill muttered under his breath.

"We told him that we will rendezvous with his resistance, that we will help destroy the tower. If we can…" Mantis said.

"Okay," Gamora said, pacing the length of the bridge, "this is good. We were going in blind but now we have a mission. And allies."

"Are you sure we can trust them?" Peter asked, approaching her.

"No," she responded, stopping in front of the viewscreen at the front of the ship. Stars and planets streaked by, any number of them already plagued by the Phalanx. "But Ultron is too confident to anticipate this kind of attack. I'm betting he's already forgotten about us. He's already moved on to the next phase of his plan."

Rocket appeared next to them.

"We can all hear you mumbling over here," he said, spreading his arms out in exasperation. "Feel like clueing everyone else into what you're thinking?"

"May I?" Gamora asked Peter.

"Of course," he responded.

Gamora faced the Guardians. She had always been a loner, had been raised by Thanos to only think about herself. But in the past few days, she'd found herself thrust into a position of leadership, but also of dependence and trust. And though it was not something that made her feel comfortable, she had to admit on some level that she liked it. She liked being a part of this motley team.

"We now have two objectives. First, take the fight to Ultron. He won't be expecting it. From what I can tell, everyone who's gone up against him has fallen. He thinks we're all still on Kvch. And he thinks he's unstoppable now that he wields the power of Adam Warlock. Even if it's hopeless, we have to show him he's still vulnerable. And distract him while the B-team takes out that damn tower."

"The *what* team?!" Rocket objected.

"I am Groot!" his best friend agreed.

"You know what I mean," Gamora said, smiling.

"Our second objective," Gamora continued, "is to meet up with this resistance and figure out a way to get to the tower without being infected by the Phalanx. And once we get to it, we blow it sky high. We don't know what it's for, but there's no question now that it's part of Ultron's scheme to conquer the entire universe."

"I do have to admit that I love blowing stuff up," Rocket said cheerfully, raising his hand as if he was in a classroom.

"You are forgetting one important thing," Drax said, confused by everyone's confidence. "How do we get there before Ultron activates the tower?"

"We don't need to get there before him," Star-Lord said, glancing at Rocket. "We just need to get there at the same time as him."

"I am not hearing the solution," Drax retorted, shaking his head. He did not like to play games with words and was getting annoyed.

"Let's just say I know a shortcut to Hala," Rocket said, waggling his eyebrows. "A little-known wormhole that I used once to smuggle an Infinity Stone. Heh heh."

"I am not a big fan of wormholes," Wraith admitted. "But if it gets us there faster… I'm all in favor of it."

Gamora heard the fear in the Nameless Kree's voice, probably the first time she'd heard that from him. She nodded, appreciative. "Peter and I will decide on the two teams, and then…"

"Then *what*?" Nova asked, putting his helmet on and powering up.

"And then we save the universe."

CHAPTER TWENTY-NINE

ABOVE THE PLANET HALA—SOME TIME LATER

ULTRON WATCHED as Hala came into view and he smiled.

He touched his cheek gently—it was still such an odd experience for emotion to become a physical response. He liked it, and hated it. His Phalanx slaves scurried about the bridge of his flagship, lost in their duties, their circuits processing data and then acting on it, no emotion involved in their decisions whatsoever.

On some level, he missed that purity. But this new form allowed him to enjoy the best of both worlds. Perhaps someday, once every single being in the universe was under his cybernetic control, he would attempt to create new organic life, modeled after this new version of himself. A race that could avoid the sins of humans like Hank Pym.

But first, he had one last thing to do on Hala—the final part of his plan. And then he would make his way to Earth. To kill Pym himself.

An alarm suddenly blared, and he sat up, looking at the data that was scrolling on his control panel. What he saw didn't make any sense.

"I thought you had cleared this section of Kree orbit," he shouted at the closest Phalanx robot.

"We did, my lord," it responded.

"Then what is *that*?" He pointed at the viewscreen. Arcing around the planet, a tiny, illuminated dot was approaching their ship. Fast.

"We do not know," the Phalanx responded, computing the evolving data as he spoke. "But it appears to be humanoid."

Another alarm starting blaring, startling Ultron. He needed to work harder to keep these unfamiliar emotions in check.

"Report!" he shouted.

"There is a second humanoid coming from the other side of Hala. Both approaching at significant speed, my lord," the robot said dispassionately.

Ultron reached over and ripped the Phalanx's head off. The body fell to the ground while he pointed the metallic cranium at the nearest still-functioning robot.

"Tell me who they are. *Now*."

The Phalanx paused for the slightest moment, running data, then responded.

"One is Phyla-Vell, otherwise known as Quasar. The other is Richard Rider, otherwise known as Nova."

"Then they managed to escape... and somehow beat me here..." Ultron said mostly to himself, both impressed and annoyed. It was discomfiting to experience these two emotions at the same time. Difficult to process. How did humans do this? he wondered. No wonder they were so weak. But he would learn how to master both of these, and all of them. He was Ultron, in the body of one of the most powerful organic beings ever to exist. Humanoid emotion was simply one more foe to conquer.

"Obliterate them," he commanded.

THE GUARDIANS of the Galaxy moved through the shadowy alleyways of Hala, weapons drawn, alert for danger, aware that it could come in many different forms.

When they'd disembarked from the ship a few minutes earlier and said goodbye to Nova and Quasar, who rocketed into the sky, they'd headed quickly towards the coordinates the Kree resistance leader had given to the two empaths.

"How much farther?" Gamora whispered to Mantis as they followed Moondragon, who led them down yet another dark passageway. It was nighttime, though Phalanx drones flew overhead every few minutes, searchlights illuminating patches of destruction, then moving off.

"Just a couple more turns," Mantis responded after touching her head for a moment. "Apparently they're holed up in the basement of a store that was destroyed early in the invasion."

Gamora nodded, then pressed herself against the wall behind her when yet another drone passed through the sky above. The others did the same, each one holding their breath as they did so.

After a few moments it moved on, and they exhaled then continued their journey, as silently as possible—not an easy task, since the alleys were cluttered with singed remnants from the battles that had been transpiring since the last time Star-Lord had set foot on Hala.

It had been a week at most, but for Peter it felt like years. The only good part was that he'd left as a loner. And now he had returned as the leader of this amazing team. He just needed to figure out how to save them—and the rest of the universe as well.

Finally, a few minutes later, they reached the back entrance to the store. The door was pockmarked with laser blasts and hung unceremoniously on its hinges. On the other side of this flimsy entrance was pitch blackness.

"Are you sure this is the right place?" Drax whispered harshly. "If I was running a resistance, I would not allow such an easy entrance for my foes to utilize!"

"I believe that's exactly why they leave it like this," Moondragon responded.

"Who would ever suspect what's really here?" Mantis added.

Star-Lord silently agreed with Drax. This did seem too easy. Regardless, he moved forward and gently pushed the door open, making his way into the darkness. The others, one by one, followed.

NOVA AND Quasar slammed into the Phalanx flagship simultaneously, from opposite directions.

Inside the vessel, on its bridge, several of the robots and Ultron himself were rocked almost off their feet. The entire ship began to pitch at an odd angle and alarms echoed through the halls, especially loud in Ultron's command center.

"Report!" he shouted.

"Significant damage to the hull where each humanoid struck," one of the Phalanx reported, "but no breach yet."

Ultron reduced the robot to slag for including the word 'yet.'

"Fire!" he screamed.

The other Phalanx looked at their melted comrade, then some continued their work to right the vessel while others opened fire on the two streaks of light that zigzagged across the viewscreen, somehow avoiding the hundreds of laser attacks coming from the flagship and the rest of the armada.

Rather than seeming intimidated by the attack, one of them—it seemed to be Nova, based on the light glinting off what looked like a helmet—punched a hole through one of Ultron's smaller ships, resulting in a massive, silent explosion.

"Why aren't you destroying them?" Ultron demanded.

"We are unable to hit them, my lord," one of the Phalanx said as it continued its attempts to take Nova and Quasar down. "They are moving faster than our targeting systems can react or anticipate."

"Fine," Ultron said, his eyes glowing with immense power. "I will simply have to do this myself."

 STAR-LORD SLOWLY made his way through the destroyed store.

Kree clothing and uniforms were strewn everywhere, along with what looked like ornate jewelry. This must have been a high-end fashion shop at one time. Reduced to little more than landfill.

Peter sensed his companions behind him but was impressed by how silent they were, even with all the debris strewn on the floor everywhere they looked. Either a battle had occurred here, or the Phalanx were simply destroying anything they came across. Luckily, there were no dead bodies. *Or maybe not so lucky…?* Peter thought. That meant Ultron's technological oppressors were making more slaves, not killing indiscriminately. He wondered how many Kree were under the sway of the Phalanx. It was probably better not to know.

"There's no one here," Gamora whispered, directly into his ear. He had to stop himself from jumping. It was unsettling that she had been able to creep that close to him without him knowing. Part of him was thrilled by her proximity; the other part chastised him for allowing himself to be so vulnerable.

"We should leave," Drax hissed. "This feels like a trap."

"No," Peter disagreed. "It's not like we got a coded message through a computer. This information came directly from Moondragon and Mantis. They would have sensed if the resistance leader was lying."

"That is correct," both Moondragon and Mantis said at the same time.

"You two really gotta stop doing that," Rocket commented.

"I am Groot," the tree creature whispered in agreement.

"How can we be sure you two weren't lied to?" Gamora asked. "We're dealing with a universal threat. We don't really know what Ultron is capable of."

"It's unlikely both of us could be deceived," Moondragon said.

"But not impossible," Mantis countered.

"Wraith, what do you think?" Star-Lord asked, turning to the Nameless Kree, who stood several feet away from the others, staring into the darkness.

There was a long moment of silence.

"Wraith?"

"We are not alone," he said finally.

At that moment, several figures emerged from the deep shadows of the shattered store.

They were Kree warriors and they all looked like they had been to Hell and back. Each had cuts and burn marks covering their bodies, but their eyes were like steel. In their hands, each one held a weapon of some kind, and they were all trained on the Guardians.

Drax stepped forward, his sword brandished, a dangerous scowl on his face.

"Drax! Stand down!" Star-Lord shouted.

"But—"

"Look at their eyes. They're not Phalanx."

Drax looked closer, saw that Quill was right, and lowered his blade—though it was clear to everyone in the room that he wasn't happy about it.

"Guardians," Peter continued, holstering his gun. "Put away your weapons."

Wraith complied immediately but Gamora and Rocket still held their guns up, eyeing the Kree warily.

"Gamora, Rocket," Quill said. "Please. Trust me."

Rocket rolled his eyes but complied. Gamora looked Peter in the eyes for a moment, then nodded and lowered her weapon as well. Star-Lord turned back to the Kree, who stood as rigid as statues, their guns still trained on them.

"Who are you?" the Kree at the front of their group demanded. "Identify yourselves!"

"My name is Moondragon and this is Mantis," Heather said, stepping forward with her fellow empath. "We were in psychic touch with the leader of the Kree resistance. We're here to help."

Star-Lord stepped up next to them. "And I'm Star-Lord. This is Gamora, Wraith, Drax, Rocket, and Groot. We have a plan that we think will stop Ultron and the Phalanx."

 "Who is Ultron?" the Kree asked, distrust still lining his voice.

"Like I said," Quill continued, raising his palms in supplication, "we have information that will help your battle to reclaim Hala. But we need to talk with your leader. As soon as possible."

The embattled Kree warriors were silent for several long moments, but then the one who had been talking lowered his weapon as well. He pointed towards a shadowy corner of the store.

"Our leader is downstairs. He told us you were coming but we had to be sure you were not Phalanx. Go ahead. We will follow. He also wants to meet with you immediately."

"They weren't exactly acting like they were in a rush," Gamora muttered to Quill as they headed towards the indicated area, followed closely by the others. The Kree warriors kept their distance, the majority of their weapons still aimed at the Guardians' backs.

"Did you see their eyes?" Peter responded quietly. "They're scared. They've been fighting since I escaped."

"So have we," she countered.

"True, but not everyone is as cool and collected as you and me, Gamora," he said with a wink.

She sighed but he saw that almost imperceptible smile appear on her face for a second, then disappear just as fast. Still, it had been there. Again.

They came to a wall with a smashed display case. More Kree clothing and jewelry was scattered across the floor.

"Um… maybe we're in the wrong corner…?" Star-Lord surmised, turning back to the Kree who had been speaking.

"Grab the right edge of the display case and pull it towards you," the Kree commanded.

Peter moved forward, feeling everyone's eyes on him, previously expensive Kree clothing and trinkets crunching underfoot as he did so.

For the slightest moment, he thought of his friend, Ten-Cor. Her dying moments reverberated in his mind and his body was suddenly filled with a rage so intense it nearly made him lose his breath.

Everything he had been through since that moment had been worth it—he would do it again, over and over, if necessary. He would avenge his friend's death. No matter what it took. Including moving a shattered display case.

He reached up, took hold of the corners at the top of the case. The unseen broken glass on top of it dug into his fingers through his gloves, and he welcomed the pain. It was kind of a sobering reminder that the stakes were very high. For all his witty banter with Gamora, and all the feelings that banter cloaked, he was here on a mission. And he would accomplish it, whatever it took.

He pulled, hard, and for a moment nothing happened.

"Do you need help?" Drax asked, innocently, but the question annoyed Quill, so he pulled even harder, and the case made a clacking noise, then began to swing away from the wall. A narrow staircase was revealed, descending into the darkness below.

If it *was* a trap, this was the moment of no return.

"Peter...?" Gamora asked after a moment.

"Let's go, Guardians," he said, then stepped forward, and down, into the shadows and the unknown.

CHAPTER THIRTY

JUST OUTSIDE HALA ORBIT

NOVA SMASHED through another Phalanx ship, grim, taking no pleasure in the explosion that resulted behind him as he flew through the vast expanse of outer space.

He loved this power, the utter freedom of rocketing through the cosmos, yes, but he knew Phalanx slaves were dying as a result of his attack. This was war, and there were inevitably casualties, but it was something that would echo in his mind for the rest of his life. He took none of this lightly, but also thought about his parents back on Earth. Hopefully they were still okay. His actions here might have a direct impact on that uncertainty.

He moved on to the next ship.

In his peripheral vision, he saw Quasar wreaking similar havoc on Ultron's fleet. But as he took in the full spectrum of the battle, he saw what they were up against. Hundreds, if not thousands, of ships. All moving in their direction. He and Phyla-Vell were powerful, there was no question about that, but he wondered if even they could take on an armada of this size. If he was honest with himself, he knew the answer was no.

But he still had to try. And hope the others were having success with their mission.

QUASAR TOOK a direct hit from a Skrull ship.

Their weapons were powerful, probably some of the strongest in the galaxy, but for her it wasn't much more than a slightly painful annoyance.

She formed a massive energy blade and sliced one of the Skrull wings neatly off the rest of the ship. There was a series of minor explosions, and the vessel began drifting away, clearly in distress. If there was time later, and if they were successful, she would recover as many of these damaged ships as possible, save as many lives as she could. But right now, she had to stay focused on their mission.

Stop Ultron. No matter what it took.

As she searched for her next target, she caught a movement in the corner of her eye. She looked over and saw a small dot of light approaching at incredible speed. She assumed it was Nova—maybe he needed to talk?—but then realized that whoever it was had actually launched from the flagship, which was surrounded by dozens of other vessels from a multitude of planets, all moving in to protect their master.

She stared, trying to see who it was—and for the briefest moment, she smiled. It was Warlock. Their ally, and a powerful one at that.

Then she quickly remembered that Ultron had transferred his consciousness into Adam's body, thanks in no small part to Quasar herself. Ultron was taking the fight directly to them. This was not good.

Before she could properly prepare herself, Ultron increased his speed and hit her with an impact that made her black out for a split second. She recovered quickly, but came to finding Ultron's fist hurtling towards her face. Adam Warlock's strength was nearly beyond comprehension.

Nova was there almost immediately, pulling Ultron off her.

Richard blasted their enemy in the face, full force, an attack that would have probably destroyed an entire city block back on Earth, but it barely seemed to phase the being that had taken over Adam Warlock's body.

Warlock had always been powerful, but now Ultron had been able to unlock the full potential of the High Evolutionary's pet project.

Both Nova and Quasar unloaded on Ultron, and for a moment they thought they were winning. The face that they recognized as Adam Warlock's seemed to contort in pain, but then they realized it was actually laughter. Their spirits sank. Combined, they wielded the most power of almost any two entities in the galaxy. But this single person shrugged them off—was literally mocking their efforts to stop him.

He flew forward and grabbed both of them by the backs of their necks, and smashed their heads together with incredible force.

Quasar was especially impacted by this, Nova's helmet cracking her skin open, blood coagulating immediately in the vacuum of space and drifting off in dark red clumps. A dazed Nova landed a punch in Ultron's midsection, but it had no effect. Instead, Ultron did the same to Nova, breaking several of Richard's ribs as he did so. Nova crumpled in half, attempting to breathe the oxygen that his helmet provided.

Ultron turned his attention to Quasar as Nova floated slowly away.

Phyla-Vell materialized her energy sword again and sliced Ultron across the arm, biting deep into Adam's skin. Ultron looked down at his rent flesh, pained surprise filling his eyes. He had never experienced corporeal pain like this.

And he wasn't amused.

His eyes and hands glowed bright once again and he hit Quasar with everything he had, her energy sword evaporating as she succumbed to unconsciousness.

A snarling Ultron flew over to Nova, grabbed him by his uniform, then flew to Quasar and did the same. He would infect them with the Phalanx virus soon enough. But first, he would force them to watch as the tower was completed and he extended his reach to every corner of the known, and unknown, universe.

ON HALA—SEVERAL MINUTES EARLIER

THE BASEMENT was lit with candles.

The Guardians stood in a cluster, surrounded by armed Kree warriors, hollow-faced and exhausted. They looked at the strangers with distrust, some with outright hatred.

Long minutes passed.

"This is… awkward," Quill mumbled.

"Ya think?" Rocket muttered.

After a few more moments, there was stirring amongst the crowd and an older Kree warrior appeared. Unlike most of the assembled resistance, this Kree had a beard and longer hair. He eyed Star-Lord up and down.

"Like what you see?" Peter asked.

The Kree laughed dryly.

"My name is Kra-Wen. So… you are here to help us?" he asked, sounding unconvinced.

"That's right," Star-Lord answered. "Two of our other comrades are currently taking the fight to the leader of the Phalanx in orbit. We have a plan to destroy the tower in case they aren't successful."

"Don't you think we've been *trying* to destroy it?!" Kra-Wen took offense, annoyance flashing in his eyes.

Gamora interjected, stepping towards him. "We need your help getting our people into the tower. While you've been staging your resistance here, we've been engaging with the Phalanx on their home world. Based on what we've learned, we think we know how to stop them once and for all. But we can't do it without you. You know these streets infinitely better than we do."

Kra-Wen took in her words, seemed to process them with great interest, and then nodded.

"Good," Quill responded, smiling. "So, can we move forward with our plan? We can outline it to you in detail."

"That would need approval from our leader," Kra-Wen said, nodding to someone deep in the crowd of resistance fighters.

"Your… leader? I thought you were in charge here," Star-Lord retorted, confused.

"I never said that. He simply wanted to observe you before he revealed himself."

Someone else approached, making his way through the assembled warriors.

It was a very tall Kree soldier with several stripes on his shoulder, indicating a high-level officer. He was wearing a helmet, covering most of his face in shadow as he made his way to the front of the group.

When he finally made it to the Guardians, he withdrew his helmet, a ring on his finger catching the candlelight, and stared into Star-Lord's face, his expression grim and emotionless.

"*I* am their leader," the man said. "My name is General Gor-Hax. And you will speak to me with respect."

Wraith sucked in a surprised breath, his entire body going tense. He felt like he might throw up, or pass out, or both. Drax was standing next to him and felt the Nameless Kree's sudden physical shift.

"What is it?" he asked quietly as everyone's else's attention was riveted on the new arrival.

"That's him," Wraith whispered, fury filling each word. He stared at the signet ring on the general's finger. "The man who killed my parents."

Drax's eyes went wide, and he looked at Wraith, his tattooed face filling with rage on behalf of his new friend. The Nameless Kree worked his jaw, attempting to wrestle the complex emotions that wracked his mind and body simultaneously. At last, he could mete out vengeance on the man who was responsible for the deaths of his parents and the destruction of his best friend.

But he had found something that almost felt like a new family—these Guardians of the Galaxy. He felt at home with them, felt listened to and cared about. And they were on a mission to save the entire universe. Would he risk that mission by killing perhaps their only chance at success? All these thoughts and emotions rushed through him in a matter of seconds.

Before he had a chance to make a decision, Drax rushed forward, tackling Gor-Hax to the ground in an explosion of violence. Everyone in the room yelled out in surprise as the two went down to the floor in a chaotic sprawl. Several people on both sides moved forward in an attempt to intervene, but stopped suddenly when they saw that Drax had his blade held to Gor-Hax's throat.

"Drax!" Star-Lord shouted. "What the hell are you doing?!"

"They are Phalanx!" Kra-Wen screamed, pointing his laser pistol directly at Quill's face. The Guardians unholstered their weapons and everyone took aim at someone else, silence descending on the tense room other than Drax and Gor-Hax's heavy breathing as they stared each other in the eyes.

"We are *not* Phalanx," Gamora countered through clenched teeth.

"Then tell your mindless barbarian to get off our leader now, before we kill you all!" Kra-Wen shouted.

"Uh... Drax," Quill said, keeping his voice as calm as possible. "Could you maybe explain exactly what's going on here?"

"This man killed Wraith's parents in cold blood," Drax responded, pushing the knife harder against Gor-Hax's throat, drawing a thin line of blue blood. The Kree in the room moved forward like a wave, their weapons getting even closer to the Guardians. Peter's mind swirled. He had to figure a way out of this. He quickly glanced back at Wraith, and when he saw the Nameless Kree's face, even more pale than usual, he realized Drax knew something almost no one else in this room did. Or hadn't, until now.

"Is that true?" Quill asked Gor-Hax.

"Possibly," the Kree leader managed to get out. His eyes were still locked on Drax's and there was no fear there. "I've killed *many* people."

Now Wraith stepped forward and one of the Kree placed the muzzle of her weapon directly to the side of his head. There was no fear in his eyes either.

"They just wanted to live in peace so my father could work on his energy experiments," he said, his voice betraying just the slightest hint of heartbreak that had consumed him for so long.

Gor-Hax looked over at Wraith, took in his face for a long moment.

"Ah yes. I recognize you now, though time has not been kind. You are the whelp of the scientist who betrayed his people."

Wraith took a deep, troubled breath and Star-Lord could see his finger twitching on the trigger of his strange, powerful weapon.

If this was true, would Peter blame Wraith for wanting justice for the murder of his parents? He wasn't sure. But no matter what happened in the next few moments, this was *not* good.

A long moment of charged silence passed, and then Wraith slowly holstered his weapon.

"Drax. Let him go. Even though I have dreamed of killing this man for decades, we have larger concerns..."

Drax clenched his jaw, shocked at the words he'd just heard, but he finally nodded at Wraith and withdrew his blade from Gor-Hax's throat. The Kree resistance leader inhaled a sharp breath, then quickly got to his feet, holding his hand against the wound on his neck. He leaned in close to Drax and whispered, "When this is all over, you and I will have a conversation that you will *not* enjoy."

"I look forward to it," Drax whispered back.

"Okay, that was not the way I wanted this to start," Peter said, holstering his gun as well. "But we're all on the same side. At least for now. Can we get back to discussing how to stop Ultron and the Phalanx?"

Gor-Hax looked at Quill and then nodded at his troops, who all put their weapons away, too. But the room was still filled with an almost palpable tension.

"So… your two empaths sent us a message that you have a plan," Gor-Hax said. "Let's hear it."

Quill took a deep breath. And then he spoke.

PETER FINISHED explaining his plan as quickly as possible, and Gor-Hax opened his mouth to respond when Moondragon suddenly doubled over, a pained gasp emitting from the back of her throat. Mantis also sucked in a deep breath, now connected to Heather on a psychic level.

"What is it?" Peter asked, rushing over to them.

Moondragon leaned against a nearby wall while Drax put his arm around Mantis, steadying her.

"It was Phyla-Vell," Heather said, breathless. "She was in incredible pain, and then nothing. I can't read her at all. She is no longer conscious… or alive." Tears filled Moondragon's eyes.

"Nova?" Quill asked.

"He was conscious, in battle, but now his thoughts have vanished as well," Mantis answered.

"Then they failed," Gamora said, joining them.

"I must go to her," Moondragon said to Quill, grabbing his jacket. "She needs me."

"No. *We* need you. Down here. If our mission fails, no one will be left to save Phyla-Vell. Or anyone else."

Moondragon stared at him, her eyes blazing. But she nodded, then moved away, trembling with rage and frustration.

Star-Lord let out a frustrated breath, shaking his head. The first part of his strategy had already collapsed.

"On to Plan B," he said to Gamora. "We knew this might… would probably happen." He walked over to Gor-Hax. "Our strike force wasn't able to defeat Ultron. So, the ground attack is now our only way to stop him. We've come up with a multi-pronged plan that involves entering the tower from more than one angle, and both a direct and indirect assault. Are your troops ready to help get our teams to the tower?"

"Of course they are," Gor-Hax said, utter disdain for the question bleeding through his words. Peter bit his tongue. He couldn't afford to tell the Kree general what he really thought of him. Not now. There was too much at stake.

"Great," Star-Lord said instead. He turned to face his troops, looked at them with grim determination. "Guardians, it's time."

"Let's do this thing," Rocket said.

"I am Groot!" his friend agreed.

As everyone prepared, Drax approached Moondragon. She was still recovering from experiencing Quasar's pain.

"Are you okay?" Drax asked, smiling down at her. He knew what they were about to attempt would be hugely dangerous, especially after everything they'd been through on Kvch.

"Yes, thank you," she responded, unsure what else to say. So much had happened between them over the years.

"I wanted to say…" Drax started. "I wanted to say how much I miss your mother."

Heather felt like she suddenly lost her breath. She hadn't thought about her mom in a long time, hadn't allowed herself. It still hurt too much.

"So do I," she finally whispered.

"I know things have been hard for you, for both of us, since that day. But I wanted to tell you, Heather, that I'm proud of you. Of the woman you've become. And I love you."

Moondragon fought against tears, then suddenly reached out and hugged her father. The first time she'd done so since she was a little girl.

"I love you, too," she whispered into his ear.

CHAPTER THIRTY-ONE

ROCKET JUMPED from one rooftop to the next, tumbling as he landed, and continuing his sprint across the city.

The rest of his sub-team—Groot, Moondragon, and Mantis—were making their way to the tower via the maze-like city streets, led by a handful of the Kree resistance's best fighters. They knew how to avoid the many Phalanx that had overrun the city.

But Rocket could get there faster (and have more fun) by doing things his own way.

He wanted to get eyes on this tower as soon as possible, see what they were dealing with. He had a photographic memory and his boast about loving to blow things up had shrouded a more basic truth: he could look at any structure and know exactly how to take it down. Provided he had the right equipment and explosives to do so.

Blowing it up was a final measure. Maybe it wouldn't even be necessary. If it was, that meant their initial strike force had confronted Ultron and lost.

After several more miles, crossed in record time for a being of his size, he found himself in viewing distance of the Phalanx tower. The sight nearly caused his mouth to fall open.

It was the largest mechanical structure he had ever seen. It reached into the sky so far that he couldn't see the top, and drones continued to work on it as he watched, though he couldn't tell from this distance exactly what they were doing. Streaks of lightning exploded out of the sky, hitting the tower, and the building seemed to literally pulse with energy. For all Rocket knew, it was doing exactly that.

He studied it for long moments, taking in as much of it as possible. Then he hit the radio unit that was strapped to his arm.

"This is C-Team leader. Come in."

After a long moment, his radio crackled to life.

"This is B-Team," Star-Lord's voice responded. "We're on our way to the tower from the opposite direction. Have you reached it yet?"

"I have eyes on it now," Rocket answered, letting out a low whistle as well. "It's crazy ginormous. *Lots* of activity. And massive bursts of lightning hitting it… or maybe the lightning is coming from it…? It's hard to tell. Either way, it looks like bad news."

"Well, Ultron wouldn't be coming all the way back here in Adam's body unless it was for a very specific reason. Which means if we don't stop him, or blow that thing to bits, it's probably lights out for every living thing in the entire universe."

"Is that your idea of a pep talk?" Rocket said, smiling.

"Heh," Quill laughed, though it sounded mirthless. "You seem like the kind of raccoon who can handle a little bad news."

"True, true. Anyway, I'll plant the explosives then meet up with the others once they catch up with me, and then we'll get Moondragon and Mantis in position within the tower."

"We'll be there in probably twenty minutes," Moondragon's hushed voice confirmed.

"Okay," Star-Lord said. "Good luck to all of you."

"You too, Quill," Rocket responded, then clicked off. "I get the feeling we're all gonna need it."

MOONDRAGON AND Mantis watched as the resistance fighters slipped back into the shadows.

Now that the Kree had accomplished their mission, getting them to the base of the tower, they took their leave, not enthused in the first place to be helping a group of people who had just threatened their leader.

"Where's Groot?" Mantis asked, looking around. "He was right behind us."

"I... don't know," Moondragon answered. "I have trouble locking onto his mind even under the best of circumstances."

"Same. I hope he's okay."

"He's pretty resourceful, even in his current form," Moondragon opined.

"And very cute," Mantis said, leaning against the alley wall. She let out a long sigh, stared at the Phalanx soldiers who were guarding the base of the tower. Several of them began what looked like a regular sweep of the area, and started to head in their direction.

"Ready?" Moondragon asked, taking hold of Mantis's hand.

"Not really," Mantis replied, but she nodded anyway, and they both engaged their psionic powers once again.

Neither of them was anywhere near full power, which is why it took their total effort to keep the Phalanx-controlled Kree that soon stood right in front of them from being aware they were even there. Under normal circumstances, this kind of significant mental illusion would not have been difficult. But after suffering so greatly on Ultron's transfer machine, they could barely manage, even together.

Moondragon grimaced in pain.

"Heather, are you okay?" Mantis thought as the Phalanx began to move away, straining to maintain the illusion while also speaking even the simplest sentence.

"I'm fine," Moondragon responded telepathically, taking a deep breath and letting it out slowly. "Let's just get into position so we're ready when Rocket gets here. I hope he—and Groot—are all right."

Mantis gazed at her new friend for a moment, then put her hand gently on Heather's shoulder. Moondragon looked extremely pale.

"I'm sure they're fine," Mantis thought. "I'm actually more worried about you right now. If you need anything—and that includes me taking this over by myself if you feel you are doing your mind irreversible damage—just say the word."

"Thank you," Moondragon responded, deeply appreciative for the connection she now shared with Mantis. "But you and I are finishing this mission and stopping Ultron together. He deserves to suffer for what he's done to us… and what he's done to millions more since this all started."

Mantis nodded, and the two waited, knowing that Rocket had to accomplish the first part of his mission, and hoping he would arrive soon. Time was running out.

ROCKET KICKED one of the Phalanx-controlled Kree right in the jaw, watching with satisfaction as the man's head snapped back and he collapsed with a loud grunt of pain.

He'd always prided himself on his stealth, but his luck had run out as he'd approached the tower. He was now facing a half-dozen Phalanx-controlled Kree, who stared at him, ready to infect.

"So much for keeping things quiet," Rocket mumbled, then unholstered his weapon and shot one of the Kree-Phalanx slaves directly in the face as it lunged towards him, hands outstretched. Rocket had modified the weapon on the way from Kvch and the modifications had clearly worked.

As that one fell, Rocket fired indiscriminately at the others, realizing this little battle was attracting the attention of other Phalanx slaves nearby. He was a crafty fighter but the odds here were not looking good.

"Crap," he said as he continued shooting, watching as more Kree-Phalanx started to swarm him.

This was it. It had been a good run. And if he was going to

go out, at least it would be while trying to save the whole dang universe.

Just as one of the Phalanx slaves' fingers was about to make contact with Rocket's fur, the technology-filled Kree's eyes widened, and then its entire body went slack. Rocket noticed what looked like a branch that had gone through one side of the Phalanx and out the other. In fact, the branch had skewered every single Kree in the immediate vicinity, incapacitating them immediately.

A tiny voice came from nearby.

"I am Groot!"

"Buddy!" Rocket shouted, watching as the Kree-Phalanx slaves collapsed while the branch retracted back to its normal arm size. Groot came running up and hugged his best friend.

"What are you doing here?" Rocket asked, in shock. "You're supposed to be with Mantis and Moondragon!"

"I am Groot…?" he said, shrugging.

"Yes, I know. You play by your own rules, just like me. Okay, fine, you saved my life. I forgive you," Rocket responded, shaking his head and laughing. "You wanna go plant some explosives with me?"

"I am Groot!!" the small tree creature said excitedly, his already huge eyes widening even more.

"All right! Let's go! And then we need to get Mantis and Moondragon into position ASAP!" Rocket shouted, heading towards the tower, chattering quietly to Groot as they did so.

STAR-LORD WATCHED the Kree resistance fighters depart, appreciative of their help.

They'd gotten them within striking distance of the tower, and now it was up to him and his sub-team to make their way up to where they would hopefully confront, and stop, Ultron. They knew he was coming. It was just a matter of when.

Quill looked over at Gamora, Wraith, and Drax. They were all grim-faced as they took out the few Phalanx slaves that were guarding this back entrance, and entered the tower, moving towards an elevator. The Phalanx must have been distracted by something else, or busy elsewhere preparing for the arrival of their master. Maybe both. Just as he was starting to worry that maybe his teammates were the thing that had been distracting the Phalanx, his radio crackled to life.

"Talk to me, Rocket," he said, the desperation sounding in his voice.

"We planted the explosives and we're in," the raccoon said. "Mantis and Moondragon are in position and we've got their backs. Which is good… 'cause Ultron's ship just docked on top of this thing."

"Roger that," Peter responded. "We're in, too, and heading up. Protect them with your life, Rocket."

"Our pleasure," Rocket said.

"I am Groot!" his best friend confirmed.

Star-Lord smiled for the slightest moment, then took a deep breath as the doors closed him in with his three comrades. The elevator shot upwards at incredible speed.

THE BRIDGE OF THE PHALANX FLAGSHIP—A FEW MINUTES LATER

"MY LORD."

Ultron stood. His flagship had done its job, had fit perfectly into the top of the tower, just the way he'd planned it. He was now connected to the entire structure and could finally enact the last part of his plan. This was where everything would change, where he would become the master of every living thing in the universe.

Although his Phalanx slave had only said two words, Ultron sensed what had just happened as the ship's sensor array extended into the tower. Maybe it was because of Adam Warlock's incredible powers. Or maybe because he had been waiting for this since the moment Hank Pym had brought him online. But he immediately knew the weight of what had transpired.

"The intergalactic transmission lens is ready. We await your order."

Ultron smiled and took a seat in the chair that had been constructed for this moment. He felt something strange in his stomach, and then realized it was what humans called 'butterflies.' For once, they had gotten something exactly right.

"Bring it online," he said simply, then sat back down and waited.

The change was almost instantaneous. He felt the energy rush up from the tower and enter his body. There was no flash of light, no physical indication that anything had changed. But for Ultron, sitting there in Adam Warlock's body, *everything* changed. He felt his senses expand in a way that was beyond description, and he nearly laughed at the sensation. So many things made sense now, and he felt justified in his plan, more than he ever had before.

He was bringing peace to the universe. Giving organic beings something they had always lacked, even if they hadn't known it.

Order. Logic. A definitive and singular way to look at any- and everything. And the destruction of pointless emotion. Things would finally make sense, for all of them. Even if it took them time to truly understand it.

He reached out into the cosmos, felt the planets being infected one by one—the universe was so much bigger than he himself had ever truly conceived. He made sure to avoid Earth. They would have to wait, have to watch the universe fall around them. He was saving them for last, just as he'd promised himself.

And he would relish the look in Pym's eyes when the frail human realized what his creation had wrought.

ACROSS THE universe, planets were instantly infected by the Phalanx virus, entire populaces turned to cybernetic slaves as their technology mobilized against them. Individuals stopped what they were doing, now part of the collective, and waited for orders from their new master: Ultron.

"OKAY, WE'RE going to reach the top of the tower in a few minutes," Peter said, looking at a data pad that Gor-Hax's troops had provided.

Based on the information he was reading, the tower had been activated and Ultron was currently enslaving planets across the entire universe, which was hard for Star-Lord to fully process.

But Ultron had made one vital mistake.

Bolstered by their presence at the center of Ultron's tower, Mantis and Moondragon were able to defend their teammates from the tower's wave of infection—though no one was sure how long they could keep this protection up. The Guardians could all feel how much strain the two empaths were under.

Drax attempted to focus on the mission, didn't dare reach out specifically to Mantis or Moondragon with his thoughts, even though he could feel them on the fringes of his brain. The last thing he wanted to do was distract them while they were helping keep any hope of victory alive for them. Still, he was worried about them.

"I'm just glad Rocket made these modifications to our weapons," Gamora responded, checking her weapon for what felt like the hundredth time, still impressed. "I'm not sure how effective they would have been otherwise."

"I'm gonna buy Rocket many drinks if we get out of this in one piece," Quill said.

"When," Gamora corrected, touching Quill's hand.

He looked at her fingers on top of his, then into her eyes. They smiled at each other, a smile that said so many things.

"When," he confirmed.

There was a loud clanking sound as the elevator reached the top floor, then it went still and silent. They all looked at each other.

"Okay," Quill said. "It's now or never."

ROCKET BLASTED a Phalanx robot just as it was about to touch an unmoving Mantis.

"Groot, keep them away from Moondragon!" he shouted.

They were in the heart of the tower as it pulsed with unbelievable energy. Several Phalanx moved towards Moondragon, who sat in the center of the room, hands clasped in Mantis's, both of them straining to keep their teammates and themselves safe from the extremely powerful transmission that was shooting out from the tower and across the universe. Sweat poured down both of their faces.

Groot shot a wooden hand out and grabbed several metal crossbeams overhead, struggling against their construction, and ultimately brought them down on the robots, crushing them into scrap. Rocket kept on shooting.

"Keep it up, buddy! We have to buy Quill and the others enough time to stop Ultron!"

"We are Groot!" he shouted back, picking up one of the beams and using it like a baseball bat against any Phalanx who dared try to touch Moondragon.

"We sure are, buddy," Rocket said, grinning, and continued his defense of Mantis. "Now all we need is a miracle."

WRAITH FOLLOWED his new friends through the bowels of Ultron's flagship.

They spoke in hushed whispers, planning, Quill sounding impossibly optimistic about their chances. Wraith envied that kind of wishful thinking, vaguely remembered those kinds of feelings from when he was a boy living on Marxhotz with his parents and Saw-Ked. But right now, at this moment, he felt nothing of the kind.

Still, these 'Guardians of the Galaxy' inspired him to fight back against Ultron, even if he personally was immune to the Phalanx, with or without the help of their empaths. These new allies made him want to be a better person, and for that alone, he would fight to the death for them.

"We're approaching the bridge," Star-Lord whispered, looking at a handheld device the Kree resistance had given them. Rocket had reconfigured it, too, so that Ultron and the Phalanx wouldn't be able to sense its presence.

"Hopefully," the raccoon had added.

Each one of them raised their energy weapons—even Drax, who generally preferred using a blade.

"Remember," Peter said, his back against the wall next to the bridge's entrance, "Ultron has the power of Adam Warlock at his disposal, so we need to move as fast as possible. Wraith, you're our heaviest hitter, so I want you to go after him with all you've got. Gamora and Drax, we'll handle any other Phalanx. Just don't let them touch you. We're immune to the virus emanating from the tower but not their physical touch. As soon as we clean those up, we'll help you, Wraith. Cool?"

Wraith wasn't sure how to respond to that Earth colloquialism, so he just nodded.

Quill nodded back, then began placing the explosives he'd brought on the door as quietly as possible. Once those were situated, he looked at each of his team members. They tightened their grips on the weapons in their hands. It was time.

Star-Lord detonated the explosives.

And all hell broke loose.

CHAPTER THIRTY-TWO

ULTRON FLINCHED as the explosion rocked the bridge, not used to having nerves, causing him to nearly trip over Nova's and Quasar's unconscious bodies at his feet.

But he quickly regained his composure and whirled, shocked to see Quill and three of his accomplices rushing into the room, firing weapons as they did. The shock almost immediately turned to amusement. Did they really think three of their least powerful members and one misfit Kree could stop Adam Warlock and a nearly endless horde of Phalanx robots? It was laughable.

As if knowing Ultron's thoughts, Wraith flicked his wrist and the gun in his hand extended into an energized whip, which wrapped around Ultron's neck, throwing him across the room and into a bank of computers, a small explosion erupting seconds later. The lights on the bridge began to flicker, creating an unsettling strobe effect.

Star-Lord, Gamora, and Drax fired at the Phalanx robots while Ultron got to his feet, grabbing the whip that was still wrapped around his neck.

"Impressive," he hissed. "I'm not sure exactly how you are avoiding the tower's signal, but it doesn't matter. This ends *now*."

He unleashed a wave of energy that ran back down along the whip and into Wraith, who screamed in pain and fell back. The other three closed ranks around their fallen teammate, continuing to decimate the Phalanx robots as they did so.

Ultron stalked forward, the whip falling away from his throat.

"*This* is your final attack?" he mocked, his eyes glowing with incredible power, causing his face to appear and disappear in the strobing lights. "Your two most powerful allies lie beaten at my feet, the entire universe is under my control, and you thought that *you four* could defeat me? Now that I wield the full power of Adam Warlock? I genuinely pity you."

His hands began to glow as he took in his last opponents. Although all his Phalanx robots on the bridge had been destroyed, he could sense more on their way from different parts of the tower. But he didn't want these four to become his slaves. He wanted them dead.

As Ultron raised his hand to obliterate them all with a single attack, Drax suddenly burst forward, dropping his gun and unsheathing his twin-bladed sword with unbelievable speed and precision. Ultron altered his attack, but the energy beam sailed over Drax as he ducked, then came charging up from below, slicing Ultron along the stomach and chest, nearly reaching his now-very-organic throat. If Drax had been only slightly faster, he might have killed Ultron in that moment.

However, Adam Warlock's natural reaction speed meant Ultron was able to pull back just in time, screaming in pain as he did so. Blood gushed from the long wound along his upper torso, but Ultron unleashed a duo of energy blasts from his eyes that hit Drax directly in the chest. He flew back through the destroyed door, collapsing in an unconscious heap in the darkness there.

As Ultron turned to face the others, he found himself being hit with laser fire from both Gamora and Star-Lord, who walked forward in lockstep, their attacks hitting the spot where Drax had already done so much damage. Ultron couldn't believe how much pain he was experiencing, and wondered vaguely how much this body could handle.

Undeterred, he stepped forward and grabbed each of his enemies' weapons in one hand, melting both instantaneously, catching a bit of their flesh as well for good measure. Both shouted in pain and crumpled, holding their hands. Ultron backhanded them both, sending them flying to separate sides of the bridge. Neither of them got back up.

He was bleeding from his stomach and chest, badly, so he raised an energized finger and cauterized the wound. The pain was remarkable, almost enjoyable on some level, but the bleeding finally stopped.

Ultron turned to face Wraith, his final enemy.

On some level, it seemed fitting. His plan had taken true form on Hala. And now here he was, fighting a Kree at the very end. Even if it was a freak Kree, an outcast.

"Are you ready to die?" he asked.

"I am not afraid of you," Wraith responded. "Or of death."

"I'm glad to hear that," Ultron said, moving closer to him. "Because your life is now over."

Ultron wrapped his hand around the Nameless Kree's neck and lifted him into the air. He slowly began to choke the life out of him.

"Back on Earth," Ultron said, "I would sometimes work with other so-called villains. They would often talk about the feeling of killing someone with their bare hands. I would try this in my different robotic bodies, and while it served a purpose, I never understood the pleasure they expressed in doing so. But now—as I feel your life draining within my grip, as I feel the breath being crushed out of your throat—perhaps I understand after all."

Wraith had never experienced this kind of strength, not even in the Exoteric Latitude, even though he had fought more battles against more enemies than he could remember. Flashes of light began to play in front of his eyes as less and less oxygen made it to his brain. He thought of his parents: wondered if he would see them again. He recalled the fact that he'd had the chance to avenge them and had chosen another road. That thought gave him comfort. Perhaps the final comfort he would ever enjoy.

Peter's eyes fluttered open.

He looked over, saw that Ultron had Wraith in a death grip. So that was it. They had failed. He looked over at Gamora, who was unconscious on the other side of the bridge. She looked like she was at peace. Good. That was the way he wanted to remember her in his final moments.

Star-Lord activated his communicator.

"Rocket, you there?"

"Uh, where else would I be?!" the raccoon shouted back in his ear, the sound of blaster fire punctuating the question. "Please tell me you have good news."

"I'm sorry, buddy," Quill responded. "I don't. We lost. It's time to push the button. It was an honor working with you."

In the heart of the tower, Rocket felt his stomach drop. But he knew what he had to do. With one hand, he continued firing; with the other, he removed the detonator. He and Groot had only placed the charges on the lower levels, but he knew they were enough to take the whole tower down.

Groot, Moondragon, and Mantis noticed the device in his hand. Groot nodded, smiled sadly. Moondragon closed her eyes and wished she could say goodbye to Quasar. It didn't seem fair to find happiness only to lose it so soon after.

Mantis shook her head, seemingly unwilling to accept their defeat. Her antennae rotated furiously as she pushed her psionic powers to their limits, reached every mind she could. And then an idea formed in her mind.

It seemed impossible. But impossible was all they had.

"Wait!" she shouted to Rocket, and the raccoon pulled his finger back, a second before he was about to activate the explosion.

"Wraith..." Mantis thought, her mind reaching to the top of the tower.

On the bridge, the Nameless Kree wondered if he was imagining the voice in his mind. Was this simply his brain playing tricks on him as it succumbed to the end of its existence?

"Wraith…" it said again.

He wasn't imagining it. Someone was saying his name. And he recognized the voice.

Wraith swiveled his eyes even as Ultron was choking the life out of him. All his allies were on the ground, defeated. More Phalanx robots were streaming onto the bridge. There was no one here who could have been calling out to him. But then he heard the voice a third time.

"Wraith, can you hear me?"

It was Mantis. She was speaking to him inside his mind.

Yes, I can hear you, Mantis, he thought. *But I'm the last one standing. And I'm dying.*

"I know," Mantis responded, sadness tingeing her voice. "I can sense that. And I'm sorry."

No, I am the one who's sorry, he thought. *I failed you. I failed everyone.*

Wraith managed to get a little more oxygen into his lungs and Ultron tightened his grip. Adam Warlock was incredibly strong, but so was the Nameless Kree. Still, it was just a matter of time.

"There is another way," Mantis said, clearly reluctant. She looked over at Moondragon, who read her thoughts and understood instantly. She opened her mind to Mantis.

I'll do anything, Wraith thought.

"Are you sure? It may kill you," Mantis responded. She shared her thoughts with him, showed him her idea. It was terrifying, and part of him wanted to say no, to just slip into nothingness—but another, more powerful part of himself responded differently.

Do it.

GAMORA BURST back into consciousness, a garbled scream filling her ears.

She sat up, grabbing at her gun, and looked around the bridge. Ultron stood in the middle of the room, shouting, holding his head. Wraith was on the floor in front of him, holding his neck, looking up in fear and sadness.

Something had happened while she was knocked out. It must have been good, if Ultron was in pain. But then, why did Wraith have that strange look on his face?

Peter was suddenly next to her, looking just as confused as she felt. As she stared up at him, she hoped they could somehow get out of this, just so she could spend more time with him—perhaps not during one of the endless battles they'd been engaged in since first meeting.

"Gamora," he said quietly.

"What's going on?" she asked.

"I don't know," he responded. "But something serious is definitely happening. And I'm guessing Mantis and Moondragon have something to do with it."

"*Be ready,*" Mantis's voice responded in their heads, and she sounded like she was in incredible pain. They had no idea what she meant but they quickly got to their feet. Nearby, Drax had also recovered and heard Mantis's words. He, too, slowly stood and readied his weapon.

Ultron continued to scream. The Phalanx robots in the room seemed paralyzed, perhaps because their master was completely overwhelmed by what was happening, but they were motionless with their arms at their sides, waiting.

Wraith stood up, his face darker than anyone in the room had ever seen it before, straining against something no one could see, dark blood trickling from one of his nostrils. He stepped up to Ultron and stood right in front of him, screaming now, too. It was a surreal tableau: two men, both screaming, one with skin of gold, the other of ash.

And then Adam Warlock's body went slack and fell to the floor, seemingly lifeless.

Wraith immediately fell to one knee, now holding his head,

taking huge breaths. Quill ran over to him, followed closely by Gamora. The Phalanx robots continued to stand stock still. Drax joined them next to the Nameless Kree.

"Wraith," Star-Lord said, helping the Kree warrior up. "What's happening? Are you okay? You did it! You defeated Ultron."

"I *am* Ultron!" Wraith screamed and shoved Quill as hard as he could. Peter fell back but Drax caught him in time, helped him stay on his feet.

"What the hell is happening?" Gamora said.

"I am Wraith!" the Nameless Kree yelled, gritting his teeth, continuing to claw at his own head.

"*Moondragon and I were able to move Ultron's consciousness from Adam to Wraith,*" Mantis said to all their minds at the same time.

"What?!" Quill responded. "How did you manage that?"

"*Ultron built this tower to give his mind access to every single organic being in the universe. It was the only way he could mass infect without physical contact. But in doing so, he left himself vulnerable in Adam's body to psychic manipulation—though it would take two empaths as powerful as myself and Moondragon, amplified by the power of this structure.*"

"Why Wraith?" Gamora asked, watching as the Nameless Kree battled himself.

"*His immunity to the Phalanx and ability to destroy the virus made him the only choice. If we had moved Ultron to any of you, it would have resulted in your death and Ultron taking over your body permanently.*"

"Okay, glad you didn't do that," Quill admitted.

Wraith unholstered his weapon and pointed it at the three Guardians.

"Uhh… Wraith, buddy, that you?"

"I am Ultron," the Nameless Kree responded. "And now you will all die."

They'd seen how powerful Wraith's weapon was. As exhausted and hurt as they all were, they suspected that one shot from that gun would be the end of them. And of everyone else in the universe.

"No!" Wraith screamed, turning the weapon towards himself, then back towards the Guardians.

"You will lose!" Ultron said to himself. "You are strong, but I am the most evolved mind ever created. I can already feel your will starting to crumble."

Peter made eye contact with Wraith and saw something there, realized that Wraith was trying to silently tell him something. He immediately understood. It was a devastating truth, but something he knew must be done.

"On my mark," he said to Gamora and Drax, aiming his own weapon, "fire on Wraith."

"What?!" they both responded, looking at their leader with confusion in their eyes.

"It's the only way," Star-Lord said grimly.

He took a deep breath, and then fired.

The blast hit Wraith directly in the chest. It clearly hurt him, or perhaps it distracted Ultron enough to allow Wraith to push back in their literal battle of wills.

"Your attack is *useless*!" Ultron screamed, managing to fire at Quill. Wraith's consciousness altered Ultron's aim slightly, and the energy beam only nicked Star-Lord's face, which immediately started to bleed.

Gamora saw this and knew what had to be done. She opened fire as well, her attack merging with Peter's. Drax did the same.

Wraith staggered back but it still wasn't enough.

"I… can't stop him…" he managed to say, and all three Guardians knew exactly who was talking, and what that meant. Their weapons simply weren't powerful enough.

Nearby, Quasar abruptly sat up, Heather's voice shouting in her mind.

"Phyla-Vell, wake *up*!"

Quasar took in the room, saw three of the Guardians attacking Wraith, saw Adam's body on the floor, breathing but motionless. Nova was still unconscious next to her.

"Heather? What the hell is going on?"

"*There's too much to explain,*" Moondragon responded in her mind. "*You need to wake Nova and join the attack on Wraith. Ultron has taken over his body. There isn't much time. Wraith is fighting back, but he's losing.*"

Quasar nodded, not happy with the orders, but ready to do her part.

"Understood."

She reached over and hit Nova's arm with the back of her hand. "Wake up, Rider. Nap time is over."

He didn't respond, didn't even move. Quasar sighed.

"We don't have time for this. Okay, fine, the hard way."

Phyla-Vell put her hand on his chest and let loose with a contained energy blast, which radiated out across Nova's body, his eyes glowing last, and he sat up with a sudden, violent intake of breath.

"Quasar? What…?"

"There's no time," she said, standing and helping him to his feet. "We both need to unload on Wraith. *Now.*"

Nova looked over and saw what was happening, watched as Wraith fired shakily at Star-Lord, Gamora, and Drax, who fired back, hitting him directly, though not seeming to do enough damage to the powerful Kree.

"I don't… I can't…" he stammered.

Quasar grabbed him by his uniform, stared angrily into his eyes.

"Do you trust me?" she asked, the words clipped and serious.

"Do I…? Yes, I do. Absolutely."

"Then fire."

Quasar attacked Wraith, who staggered back in pain.

"I will kill all of you!" Ultron screamed, firing all over the bridge, hitting nothing except Phalanx robots and walls.

Nova took a deep breath, hoped he was doing the right thing, and added his energy attack to Quasar's.

"Don't stop!" Mantis and Moondragon said into each of their

minds. "You're doing it!"

Each of them stepped forward, increasing their attack as much as possible, and at length, Wraith collapsed, arms stretched out on the floor, eyes closed. All the Phalanx in the room collapsed at the same time. Immediately, the Guardians ceased their offensive. Silence filled the room.

"It's done," Mantis said.

"Ultron is gone," Moondragon confirmed.

Star-Lord rushed forward and fell to his knees, cradling the Nameless Kree's head on his leg.

"Wraith? Wraith!"

After a moment, his eyes opened and he looked up at Peter, a small smile appearing on his face. His breathing was shallow, nothing more than wet desperate rasps.

"My name… is Zak-Del…" Wraith managed to say.

"That's a great name. And you did it," Quill said quietly. "You beat him."

"We all did. Like a family…"

"Exactly," Peter responded, his eyes filling with tears. Gamora approached and put her hand on his shoulder. "You're part of our family, Zak-Del. You always will be."

"Thank you," he gasped. "For everything. I'm going to go see my mother and father now. I miss them…"

And then he was gone.

Star-Lord slowly closed Wraith's eyes as everyone in the room gathered around them.

They had won. But victory had come at a terrible price.

CHAPTER THIRTY-THREE

THE CAPITAL CITY OF HALA—A FEW DAYS LATER

STAR-LORD STARED Ronan the Accuser directly in the eyes, waiting.

The cleanup of Hala had begun but it would be a long time before the planet and its liberated people recovered from the most destructive invasion in the planet's history. Still, the mood was celebratory as the Guardians of the Galaxy waited to receive commendations for their part in Ultron's and the Phalanx's defeat.

However, Peter Quill didn't really feel like celebrating.

Still, he stood there next to his teammates, Ronan still looking at him, wondering if this was some kind of elaborate ruse so Ronan could officially blame Peter for inadvertently uploading the Phalanx into the Kree defense network what seemed like years earlier.

It had been less than a week.

The last time Quill had seen Ronan, they had dropped the Accuser off on one of his surviving ships and Ronan hadn't even said thank you. Now, being here, like this, was surreal to say the least. The Kree suns beat down on them and he could feel the sweat trickling down his back. In some ways, battling the Super-Adaptoid was preferable to this.

Behind and below Ronan, gathered in the streets of the city, throngs of Kree citizens waited for their leader to speak. At length, he turned and faced them, and they cheered as he did so.

"People of Hala!" he shouted, his voice carried out into the crowd by some unseen audio system, his ever-present hammer gripped in his right hand and now held up over his head. "Today is a day for celebration! And a day to honor your great leader, Ronan the Accuser! I myself brought together the team that helped me saved the universe, my personal guardians that you see behind me! Without my leadership and courage, our planet and our entire universe would have been lost!"

"What?!" Peter whispered harshly, starting to step forward. Gamora gently wrapped her fingers around his forearm.

"Let him have it. It doesn't change what really happened," she told him quietly.

Star-Lord worked his jaw, took several deep breaths. He was still in a lot of pain after the events of the past week and didn't have the patience for this kind of political maneuvering.

Ronan began to speak again but Quill suddenly shot forward, bumping past Ronan and raising his hand to the throngs of Kree below him. Confused, they went silent.

"Citizens of Hala!" Peter shouted, glad to hear that his voice was also picked up by the audio device. "Uh… hi!"

Ronan reached out to grab Star-Lord, rage gleaming in his eyes, when the Kree leader suddenly felt something jut into his side. He glanced down and saw Gamora standing there, her gun very inconspicuously placed against his ribs.

"Let him talk," Gamora instructed quietly.

Ronan's anger was almost palpable but all he could do was stare. After a moment, he let out a frustrated sigh and turned his head back to listen to Quill.

"My name is Peter Quill, though some of you may know me as Star-Lord!"

There were no looks of recognition in the crowd.

"Well, on other planets they know me," he muttered. "Ronan is correct!" he continued, full volume. "Today is a day for celebration. But it is also a day of mourning as you bury your loved ones, killed by the evil known as the Phalanx. I would propose that we take a moment of silence to honor those we have lost, both the innocent and those lost in the course of battle."

He lowered his head, as did the thousands below him. Ronan tensed to move forward again but was surprised to feel something press against his other side. He looked over and found himself staring into Drax's eyes.

"Hello there," Drax whispered, a malicious smile on his face. "I would not do that if I were you."

Ronan looked over at his guards, ready to signal them to attack, but was surprised to see them with their heads down, eyes closed. He scoffed. Sentimental fools. They would pay for this later.

"There are many who acted in heroic fashion over the past several days," Star-Lord continued, the masses looking up again. "But this is not about one person..." He glanced back at Ronan, shook his head in disgust slightly. "Or even any group, Guardians or otherwise. This was a team effort across worlds, across races. We came together, we overcame differences, because we saw that this threat was bigger than our petty grievances with each other. We came together because ultimately, we are stronger together. And we should remember that the next time we find ourselves at each other's throats."

The crowd cheered, much to Quill's surprise. He noticed a small Kree child down below, looking up at him with awe and wonder in her eyes. Peter smiled, then remembered a final thing he wanted to say. His smile faded.

"However, there is one person that I wish to single out, and to honor. For many years, he was only called Wraith. But his real name was Zak-Del. And he was a Kree citizen. His parents were scientists who tried to better your planet, and for that, they were hunted and killed, and Zak-Del was orphaned."

"Tread very carefully, Quill," Ronan demanded.

Peter took a deep breath, then pressed on.

"He was tortured and turned into something less than Kree, and then found himself on a mission of vengeance. But he put that aside and helped us stop Ultron and the Phalanx. In fact, he gave his life to end the threat once and for all. And when he had his chance for revenge, he instead chose a higher path. In order to save us all. So, today's celebration is for all the nameless heroes in the universe, Kree and otherwise. The nameless who fought and gave their lives. The nameless who are listening to me right now, who may feel like they are not seen or heard or believed. I see you. I hear you. I believe you. You are the future."

Peter smiled at that young Kree girl again and nodded. Maybe that girl would someday become a leader on this planet.

"Finally, I implore you, citizens and leaders of Hala..." He glanced back at Ronan again for a moment, who clenched his hammer as tightly as he could, his face registering his absolute desire to use it. "...in the name of the great Kree who have come before you, like my friend Ten-Cor, who gave her life to defend you—do not give in to tyrants, no matter what form they take. Choose kindness over violence; wisdom over fear; acceptance over hate. I think you'll be surprised at how effective those choices can be. Thank you."

Peter stepped back, past Ronan. Gamora and Drax joined their leader back in line.

The Accuser stared at them, at Star-Lord.

"You will pay for what you've done here today, Quill," he said darkly.

"I look forward to it," Peter responded. "Guardians, let's get outta here. I could use a drink."

Ronan resumed his speech, spewing propaganda at his citizens, as the Guardians made their way down and away, silent, thinking about all they had lost—and also what they had gained.

THE BAR was raucous.

It was evening in the capital city of Hala, and the Kree people were out in force, letting off steam after so many days of terror and sadness. The Guardians sat in the back, at a table that could barely be seen by most of the occupants of the establishment.

"Here's to Zak-Del," Quill said, holding up his mug of Kree ale.

"To Zak-Del," the others said, clinking their mugs against his.

They drank. Peter managed to swallow a sip and his face contorted, his eyes watering.

"This… this is terrible," he managed to cough out.

"I quite like it," Mantis said, taking another huge gulp.

"Same!" Rocket said, wiping his mouth with the back of his paw. Groot sat next to him on a booster seat, creating flowers and placing them on the table in front of him. He handed one to Quasar, who smiled at the small tree creature.

"Thank you," she said. "It's beautiful."

"I am Groot," he replied.

"So, what's next for you two?" Star-Lord asked Moondragon and Quasar. "Any interest in joining us? Gamora and I have been talking about sticking together for a little while longer, seeing where the galaxy takes us. I'm hearing the Space Knights have gone AWOL. Turns out they may have willingly helped Ultron. I'd like to have a little catch-up with Daystar."

Phyla-Vell looked at Heather, then back at Peter.

"I think we're going to take some time off. Go on a vacation. Our last one was interrupted by some nasty hunters."

"Oh man, a vacation. I've been dying for one of those," Quill responded. "How about you, Nova? Feel like star-hopping with the Guardians for a while?"

Richard looked up from his ale, which he was still struggling to drink. His helmet sat on the table in front of him, most of the dents having been hammered out of it by a local Kree blacksmith.

"*Very* tempting," Nova admitted. "But I need to get back to Earth, check in on my parents. And there's a former Nova that I need to visit in prison. See if I can help him out. But maybe I'll meet up with you later."

"Totally get it. I'm due a trip to Earth one of these days, too," Peter said. "There's a pizza place at West 3rd and MacDougal that I've been dying to get back to. Adam?" he asked, turning to the quietest member of their party, who sat in the corner, staring at the untouched drink in front of him.

"I… do not know," Adam Warlock responded. "I am still trying to work through all that has happened since I awoke from my cocoon on Morag IV. I watched helplessly while Ultron used my body to further his evil plan. Part of me feels guilty about that, even though it was beyond my control. And now that I am back in control of my own body, I do not know exactly what to do with myself. My memories are still only a patchwork, at best. I feel… I feel lost."

They all stared at him, not quite sure how to answer.

Finally, Quasar spoke.

"I understand what you mean. I never expected to have these incredible powers that were thrust on me. And I've struggled with being Quasar… with my desire to honor the legacy of Wendell Vaughn."

"You have more than lived up to that legacy, my love," Moondragon said quietly, putting a hand on Phyla-Vell's.

"That's debatable," Quasar responded, keeping her eyes on Warlock's. "But what I'm saying, Adam, is this: you are not alone. You have a network of new friends who care about you, who are here for you if and when you need us. In fact… why don't you come with me and Heather on vacation? We're heading to an ocean planet with amazing beaches. I think you've earned a little time in the suns." She looked over at Heather. "If… if that's okay with you…?"

"Of course it is," Moondragon responded immediately.

Adam looked surprised for a moment, and then a smile slowly crept onto his face. "I would love that, thank you. I am not sure that I, or any of my past selves, have ever relaxed."

"As long as you don't mind going on some adventures afterwards," Quasar added.

"Sounds even better," Adam said, finally taking a sip of his drink. He seemed to like it, because he took several more in rapid succession.

"What's your plan, Rocket? Groot?" Gamora asked, trying her drink too. She found the taste pleasant and sat back in her seat. She had been fighting for so long, and against so many enemies. It felt nice to sit here, to drink with her friends, to have Peter Quill next to her.

"I kinda like hanging with you guys," Rocket said. "Let's keep this party going!"

"I am Groot!" his best friend agreed, throwing flowers up into the air.

"Ha, nice," Peter said, turning to Mantis. "How about you, Mantis? You need a vacation too?"

"Not at all," she responded, her antennae turning towards a nearby waiter, who immediately looked at her, cocked his head, and nodded.

That's one way to order a drink, Quill thought.

"I love spending time with all of you and would like to continue to do so!" she finished, looking at the bottom of her mug as if there was still some liquid hiding there.

"Awesome," Star-Lord responded, nodding. He had hoped he'd still have a team at the end of this. "And last but not least... Drax?"

No one answered. They all looked around.

"Wait..." Peter said. "Where's Drax?"

CHAPTER THIRTY-FOUR

GENERAL GOR-HAX stood in his luxurious apartment that overlooked the city, sipping at a cold drink, his mind racing.

Though damaged, his home had been spared from the utter destruction wrought by the Phalanx and was merely mildly wrecked, but livable for the time being. He suspected this was divine intervention. After all, he had been the one to lead the Kree resistance during the invasion, had been integral to the plan to stop Ultron. Not Ronan. No, the 'Accuser' had been hiding in space like the weakling Gor-Hax knew he was.

In fact, the invasion could not have come at a better time. While he had lost some excellent warriors, it had also accelerated his long-gestating plan to supplant Ronan as the leader of the Kree Empire.

He walked over to a nearby table and picked up his personal handheld communicator. This particular device was illegal under Ronan's laws, but Gor-Hax had been using it for quite some time to coordinate his plans against the Accuser.

"Kra-Wen, report."

"I am here, General," Kra-Wen's voice responded. "Our plans were obviously disrupted by the events of the past week, but I have been putting together a list of survivors, and a new timeline for our operation against Ronan and his supporters."

"Excellent," Gor-Hax said. "Make sure you have all of that ready, but I do not want you to do anything until we see each other again in person. I trust only myself in this matter and I do not want you going off unprepared like you have in the past. You will do nothing until you see me again. Is that understood?"

"Yes sir, of course," the voice responded after a moment, laced with fear. Just the way Gor-Hax wanted it. "I will await your word."

"Good."

He clicked off and put the communicator back down on the table.

"Moron," he muttered, then walked back over to his huge window, the lights of the city twinkling below, the distant sound of cheers and laughter barely reaching him.

All these people were morons. *Which is a good thing*, he thought. *Easier to manipulate, to control.* He would start small, take advantage of the chaos that would linger for many months after so much destruction. Place his people in key positions both in the government and in the business community. He would do all the right things, at least in public view—would grovel at Ronan's feet as necessary.

But behind the Accuser's back, Gor-Hax would slowly be killing the great and powerful Ronan, one small cut at a time. He would turn everyone against him until the leader of Hala was utterly alone, and then Gor-Hax would assume control—reluctantly, of course. And he would take immense pleasure in the act.

After that, his grip would reach beyond Hala, beyond the Kree Empire, and out to all the infidels beyond. The Skrulls. The Earthlings. They would all come to understand his greatness, the superiority of the Kree. Even these so-called Guardians of the Galaxy would fall, and they would never even see him coming.

He would get everything he deserved. Everything he had been fighting so long to attain.

Gor-Hax stood at his window for a long time, taking in the city, a city that would soon be under his utter control.

A noise in the shadows of his apartment caught his attention, and after a moment, a figure melted out of the shadows, the stranger's face a tableau of rage and intent.

No, not a stranger.

It was one of the Guardians. Drax. The one who had attacked him in that disgusting basement. He held a sword in his right hand, that same damn double-bladed sword.

"I'm ready to have that conversation," Drax said quietly.

Gor-Hax laughed and finished his drink, placing it down. He sucked his teeth, enjoying the taste of the alcohol. It was from the most expensive bottle on the planet. And he planned on finishing it. As soon as he'd dealt with this insect.

"Am I supposed to be impressed?" he asked. "That you broke into one of the most secure homes on this entire planet? Well, I am not. But you will be impressed by how quickly I dispatch you, without even laying a finger on you. Impressed, as you lie dying on my carpet, a carpet you could never afford in your pathetic life."

Drax took a step forward, tightened his grip on his sword.

"I am going to enjoy this," Gor-Hax hissed.

He quickly reached over and touched a button on the wall. Immediately, a gun turret unfolded there, tracked Drax's heat signature, and opened fire. The Guardian was too fast, however, and dodged the bullets, flipping over the nearby couch and rolling along the floor, out of sight.

Gor-Hax reached under the table upon which his perspiring glass still sat, withdrew a nasty looking laser weapon, and began firing at the couch. The shots were so powerful that they ripped huge holes in the high-end furniture, though Gor-Hax could see no evidence of Drax through those holes.

There was silence as Gor-Hax stopped firing and waited.

"That couch was worth more than your entire existence," he said, taking a step forward. "Do you understand me? You are less than worthless. After I kill you, I—"

Drax came bursting up and over the couch, his weapon strapped to his back, with a speed that shocked Gor-Hax. He still managed to get off a shot as the massive Guardian came flying towards him, puncturing his shoulder clean through one side and out the other. Blood went flying across the smartly appointed apartment, splattering an obscenely expensive painting that Gor-Hax had won in a high-stakes card game years earlier—though no one had realized he'd been cheating the whole time.

Drax barely flinched.

He tackled Gor-Hax without uttering a sound, and the two men tumbled across the carpet, laser blasts arcing wildly across the room, creating a series of holes.

They ended up next to the table where Gor-Hax had stored his weapon, on top of which his finished drink still rested, and the Kree commander reached up in desperation as Drax straddled him, holding his weapon over his head and hitting the button that engaged the blades, a smile starting to creep onto his face.

Gor-Hax managed to grab hold of the glass, then smashed it with as much strength as he could across Drax's head. More blood flowed, dripping down onto Gor-Hax's face, creating an insane-looking Rorschach inkblot on his skin.

Drax's grin widened further, the blood running down on both sides of his mouth, and also between his teeth. A madman's smile.

He brandished the sword so that Gor-Hax could see it. The blade caught the light, looked almost beautiful from this angle.

"I'll give you anything you want," he said, his voice suddenly fearful. "I have money… more than you can possibly imagine. Please. I'll make you the most powerful man on Hala… in the entire galaxy. Just spare my life. I beg you."

Drax simply shook his head, silent, but his eyes said: *Not gonna happen.*

"If you go down this path, you will pay," Gor-Hax said, switching tracks, desperate. "My soldiers will find you. And they will kill you very, very slowly. And then they will find and kill everyone you care about. Think carefully about your decision."

Drax seemed to consider this for a moment, then let out a long breath, at peace with where the evening was about to go.

"Here is what I think, General Gor-Hax. This is for Zak-Del's parents," Drax said quietly, then brought the sword down.

Gor-Hax's screams filled the most expensive apartment on the planet, and then, after what must have felt like a very long time, suddenly went silent.

EPILOGUE

THE HIGH EVOLUTIONARY'S SANCTUARY—
SOME TIME LATER

THE HIGH Evolutionary sat in his throne, gazing out upon the cosmos.

He had watched the recent conflict from here, pleased that his machinations had resulted in the conclusion he had desired from the start. He generally disdained being drawn into the affairs of lesser beings but this time had been slightly different. Still, in retrospect, he found the entire thing amusing.

He had studied the evolution of different species ever since he himself had evolved into his current state; had found it fascinating that each one seemed to think itself immortal. And each one wrong, every single time. Species continued to die every day, all across the universe. But what difference did it make to him if one survived or another? Organic or technological? For the High Evolutionary, it was all the same. As long as he survived, of course.

Now the invasion was over, and his 'son' had survived, the High Evolutionary could go back to his quiet life inside this massive star, experimenting on different species and races, discovering—

"I gotta say, purple is not a very intimidating color," a voice rang out, breaking his reverie.

He looked over and was shocked to see the so-called Guardians of the Galaxy standing in his private quarters, looks of displeasure on their faces.

Star-Lord. Gamora. Drax. Mantis. Rocket. And Groot.

"How did you get in here?" he demanded, unhappy with the interruption and rattled by their appearance in what was one of the most secure locations in the galaxy. It shouldn't have been possible.

"Meh," Rocket said, revealing a dozen or so severed cables in his paw. "Once you've hacked Ultron and stopped his never-ending horde of Phalanx robots, breaking into a star ain't such a big deal."

"And you didn't have Mantis to contend with the last time we were here," Gamora said, nodding at her friend, whose antennae were swiveling furiously.

The High Evolutionary stood and approached them. He was tempted to grow taller as he walked, to scare them, but he knew this group wasn't easily frightened. Besides, they were not worth the energy.

"What do you want?" he asked.

"We don't want anything," Star-Lord said, stepping up to him, staring him straight in the eyes. "We're just here to give you a warning."

"Is that so?" the High Evolutionary asked, a rare smile slipping onto his face. Humans were always so amusing.

"Yeah. It is," Quill confirmed. "We know you helped Ultron. You basically handed your 'son' over to him as a sacrifice."

"That is true," the High Evolutionary said. "But even I was in danger from the Phalanx. I am a technological being, just as vulnerable as you to their virus. If I had not made that deal with Ultron before his invasion even began, if I had not further evolved Adam after you brought him to me, Ultron would never have left his mechanical body, and would never have ended up inside Wraith. If I had not done what I did, Ultron would have won. We all would have died, even me."

"Maybe," Star-Lord said, anger creasing his face. "Maybe not. The point is, you didn't give us a choice. You didn't give Adam a choice, either. His body was hijacked by an evil entity and used to kill who-knows-how-many people. And to you, it's just some kind of abstract game that you watch play out, and then move on."

"You are not incorrect," the High Evolutionary commented. "Your point?"

"My point is this," Quill continued, the others stepping forward too, silent but menacing. "If you mess with us again, I promise you'll regret it."

The High Evolutionary looked each of them in the eyes. Individually, they were nothing significant—lower life forms that strutted and fretted their way across the galaxy.

But together, there was something else about them, an almost palpable energy that even he, the most evolved being in the universe, couldn't ignore. After all, they had somehow broken into his highly guarded sanctuary, bypassing both physical and mental safeguards.

He felt what seemed almost like fear.

The empath, Mantis, seemed aware of this and nodded, almost imperceptibly.

"Very well," he said after a long moment. "I will refrain from involving myself in your matters. Are you satisfied?"

"Works for me," Star-Lord said, then turned and walked off without another word. The rest of the Guardians followed, except Rocket, who lingered for an additional moment.

"And I'm tellin' ya... lose the purple. It is *not* working for you," the raccoon said, then followed his teammates back to Ship.

GAMORA WATCHED the monitor as the High Evolutionary's star receded into the distance behind them.

She had the bridge to herself and was struck by the beauty of outer space, the silence. It was something that was easy to forget. But for now, in this moment, she took it in. And smiled.

After a moment she heard someone behind her, and knew immediately who it was.

"How was your inspection?" she asked without looking back.

"All things considered, this ship is in amazing shape. She may be a little rough around the edges, but she'll get the job done in a pinch," Star-Lord responded, taking the co-pilot seat next to Gamora and gently patting the computer terminal in front of him as if the ship was an especially loved pet.

"Sounds like a certain team I know," Gamora said, still staring out into the vast beautiful darkness splayed out before her.

"We can… we can come up with a different name for our group," he said after a long moment of silence. "You've made it clear that you don't love the one I came up with. Which is fine. I get it."

Gamora finally glanced over at Peter, pleasantly surprised to find him already looking at her. After the last several days of battles, he suddenly looked younger than before.

"You know what?" she said. "I got used to it. I might even… *like* it now."

"Really?!" Quill asked, then nodded, pleased with himself. "I knew it would stick eventually," he said, looking at his computer console.

"I guess I can live with it, too," a voice said from behind them. They looked and saw Rocket and Groot, who took seats behind them. "But I reserve the right to change my mind."

"I would expect nothing less, Rocket," Star-Lord said.

"I am Groot," the tree creature said. He'd grown a few inches since the events on and above Hala.

"That's a good point," Gamora responded.

"Wait," Quill said, looking up at her. "You can understand him now, too?"

"It isn't that hard, Peter. You just have to listen a little harder."

"Okay," he conceded. "I'll keep trying. Go ahead, hit me again."

"I am Groot!"

"You…" Quill said, thinking carefully. "You're hungry…?"

"Very impressive," Gamora mused, reaching over and patting Star-Lord on the shoulder.

"I may learn slowly," Peter said, "but I do learn."

"I am hungry, too," Drax said, entering the bridge with Mantis. They sat in the back row. Drax withdrew his sword, engaged the blade, and began sharpening it. The wound in his shoulder had already started healing.

"I don't think you're going to need your sword just to get some food," Gamora observed.

"You never know..." he responded.

Quill punched a series of coordinates into the computer. Ship's engines began to hum as they prepared for a hyperspace jump.

"Okay, Guardians, let's do this thing," he said.

"Where are we going?" Gamora asked.

"I think everyone has earned a great meal," Star-Lord responded. "There is a great Acanti restaurant on Sakaar."

"Ah yes," Drax said, "as well as some of the most dangerous taverns in the galaxy."

"I once fought a couple of bad-tempered Brood in a bar on that planet," Rocket said, sounding excited. "Count me in."

"I am Groot!"

"I, too, am excited to eat a meal with you," Mantis added, smiling widely at her friends.

"Sounds like everyone's on board," Gamora confirmed, looking at Peter. "Shall we?"

Star-Lord nodded, engaged the engines, and after the briefest moment Ship burst forward, carrying the Guardians of the Galaxy into a new, and most likely dangerous, part of the universe.

POST-SCRIPT

I GREW up reading comic books. My oldest brother is nine years older than me, so in the late 1970s I was lucky enough to read every single one of his proverbial hand-me-downs, which were almost all Marvel titles. Despite how long ago that was, my memories of those issues are crystal clear: *Spider-Man* #200 and *Fantastic Four* #200 were especially memorable, but so were the handful of Avengers comics that were peppered in there. This was the era of George Perez and John Byrne, so of course I fell in love with those issues and characters.

One issue that I really adored was *Avengers* #167, which featured an appearance by the Guardians of the Galaxy. Now, the Guardians at that time were not the Guardians we know and love today. Back then, they were comprised of Starhawk, Vance Astro, Martinex, Charlie-27, Yondu, and Nikki. This was the start of the legendary Korvac Saga, arguably one of the best Avengers stories ever published. That entire storyline blew me away as a kid. I thought the Guardians of the Galaxy were extremely cool.

Now, one thing that's constant in comic books is change. The Avengers altered their lineup as early as issue #2, when the Hulk left the roster. While having a core group for its first several years, the X-Men cycled through many, many mutants once it was relaunched in 1975. Heck, even the Fantastic Four has swapped out members now and then. So, it's no surprise that the Guardians of the Galaxy have gone through several different permutations.

One of those is the version of the group that was thrown together for the first *Guardians* movie, a character formula that clearly worked. So, when I was approached to write *my* version of how these characters came together, inspired by the events of the 2008 Marvel Comics crossover event which had many of the elements that ended up in the first *Guardians* film, I jumped at the chance. My book wouldn't be the same as the original book storyline, though it would certainly draw from it. It is a privilege to write my own take on how the Guardians formed, all these decades after reading *Avengers* #167.

And I would be remiss not to mention the fact that I was already somewhat associated with the Guardians of the Galaxy…

In 2013, while I was with my family in an Anthropologie in Montclair, NJ, I noticed this clothing store sold some books. I'm not much of a shopper, so I checked out their literary selection and noticed one book called *Good Night iPad*. It was a parody of *Good Night Moon*, a book I had loved as a kid and one that I often read to my own two daughters.

A couple of nights later, I was reading *Good Night Moon* to my younger daughter and my brain played around with the title, transforming it to *Good Night Doom*. I thought the idea of a baby Doctor Doom would be hilarious, so I cold emailed Disney Publishing and pitched them *Good Night Doom*. They loved it but didn't have the rights to publish the Fantastic Four (yet), so they asked if I would consider using a different character. Eventually, we landed on Groot.

Night Night Groot (with phenomenal art by Cale Atkinson) came out one month before *Guardians of the Galaxy Volume 2* and the book was a monster hit. One friend from high school even thought I had created Groot (I realize how ridiculous that sounds). It did so well that Cale and I did three more Groot picture books, *First Day of Groot*, *Snow Day for Groot*, and *Summer Adventure for Groot*. I loved writing these characters, even if I didn't get to dig too deep into their personalities or motivations.

But now, with *Annihilation: Conquest*, I got to dig in *deep*. And I had a ton of fun doing so. I am deeply appreciative for the opportunity. And I hope you have enjoyed my take on how the Guardians became a team, and a family.

ACKNOWLEDGMENTS

BEING CHOSEN to write a novel like *Guardians of the Galaxy – Annihilation: Conquest* doesn't happen in a vacuum. There are a series of events, usually ones that transpire over years or even decades, that lead to this kind of opportunity.

With that in mind, I want to thank two of my teachers specifically, neither of whom are still alive, unfortunately. The first is Mrs. Morganthaler, my third-grade teacher, who recognized that I loved writing and actively encouraged me to follow my passion. The second is Mr. Murphree, who was my AP English teacher during my senior year of high school. He was as close to John Keating from *Dead Poets Society* as I've ever seen, and he inspired me to more fully immerse myself in literature during college and for the rest of my life.

I wrote my first novel when I was 18 (while Mr. Murphree was my teacher), and it was terrible. I wrote my second novel when I was 21, and it was slightly less terrible. I wallpapered my bathroom in college with rejection letters for those two novels. My next novel was a kids' book, and it was pretty good, and it eventually morphed into a stage play (which got a glowing *New York Times* review) and then a graphic novel.

My fourth novel, which was eventually titled *The Ninth Circle*, took me fifteen years to write, and that's the one that got published.

Getting my first novel published, after so many years of writing and rejection, was a literal dream come true. And for that, I have to thank Richard Pine, Charlie Olsen, and Anthony Ziccardi.

That novel led to the sale of my next novel, *The Chrysalis*, and for that I have to thank editor extraordinaire, Melissa Singer. The publication of that book led to me getting hired to write *Morbius: Blood Ties*, which was my first Marvel novel. It was an absolute delight to write a novel set in the Spider-Man universe, and for that I have to thank Steve Saffel at Titan.

The success of my Morbius novel led Titan to reach back out to me and ask if I would want to write the novel you are currently holding. It was an offer I couldn't refuse. As I've said elsewhere, I love these characters, and I feel a deep connection with them. So, thank you Fenton Coulthurst for giving me this opportunity.

And thanks to Marvel for allowing me to write six (!) books starring your characters. Speaking of Marvel, I would like to sincerely thank Dan Abnett, Andy Lanning, Keith Giffen, Christos N. Gage, and Javier Grillo-Marxuach for laying the foundation upon which I was able to build this novel. And of course, I need to thank James Gunn and Nicole Perlman for their inspired work on the *Guardians of the Galaxy* films.

Finally, and most importantly, I have to thank my wife, Kim, and my daughters, Eloise and Charlotte, for supporting and loving me. They are my real-life super heroes.

ABOUT THE AUTHOR

BRENDAN DENEEN is the author of the award-winning coming-of-age novel *The Ninth Circle*, as well as the critically acclaimed horror novels *The Chrysalis* and *Morbius: Blood Ties*. He's also the author of the four volume *Rocket and Groot* picture book series for Marvel/Disney, and *Green Arrow: Stranded*, an original middle grade graphic novel for DC Comics. His other graphic novel work includes multiple volumes of *Flash Gordon*, an original *Island of Misfit Toys* book, and the dark superhero tale *Scatterbrain*. Upcoming graphic novels include *The Bones of the Gods* and *Mortimer the Lazy Bird*. His short stories and essays have been published by St. Martin's Press, Reader's Digest Books, 13Thirty Press, and Necro Publications.